continued on next page . . .

Don't miss Nora Roberts's bestselling sagas . . .

Key of Light • *Key of Knowledge* • *Key of Valor*
The captivating Key trilogy about three women who embark on three dangerous quests that could fulfill each woman's destiny . . . or forever destroy their lives.

Dance Upon the Air • *Heaven and Earth* • *Face the Fire*
The bewitching Three Sisters Island trilogy about the lives of three passionate and powerful women on the haunting shores of New England.

Jewels of the Sun • *Tears of the Moon* • *Heart of the Sea*
The enchanting Gallaghers of Ardmore trilogy featuring the secret dreams and enduring passions of these Irish siblings.

Sea Swept • *Rising Tides* • *Inner Harbor* • *Chesapeake Blue*
Four novels about the lives and loves of the Quinn brothers on the windswept shores of the Chesapeake Bay.

Born in Fire • *Born in Ice* • *Born in Shame*
Three novels featuring the Concannon sisters of Ireland—women of ambition and talent, bound by the timeless spirit and restless beauty of their land.

Daring to Dream • *Holding the Dream* • *Finding the Dream*
The saga of three women who shared a home and a childhood—but grew to fulfill their own unique destinies.

Turn the page for a complete list of titles by Nora Roberts and J. D. Robb from the Berkley Publishing Group . . .

Nora Roberts

A Little Fate

NORA ROBERTS

BERKLEY BOOKS, NEW YORK

THE BERKLEY PUBLISHING GROUP
Published by the Penguin Group
Penguin Group (USA) Inc.
375 Hudson Street, New York, New York 10014, USA
Penguin Group (Canada), 10 Alcorn Avenue, Toronto, Ontario M4V 3B2, Canada
(a division of Pearson Penguin Canada Inc.)
Penguin Books Ltd., 80 Strand, London WC2R 0RL, England
Penguin Group Ireland, 25 St. Stephen's Green, Dublin 2, Ireland (a division of Penguin Books Ltd.)
Penguin Group (Australia), 250 Camberwell Road, Camberwell, Victoria 3124, Australia
(a division of Pearson Australia Group Pty. Ltd.)
Penguin Books India Pvt. Ltd., 11 Community Centre, Panchsheel Park, New Delhi—110 017, India
Penguin Group (NZ), Cnr. Airborne and Rosedale Roads, Albany, Auckland 1310, New Zealand
(a division of Pearson New Zealand Ltd.)
Penguin Books (South Africa) (Pty.) Ltd., 24 Sturdee Avenue, Rosebank, Johannesburg 2196,
South Africa

Penguin Books Ltd., Registered Offices: 80 Strand, London WC2R 0RL, England

This is a work of fiction. Names, characters, places, and incidents either are the product of the author's imagination or are used fictitiously, and any resemblance to actual persons, living or dead, business establishments, events, or locales is entirely coincidental.

PRINTING HISTORY
Jove mass-market edition / June 2004
Berkley trade paperback edition / April 2005

Library of Congress Cataloging-in-Publication Data

Roberts, Nora.
    A little fate / by Nora Roberts.—Berkley trade pbk. ed.
        p.   cm.
    Contents: The witching hour—Winter rose—A world apart.
    ISBN 0-425-20132-5
    1. Fantasy fiction, American.   2. Love stories, American.   I. Title.

PS3568.O243L57   2005
813'.54—dc22

                                                                                        2004054248

PRINTED IN THE UNITED STATES OF AMERICA

10   9   8   7   6   5   4   3   2   1

CONTENTS

✳

The Witching Hour

Prologue

In a distant time, in a distant place, the great island of Twylia swam in the vast blue Sea of Wonders. It was a land of mountains and valleys, of green forests and silver rivers, of wide fertile fields and quiet lakes. To those who lived there, it was the whole of the world.

Some said that once, in the dawn of beginnings, there was a bridge of land that led to other worlds, and back again to Twylia. A bridge of rock and earth conjured by the great wizard-god Draco, and so destroyed by him when the world beyond became a battlefield of greed and sorrow.

For on Twylia peace and prosperity prevailed for a thousand seasons.

But a time came when men—some men—sought more. When the more they sought was riches not earned, women not wooed, land not honored. And power, most of all—power not respected.

With this avarice, war and death, treachery and fear infected Twylia so that Draco, and those who came from him, wept to see the green fields stained with blood and the valleys echoing with the cries of starving children. He vowed, as he stood on the peak of Sorcerer's Mountain, in the light of the moon, on the night of the solstice, that peace would return to the world.

It would come through blood, and courage, through pure love and willing sacrifice. After dark days, the light would shine again. And so he cast his spell.

There will be one born in the darkest hour of the darkest night who will wield the power and bring the light. The Crown of Stars only one will wear to prove this be my one true heir. Through blood and valor, through grief and joy, the True One shields what greed would destroy. But one seeks another, woman to man, heart to heart, and hand to hand. So warrior, witch, daughter, and son, will complete what has begun. If there is strength and hearts are pure, this land of Twylia will endure.

The midnight hour will forge their power to free this world of tyranny. As I will, so mote it be.

From the peak of Sorcerer's Mountain, to the Valley of Faeries far below, across the fields and lakes and forests, the length and breadth of the island trembled from the might of the spell. Wind swirled and lightning spat.

So Draco sat atop his mountain and watched in glass and fire, in star and water as years passed.

As Draco bided, the world struggled. Good against evil, hope against despair. Magic dimmed in all but the secret places, and some grew to fear as much as covet it.

For a time, a short time, light bloomed again when good Queen Gwynn took the throne. The blood of the sorcerer ran in her veins, as did his love for the world. She was fair of face and of heart and ruled with a firm and loving hand beside her husband, the warrior-king Rhys. Together, they worked to heal the world, to rebuild the once grand City of Stars, to make the forests and fertile valleys safe again for the people of the world.

Hope shimmered into light, but its opposite lurked, and plotted. The shadows of envy and greed slithered in the corners and the caves of Twylia. And those shadows, under the guise of peace and reconciliation, armed for war and treachery. They marched into the City of Stars on a cold December morning, led by Lorcan, whose mark was the snake. And he would be king at any cost.

Blood and smoke and death followed. Come the dawn, the valiant Rhys lay dead and many who had fought with him slaughtered. Of the queen there was no sign.

On the eve of the solstice, Lorcan proclaimed himself king of Twylia and celebrated in the great hall of the castle, where royal blood stained the stones.

1

Snow fell in streams of icy white. It chilled to the bone, but she didn't curse it. It would blind any who pursued, and cover the trail. The bitter white cold was a blessing.

Her heart was broken, and her body nearly done. But she could not, would not yield. Rhys spoke to her, a spirit whisper in her mind that urged her to be strong.

She did not weep for his death. The tears, a woman's tears for the man she loved, were frozen inside her. She did not cry out against the pain, though the pain was great. She was more than a woman. More even than a witch.

She was a queen.

Her mount plowed through the snow, surefooted and loyal. As loyal, she knew, as the man who rode in silence beside her. She would need the loyalty of the faithful Gwayne, for she knew what was coming, what she could not stop. Though she hadn't seen her beloved Rhys's death, she knew the instant the usurper's sword had struck him down. So inside her cold and shattered heart she was prepared for what was to come.

She bit back a moan as the pain tore through her, breathed fast through her teeth until it eased again and she could say what needed to be said to Gwayne's silence.

"You could not have saved him. Nor could I." Tears stung her eyes and were viciously willed away. "Nor could I," she said again. "You served him, and me, by obeying his last order to you. I regret . . . I'm sorry that I made it difficult for you to do so."

"I am the queen's man, my lady."

She smiled a little. "And so you will continue to be. Your king thought of me. Even in the heat of battle, he thought of me, and our world. And our child." She pressed a hand to her heavy belly, to the life that beat there. "They will sing songs of him long after . . ." The pain ripped a gasp from her, had her fumbling the reins.

"My lady!" Gwayne grabbed her reins to steady her mount. "You cannot ride."

"I can. I will." She turned her head, and her eyes were a fierce and angry green in a face as pale as the snow. "Lorcan will not find my child. It's not time. It's not yet time. There will be a light." Exhausted, she slumped over the neck of her horse. "You must watch for the light, and guide us to it."

A light, Gwayne thought, as they trudged through the forest. Night was falling, and they were miles from the City of Stars, miles from any village or settlement he knew. Nothing lived in these woods but faeries and elves, and what good were they to a soldier and a woman—queen or no—who was great with child?

But here, into the Lost Forest, was where she'd ordered him to take her. She'd fought him, that was true enough, when he bowed to the king's command and dragged her from the castle. He had no choice but to lift her bodily onto the horse and whip her mount into a run.

They fled from the battle, from the stench of smoke and blood, from the screams of the dying. And royal command or not, he felt a coward for being alive while his king, his people, his friends were dead.

Still, he would guard the queen with his sword, with his shield, with his life. When she was safe, he would go back. He would slay the murderous Lorcan, or die trying.

There was murmuring under the wind, but it was nothing human, so didn't concern him. Magic didn't worry him. Men did. There may have been sorcery in Lorcan's ambush, but it was men who had carried it out. It had been lies as much as spells that had opened the doors for him, allowed him to walk into the castle under the flag of diplomacy.

And all the while his men—those as vicious as he, and others he'd gathered from the far edges of the world and paid to fight in his name—had prepared for the slaughter.

Not war, Gwayne thought grimly. It wasn't war when men slit the throats of women, stabbed unarmed men in the back, killed and burned for the joy of it.

He glanced toward the queen. Her eyes stared straight ahead, but seemed blind to him. As if, he thought, she was in some sort of trance. He wondered why she hadn't seen the deception, the bloodbath to come. Though he was a queen's man in spite of her reputed powers rather than because of them, he figured sorcerer's blood should have some vision.

Maybe it had something to do with her condition. He didn't know anything about increasing women, either. He hadn't wed, and didn't intend to. He was a soldier, and in his mind a soldier had no need of wiving.

And what would he do when the time came for the babe? He prayed to every god who walked or flew that the queen would know what to do—in the way he assumed a woman knew of such matters.

The heir to Twylia born in a snowbank in the Lost Forest during a winter storm. It wasn't right. It wasn't seemly.

And it terrified him more than any enemy's sword.

They must stop soon, for their mounts were near exhaustion. He would do what he could to make a shelter for her. Build a fire. Then, gods willing, things would . . . progress as nature demanded they progress.

When it was done, and they'd rested, he would get them—somehow—to the Valley of Secrets, and the settlement of women—some said enchantresses—who lived there.

The queen and the child would be safe, and he would go back—go back and drive his sword through Lorcan's throat.

He heard a sound—it was like music through the soughing wind. And looking to the west, he saw a glimmer of light through the stormy dark.

"My lady! A light."

"Yes. Yes. Hurry. There isn't much time."

He pushed the mounts off the path, so they were forced to wade through the sea of snow, to wind around ice-sheathed trees toward that small flicker of light. The wind brought the smell of smoke to him, and his fingers gripped the hilt of his sword.

Ghosts slipped out of the dark, with arrows notched.

He counted six, and his soldier's sense warned him there were more. "We have no gold," he shouted. "We have nothing to steal."

"That's your misfortune." One of the ghosts stepped forward, and he saw it was a man. Only a man, and a Traveler at that. "Why do you journey here, and on such a night?"

Travelers might steal, Gwayne knew, for the sport of it. But they wouldn't attack unprovoked, and their reputation for hospitality was as renowned as their love of the road.

"Our business is our own, and we want no trouble from you,

but only some of the warmth of your fire. I have a lady with me. She is near her time. She needs women to help her with the birthing."

"Throw down your sword."

"I will not, nor will I raise it against you unless you seek to harm my lady. Even a Traveler should honor and respect a woman about to give birth."

The man grinned, and under his hood his face was brown as a nut and just as hard. "Even a soldier should honor and respect men with arrows pointed at his heart."

"Enough." Gwynn threw her hood back, gathered her strength to raise her voice. "I am Gwynn, Queen of Twylia. Have you not seen the portents even through the storm of snow? Have you not seen the black snake slither over the sky this night to snuff out the stars?"

"We have seen, Majesty." The man and those with him lowered to one knee in the snow. "My wife, our wisewoman, told us to wait, to watch for you. What has happened?"

"Lorcan has overthrown the City of Stars. He has murdered your king."

The man rose, laid a fist on his heart. "We are not warriors, my lady queen, but if you bid it, we will arm and band and march against the snake in your name."

"So you will, but not tonight, and not in my name but in the name of one yet to come. Your name, sir?"

"I am Rohan, my lady."

"Rohan of the Travelers, I have sought you for a great task, and now I ask your help, for without it, all is lost. This child seeks to be born. Draco's blood runs through me, and through this baby. You share this blood. Will you help me?"

"My lady, I and all I have are yours to command." He took her horse's halter. "Go back," he shouted to one of his men.

"Tell Nara and the women to prepare for a birth. A royal birth," he added, his teeth flashing in a smile. "We welcome a cousin." He pulled the horse toward the camp. "And enjoy a fight. Though Travelers pay little mind to the changing wind of politics, you will find none among us who has love for Lorcan."

"Politics play no part in murder done under a flag of truce. And your fate is tied to what happens this night."

He looked back at her and fought off a shudder. It seemed her eyes burned through the dark and into him. "I give you my sympathies for the loss of your husband."

"It is more than that." She reached down, gripped his hand with an urgency that ground bone to bone. "You know the Last Spell of Draco?"

"Everyone knows it, my lady. The song of it is passed generation to generation." And he, a man who feared little, felt his hand tremble in hers. "This child?"

"This child. This night. It is destiny, and we must not fail to meet it."

The pain seized her, and she swooned. She heard voices, dim and distant. A hundred voices, it seemed, rising up in a flood. Hands reached for her, lifted her down from her mount as the birth pangs ripped a cry from her throat.

She smelled pine, and snow and smoke, felt something cool pressed to her brow. When she came back to herself, she saw a young woman with bright red hair that gleamed in the firelight. "I am Rhiann, sister of Rohan. Drink a little, my lady. It will ease you."

She sipped from the cup held to her lips and saw she was in a rough shelter of branches. A fire burned nearby. "Gwayne?"

"Your man is just outside, my lady."

"This is women's work, and men are useless here, be they warrior or scholar."

"My mother," Rhiann said. "Nara."

Gwynn looked at the woman busily tearing cloth. "I'm grateful to you."

"Let's get this baby into the world, such as it is, then you can be grateful. Get that water on the fire. Fetch my herbs." The orders were snapped out as Gwynn felt the grip of the next pang.

Through the blurring of her vision she saw movement, heard chatter. More women. Women's work. Birth was the work of women, and death, it seemed, the work of men. Tears she'd conquered earlier now began to spill.

More voices spoke to her, inside her head, and told her what she already knew. But they were small comfort as she fought to give her child life.

"Midnight approaches." She turned her head against Rhiann's bracing shoulder. "The solstice. The darkest hour of the darkest day."

"Push," Nara ordered. "Push!"

"The bells, the bells strike the hour."

"There are no bells here, my lady." Rhiann watched the cloths go red with blood. Too much blood.

"In the City of Stars, Lorcan has the bells rung. For his celebration, he thinks. But they ring out for the child, for the beginning. Oh! Now!"

Rearing back, she pushed the child into life. She heard the cries and laughed through her own weeping.

"This is her hour, this is her time. The witching hour between night and day. I must hold her."

"You're weak, my lady." Nara passed the squalling baby to Rhiann.

"You know as well as I, I'm dying. Your skill, Nara, your herbs, even your magic can't stop my fate. Give me my child."

She held out her arms, and smiled at Rhiann. "You have a kind heart to weep for me."

"My lady."

"I must speak to Gwayne. Quickly," she said as Rhiann put the baby in her arms. "There's little time. Ah, there you are. There you are, my sweet girl." She pressed a kiss on the baby's head. "You've healed my heart, and now it tears in two again. Part to stay here with you, part to go to your father. How I grieve to leave you, my own. You will have his eyes, and his courage. My mouth, I think," she murmured and kissed it, "and what runs in my blood. So much depends on you. Such a small hand to hold the world."

She smiled over the baby's head. "She will need you," she said to Nara. "You will teach her what women need to know."

"You would put your child into the hands of a woman you don't know?"

"You heard the bells."

Nara opened her mouth, then sighed. "Yes, I heard them." And she had seen, with a woman's heavy heart, what would pass this night.

Gwayne came into the shelter, fell to his knees beside her. "My lady."

"She is Aurora. She is your light, your queen, your charge. Will you swear your fealty to her?"

"I will. I do."

"You cannot leave her."

"My lady, I must—"

"You cannot go back. You must swear to me to stay beside her. Keep her safe. You must swear on my blood that you will protect her as you have protected me." She took his hand, laid it on the child. "Gwayne, my white hawk. You are hers now. Swear it."

"I swear it."

"You will teach her what a warrior needs to know. She will stay with the Travelers. Hidden in the hills, and in the shadows of the forest. When it is time . . . you will know, you will tell her what she is." She turned the child so he could see the birthmark, a pale star, on the baby's right thigh. "All she is. Until then, Lorcan must not know of her. He will want her death above all things."

"I will guard her, on my life."

"She has her hawk, and her dragon watches from the highest point of the world," she murmured. "Her wolf will come when he's needed. Oh, my heart, my own." She pressed her lips to the child's cheeks. "This is why I was born, why I loved, why I died. And still, I grieve to leave you." She drew a trembling breath. "I give her into your hands." She held the baby out to Gwayne.

Then she held out her own hands, palms up. "I still have something left in me. She will have it." Light spun over her hands, whirled and caught the red, the gold from the fire. Then with a flash, what lay in Gwynn's hands became a star and a moon, both clear as ice.

"Keep them for her," she said to Nara.

The good queen closed her eyes and slipped away. The young queen wailed in the arms of a grieving soldier.

2

Seasons passed, and the world suffered under the harsh reign of King Lorcan. Small rebellions were crushed with a brutality that washed the land with blood and sent even the valiant into hiding. Faeries, witches, seers, and all who dwelt within the Realm of Magicks were outlawed and hunted like wild beasts by the mercenaries who came to be known as Lorcan's dogs.

Those who rose up against the usurper—and many who didn't—were executed. The dungeon in the castle filled with the tortured and forgotten, the innocent and the damned.

Lorcan grew rich, lining his coffers with taxes, increasing his holdings with land taken by force from those who had held it, worked it, honored it for generations. He dined off plates of gold and drank his wine from goblets of crystal while the people starved.

Those who spoke against him during the dark times spoke in whispers, and in secret.

Many of the displaced took to the high hills or the Lost Forest. There magic was practiced still, and the faithful searched the sky for portents of the True One who would vanquish the snake and bring light back to the world.

There, among the farmers and merchants, the millers and artists who had become outlaws, among the faeries and elves and witches with bounties on their heads, the Travelers roamed.

"Again!" Aurora thrust with the sword and thrilled to the ring of steel against steel. She drove her opponent back, parried, pivoted.

"Balance," Gwayne warned.

"I have my balance." To prove it, she leapt nimbly over the sword swept at her feet, landed lightly.

Swords crossed, slid hilt to hilt. And she came up with a dagger, pressing the point to his throat. "And the kill," she added. "I like to win."

Gwayne gave her a little poke with the dagger he held to her belly. "So do I."

She laughed, stepped back, then gave him a courtly bow. "We both died well. Sit. You're winded."

"I am not." But he was, and he rested on a stump while she fetched a skin of water.

She has her father's eyes, he thought. Gray as woodsmoke. And her mother's soft and generous mouth. Gwynn had been right—about so many things.

The child had grown into a lithe and lovely young woman, with skin the color of pale, pure honey, hair black as midnight. A strong chin, he judged, murmuring a thanks when she offered the water. Stubborn. He hadn't known a girl-child could *be* so stubborn.

There was a light in her, so bright he wondered that those who looked on her didn't fall to their knees. She was, though garbed in hunting green and worn boots, every inch a queen.

He had done what he had been asked. She was trained in the

ways of a warrior. In sword and arrow and pike, in hand against hand. She could hunt and fight and ride as well as any man he'd trained. And she could think. That was his pride in her.

Nara and Rhiann had schooled her in women's work, and in magicks. Rohan had tutored her in scholarly matters, and her mind, her thirsty mind, soaked up the songs, the stories of their people.

She could read and write, she could cipher and chart. She could make the cold fire with a thought, stitch a wound, and— these days—take him in a sword fight.

And still, how could a girl of barely twenty seasons lead her people into battle and save the world?

It haunted him at night when he lay beside Rhiann, who had become his wife. How could he honor his vow to keep her safe and honor his vow to tell her of her birthright?

"I heard the dragon in the night."

His fingers squeezed the skin. "What?"

"I heard it roar, in my dreams that were not dreams. The red dragon who flies in the night sky. And in his claws was a crown of stars. My wolf was with me." She turned her head, smiled at Gwayne. "He is always with me, it seems. So handsome and strong, with his sad eyes green as the grass on the Hills of Never."

Even speaking of the man she thought of as her wolf had her blood warming. "We lay on the floor of the forest and watched the sky, and when the dragon came with his crown, I felt such a thrill. Fear and wonder and joy. As I reached up, through a great wind that blew, the sky grew brighter than day, stronger than the faerie fire. And I stood beside my wolf in the blinding brightness, with blood at my feet."

She sat on the ground, resting her back against the stump. With a careless gesture, she flipped the long, fat braid she wore behind her shoulder. "I don't know what it means, but I wonder if I will fight for the True One. If his time draws near. I wonder if I will, at last, find the warrior who is my wolf and stand with him to lift my sword for the true king."

She had spoken of the wolf since she could form words—the boy, and now the man, she loved. But never before had she spoken of seeing the dragon. "Is that all the dream?"

"No." Comfortably, she rested her head against his knee. "In the dream that was not a dream, I saw a lady. A beautiful lady with green eyes and dark hair, and she wore the robes of royalty. She was weeping, so I said, My lady, why do you weep? She answered, I weep for the world while the world waits. It waits for the True One, I said to her, and asked, Why doesn't he come? When will he strike at Lorcan and bring peace to Twylia?"

Gwayne looked into the forest, gently stroking her hair. "What did she say to you?"

"She said the True One's hour is midnight, in birth, in death. Then she held out her hands, and in them were a globe, bright as the moon, and a star, clear as water. Take them, she told me. You will need them. Then she was gone."

She rubbed her cheek against his knee as the sadness she'd felt came back on her. "She was gone, Gwayne, and I ached in my heart. Beside me stood my wolf with his green eyes and dark hair. I think he was the True One, and that I'll fight for him. I think this dream was a portent, for when I woke, there was blood on the moon. A battle is coming."

Gwynn had said he would know when it was time. He knew, sitting in the quiet forest with spring freshening the air. He knew, and it grieved him.

"Not all battles are fought and won with the sword."

"I know. Mind and heart, vision and magic. Strategy and

treachery. I feel . . ." She rose, wandered away to pluck up a stone and cast it into the silver water of the river.

"Tell me what you feel."

She looked back. There was silver, bright as the river water, mixed with the gold of his hair, and in his beard. His eyes were a pale blue, and it seemed to her there was a shadow in them now. He was not her father. She knew her sire had fought and died in the Battle of the Stars, but Gwayne had been her father in all but blood all of her life.

There was nothing she couldn't tell him.

"I feel . . . as if something inside me is waiting, as the world is waiting. I feel there is something I must do, must be beyond what I am, what I do know." She hurried back to him, knelt at his feet. "I feel I must find my wolf. My love for him is so great, I will never know another. If he's the one of prophecy, I want to serve him. I honor what you've given me, Gwayne. You and Rhiann, Nara, and Rohan and all my family. But there's something inside me, stretching, growing restless, because it *knows*. It knows, but I can't see it."

She rapped a fist against his leg in frustration. "I can't see. Not yet. Not in my dreams or in the fire or the glass. When I seek, it's as if a film covers my vision and there are only shadows behind it. In the shadows I see the snake, and in the shadows my wolf is chained and bleeding."

She rose again, impatient with herself. "A man who might be king, a woman who was a queen. I know she was a queen, and she offered me the moon and a star. And while I wanted them with a kind of burning hunger, I feared them. Somehow, I know if I took them, everything would change."

"I have no magic. I'm only a soldier, and it's been too long since my courage was tested. Now I taste fear, and it makes me an old man."

"You're not old, and you're never afraid."

"I thought there would be more time." He got to his feet, just looked at her. "You're so young."

"Older than your Cyra, and she marries at the next equinox."

"The first year of your life I thought the days would never end, and time would never pass."

She laughed. "Was I so troublesome an infant?"

"Restless and willful." He reached out to touch her cheek. "Then time flew. And here we are. Come, sit with me on the riverbank. I have many things to tell you."

She sat with him, and watched a hawk circle in the sky. "There is your talisman. The hawk."

"Once, long ago, and most often behind my back, I was called the queen's hawk."

"The queen?" Aurora looked back sharply. "You were the queen's man? You never told me. You said you fought with my father in the great battle, but not that you were the queen's man."

"I told you that I brought your mother out of the city, into the Lost Forest. That Rohan and the Travelers took us in, and you were born that night in the snow."

"And she died giving me life."

"I didn't tell you that it was she who led me, and that I left the battle with her on orders from the king. She did not want to leave him." Though his words were spoken softly, his gaze was keen on her face. "She fought me. She was heavy with you, but still she fought like a warrior to stay with her king. With her husband."

"My mother." The breath caught in her throat. "In my dream. It was my mother."

"It was cold, and bitter, and she was in great pain. Body and heart. But she would not stop and rest. She guided me, and we came to the camp, to the place of your birth. She wept to leave you, and held you to her breast. She charged me to keep you safe, to train you, as she charged Nara to train you. To keep the truth of your birth from you until the time had come. Then she gave you to my hands, she put you in my hands."

He looked down at them now. "You were born at midnight. She heard the bells, miles away in the city. Your hour is midnight. You are the True One, Aurora, and as I love you, I wish it were another."

"How can this be?" Her heart trembled as she got to her feet, and she knew fear, the first true fear of her life. "How can I be the one? I'm no queen, Gwayne, no ruler."

"You are. It is your blood. From the first moment I held you in my hands, I knew this day would come. But beyond this I can see nothing." He rose, only to kneel before her. "I am the queen's man, and serve at your hand."

"Don't." Panicked, she dropped to her knees as well, gripped his shoulders. "By Draco and all the gods, what will I do? How could I have lived all my life in comfort, never knowing true hunger or hurts while the people of the world waited? How can I stand for them, free them, when I've hidden away like a coward while Lorcan rules?"

"You were kept in safety, your mother's dying wish." He stood, taking her arm to pull her up with him. "You have not been a coward. Nor will you shame the memory of your mother, your father, and play the coward now. This is your fate. I have trained you as a warrior. Be a warrior."

"I would fight." She slapped a hand to her sword as if to prove it. "I would pledge sword and magic, my *life*, without reserve. But to lead?" She drew a shaky breath and stared out over the river. "Nothing is as it was only a moment ago. I need time to think." She shut her eyes tightly. "To breathe. I need to be alone. Give me *time*, Gwayne," she said before he could argue.

"If you must break camp and move on, I'll find you. I need to find my way. Leave me." She stepped aside as he reached out to touch her. "Go."

When she knew she was alone, she stood by the banks of the silver river and grieved for her parents, her people, and herself.

And longed for the comfort of the lover she called her wolf.

✶

She walked deep into the forest, beyond the known and into the realm of faeries. There she cast the circle, made the fire, and sang the song for vision. She would see what had been—and what would be.

In the flames, while the moon rose and the single star that dogged it blinked to life, she saw the Battle of the Stars. She saw the bodies of servants, of children as well as soldiers. She saw the king—her father—fight like a demon, driving back the greater forces. She heard the screams, and smelled the blood.

Her father's voice came to her ears, a shouted order to Gwayne, who fought beside him, to get the queen, and the child she carried, to safety. To do this thing, as a soldier, even against the queen's orders, for the world. For the True One.

She saw her father's death, and her own birth. She tasted her mother's tears, and felt the force of love beam through the magic.

And with it, the force of duty.

"You will not shirk it."

"Am I enough?" Aurora asked the image of her mother.

"You are the True One. There is no other. You are hope, Aurora. And you are pride. And you are duty. You cannot turn from this."

Aurora watched the battle, and knew it was what would come, not what had. This blood, this death, would be by her own hands. On her own hands. Even if it meant her end, she must begin. "I have power, Mother, but it is a woman's power. Small magic. I'm strong, but I'm not seasoned. How can I lead, and rule, with so little to offer?"

"You will be more. Sleep now. Dream now."

So she dreamed again of her wolf, her warrior with eyes as green as the hills. He was tall, and broad of shoulder. His hair, dark as her own, swept back from a face of sharp planes and angles, and a white scar slashed through his left brow like a bolt of lightning. She felt a curling in her belly that she knew for desire, one she had felt for no one but him.

"What will you be to me?" she asked him. "What will I be to you?"

"I know only that you're my beloved. You and you alone. I've dreamed of you through my life, waking and sleeping, only of you." He reached out, and she felt the brush of his fingers over her cheek. "Where are you?"

"Close, I think. Close. Are you a soldier?"

He looked down at the sword in his hand, and as disgust rippled over his face he shoved its point into the ground. "I am nothing."

"I think you are many things, and one of those is mine." Giving in to curiosity, following her own will, she pulled him to her and pressed her lips to his.

The wind swirled around them, a warm wind stirred by the great beating of faerie wings. The song rose up inside her, and beat in her blood.

She would have love, she thought, even if death followed.

"I must be a woman to become what I am to become." She stepped back, drew off her hunting tunic. "Teach me what a woman knows. Love me in visions."

His gaze swept down her as she stood before him, dressed only in moonbeams within the shimmering circle of magic. "I've loved you all my life," he said. "And feared you."

"I've looked for you all of mine, and come to you here, fearing everything. Will you turn from me? Will I be alone?"

"I'll never turn from you." He drew her to him. "I'll never leave you."

With his lips on hers, he lowered her to the soft floor of the forest. She knew the thrill of his hands, the taste of his skin, and a pleasure, a deep and drugging pleasure that caused her body to quake. Flames leapt beside them, and inside her.

"I love you." She murmured it as she raced her lips over his face. "I'm not afraid."

She rose to him, opened to him, entreated. When he joined with her, she knew the power of being a woman, and the delights.

When she woke at dawn, alone, with the fire gone to ash, she knew the cold kiss of duty.

✶

"You should not have let her go alone."

Gwayne sat honing his sword while Rhiann scolded and made oatcakes. The morning sounds of the camp stirred around them. Horses, dogs, women cooking at pots, children chattering, and men readying to hunt.

"It was her wish." He spoke more sharply than he intended. "Her command. You fret over her like a mother."

"And what am I to her if not a mother? Two days, Gwayne, two nights."

"If she can't stay two nights alone in the forest, she can hardly rule Twylia."

"She's just a girl!" Rhiann slammed down her spoon. "It was too soon to tell her of this."

"It was time. I gave my oath on it, and it was time! Do you think I have no worries? Is there anything I would not do to keep her from harm, even to giving my life?"

She blinked back hot tears and took his hand. "No. No. But she is like our own, as much as Cyra and young Rhys are. I want her here, sitting by the fire, putting too much honey on her oatcake, laughing. It will never be like that again."

He set aside his sword to rise and take his wife in his arms. "She is not ours to keep."

Over Rhiann's head, he saw her come out of the forest, through the mists of the morning. She was tall—tall for a girl, he thought now. Straight as a soldier. She looked pale, but her eyes were clear. They met his, held.

"She is come," Gwayne said.

Aurora heard the murmurs as she walked through camp. They had been told, she thought, and now they waited. Her family, her friends, stood beside their colorful wagons, or stepped out of them to watch her.

She stopped, waited until all was quiet. "There is much to be done." She lifted her voice so that it echoed through camp, and beyond. "Eat, then come to me. I'll tell you how we will defeat Lorcan and take back our world."

Someone cheered. She saw it was young Rhys, barely twelve, and smiled back at him. Others took up the shouts, so that she walked through the celebration of them on her way to Gwayne.

Rhys dashed to her. "I'm not going to have to bow, am I?"

"You might, but not just now." She ruffled his mop of golden hair.

"Good. When do we fight?"

Her stomach clutched. He was a boy, only a boy. How many boys would she send into battle? And into death? "Soon enough."

She stepped to Gwayne, touched Rhiann's arm to comfort her. "I've seen the way," she said. "The way to begin. I'll need my hawk."

"I'm yours." He bowed, deep. "Majesty."

"Don't give me the title until I've earned it." She sat, took an oatcake, and drenched it with honey. Beside her, Rhiann buried her face in her apron and sobbed.

"Don't weep." Aurora rose again to gather Rhiann close. "This is a good day." She looked at Gwayne. "A new day. It's not only because of what's in my blood that I can do this, but because of what you've taught me. Both of you. All of you. You've given me everything I need to meet my destiny. Rhys, will you ask Nara and Rohan to join us and break fast?"

She pressed a kiss to Rhiann's cheek as Rhys ran off. "I've fasted for two days. I'm hungry," she said, and with a wide grin she sat to devour her oatcakes.

3

He had known her all his life, in his mind, in his heart. She came to him first as a child, laughing as she splashed in the silver river of a deep forest.

In those days they played together, as children do. And when he knew hunger and hurt, cold and a loneliness sharper than a blade, she would comfort him.

She called him her wolf. To him she was the light.

When they were no longer children, they walked together. He knew the sound of her voice, the scent of her hair, the taste of her lips.

She was his beloved, and though he thought her only a fantasy, he clung to her for his sanity. She was the single light in a world of darkness, the only joy in a world of despair.

With her he watched the dragon roar across the sky with the crown of prophecy in its claws. Through the magic light that followed, he saw the blood stain the ground at her feet, and he felt the smooth hilt of a sword in his hand.

But he dared not hope that he would be free, at long last, to lift that sword and serve her.

He dared not hope that she was real, and that someday she would belong to him.

✱

"Will you give me the gifts from my mother?" Aurora asked Nara.

"I've kept them for you. Rohan made this box, to keep them." An old woman with a face scored by many seasons, Nara held out a box of polished applewood, scribed with the symbol of star and moon. It had been the royal seal of Twylia before Lorcan had ordered all such symbols outlawed.

"It's beautiful. You honor my mother, Rohan."

"She was a great lady."

She opened the box and saw the clear globe, the clear star lying on dark velvet. Like the moon and star she'd seen in the night sky. "Conjured from love and grief, from joy and tears. Can there be stronger magic?"

When she lifted the globe, the light exploded in her hand. She saw through it, into the glass, into the world. Green fields sparkling in summer sunlight, wide rivers teeming with fish, thick forests where game grew fat. Cities with silver towers.

Men worked the fields, hunted the forests, fished the rivers, brought their wares to the city.

The mountains speared up, white at the peaks where the snow never melted. Beyond them, the Sea of Wonders fanned out. Other lands rose and spread. Other fields, other cities.

So they were not the world, she thought. But this was hers, to guard, to rule.

She took the star in her other hand and felt its heat, the flame of its power, fly into her.

"And the star shall burn with the blood of the dragon. Come as a lamb, mate with the wolf. Under truth is lies, under lies, truth. And valor holds its light under the coward's guise. When the witching hour comes, when the blood of the true one spills on the moon, the snake shall be vanquished, torn by the fangs of the wolf."

She swayed, lowered the crystals in her hands. "Who spoke?"

"You." Gwayne's voice was thin as he stared at her. Her hair had flown out as if on a wind, and her face had been full of light, her eyes full of power. Power that struck even a warrior with edges of fear and superstition.

"I am who I was. And more. It's time to begin. To tell you, tell everyone."

★

"I had visions," Aurora said when everyone gathered around. "Waking and dreaming. Some were shown and some were told to me, and some I know because it is my blood. I must go to the City of Stars and take my place on the throne."

"When do we march?" Rhys shouted, and was lightly cuffed by his father.

"We will march, and we'll fight, and some of us will fall. But the world will not be freed by only the slice of a sword. It is not only might that will win what was taken from us."

"Magic." Rohan nodded. "And logic."

"Magic, logic," Aurora agreed. "Strategy and steel. And wiles," she added with a sly smile. "A woman's wiles. Cyra, what was most talked of in the village where we last stopped for supplies?"

Cyra, a blooming sixteen, still struggled not to stare at Aurora with awe. "Prince Owen, son of Lorcan. He seeks a bride among the ranking ladies across Twylia. Orders have gone out for any knights or lords still with holdings to send their eligible daughters to the city."

"So Owen can pick and pluck," Aurora said with disgust. "There will be feasting, and a grand ball, will there not, while ladies are paraded before the son of the snake like mares at auction?"

"So it's said, my . . . my lady."

"My sister," Aurora corrected, and made Cyra smile. "I will go as the lamb. Can you make me look the lady, Rhiann?"

"To ride into the city unarmed—"

"I won't be unarmed." Aurora looked at the crystals, and the sword she'd laid beside them. "Or alone. I'll have an escort, as befits a lady of quality, and servants." She tugged the hem of her hunting tunic. "And a wardrobe. And so . . . garbed, I will gain access to the castle. I need men."

Excitement rose in her. What had been stretching inside her had found its shape. She bounded onto the table, lifted her voice. "I need men to ride out, to find the pockets of rebels, of soldiers whose swords grow dull and rusted, of their sons and daughters who would follow the True One. Find farmers willing to set aside their plows, and craftsmen willing to forge weapons for them. They must be trained, they must be forged, even as the weapons are forged, into an army. In secret, in haste."

She looked into the forest, into the deep green of summer. "I swear to you, before the first frost bites the air we will take the city, we will take the world, and I will have the head of the snake in my hand."

She looked down at Gwayne. "Will you raise my army?"

His soldier's heart thrilled. "I will, my lady."

"When it's time to strike, I'll send you a sign. You'll know it. Rohan, I need your maps, and your logic."

"You'll have them."

"Rhiann." Aurora spread her arms. "I need a gown."

✴

She was groomed and tutored, gowned and schooled. Even as Rhiann and those she deemed could run a passable seam worked on silks and velvets, Aurora practiced with sword and arrow.

She gritted her teeth as lotions were rubbed into her skin, as Cyra practiced dressing her hair. And she planned her strategy over bowls of mead, read dispatches from Gwayne, and sent them.

It was the far edge of summer when she set out, garbed in a traveling cloak of dark blue, with Cyra and Rhiann as her handmaidens and Rohan, young Rhys, and three other men as her escorts.

She would play her part, Aurora promised herself. The gods knew she looked the pampered lady. She would charm and beguile, seduce if need be. And she would take the castle from the inside, while the army Gwayne was training came over the city walls.

It was a long journey, but she was grateful for the time. She used it to hone her vision, gather her courage, strengthen her purpose.

The fields were still green, she noted, whoever ruled. But she'd seen the fear, the distrust, and the anger in the eyes of men they passed on the road. She'd seen the crows picking at the bones of those who had been unlucky enough to be set upon by thieves, or Lorcan's dogs.

Children, their faces pinched with hunger, begged for food or coin. She saw what was left of homes that had been burned to the ground, and the desperate eyes of women with no man left to protect them.

Had she not looked so closely before? Aurora wondered. Had

she been so content to run through the forest, to sing in the hills, that she hadn't seen the utter despair of her people, the waste of her land?

She would give her life to put it right again.

"It seems so strange to see Grandfather garbed so richly," Cyra said.

"You must not call him Grandfather."

"No, I'll remember. Are you afraid, Aurora?"

"I am. But it's a good fear. The kind that tells me something will happen."

"You look beautiful."

Aurora smiled, and struggled not to tug at the confining gown. "It's only another weapon, and one I find I don't mind wielding. A sprinkle of witchcraft and . . . he'll look on me, won't he, this son of a demon? He'll look on me and want?"

"Any man would."

Satisfied, Aurora nodded. While he looked, and wanted, she would seek another. She would seek her wolf.

He was there. Waiting. She felt him in her blood, and with every league they traveled, that blood warmed.

She would find her love, at last, in the City of Stars.

And her destiny.

"Oh, look!" Cyra bounced in her seat. "The city. See how the towers shine."

Aurora saw it, in the distance, the silver and gilt that spread up into the sky. The grand towers of the castle gleamed, and on the topmost, the black flag with its coiled red snake flew.

She would burn it, she vowed. Burn it to ash and hoist her family crest in its place. The gold dragon on its white field would fly again.

"Twenty men on the castle walls," Rohan said quietly as he rode his mount sedately toward her.

"Yes, I see them. And more at the city gates. He will have a personal guard as well, others at the castle gates. Some will slip away once Lorcan is dead, some will certainly join our cause. But others will fight. We'll need to know the castle, every foot of it. Gwayne's drawings are a start, but it's likely Lorcan has changed some of it over the years."

"On the sweat and blood of the people," Rohan agreed. "Building fine rooms and thicker walls." He had to remind himself not to spit. "However fine the gilt, he's turned the City of Stars into the pit of a snake."

"And I will bury him in it."

She fixed a bored expression on her face, and watched everything, as they rode through the gates of the city.

✳

In the stables, Thane groomed the roan mare. He worked alone, and the work was endless. But he was used to that, to the aching muscles, the weary bones at the end of the day.

And he had come to prize his solitude.

He loved the horses. That was his secret. If Owen and Lorcan knew he enjoyed them, they would cast him out of the stables and the dim quiet that brought him some measure, at least, of peace. They would find him other drudgery, he thought. It pleased them to do so. He was used to that as well.

He'd learned as a very young boy to keep his words and his opinions to himself, to do his work, expect nothing—unless it was the heel of a boot in the ass. As long as he controlled his temper, his fury, his hatred, he had the gift of alone.

And those he loved were safe.

The mare blew softly as he ran a hand over her silky neck. For a moment, Thane laid his cheek to hers, shut his eyes. He was exhausted. Dreams plagued him, night after night, so that he woke hot and hard and needy. Voices and visions ran through his head and gave him no answers, and no relief.

Even his light, his love, brought a strange restlessness to him.

He could not war, could not find peace, so there seemed nothing for him but hours of work.

He stepped away from the mare, ran a hand through his unruly black hair. He would have gone to the next mount, but something stirred in his belly, a kind of hunger that had nothing to do with desire for food.

He felt his heart thudding in his chest as he walked past the stalls, toward the stable entrance, where the light fell like a curtain of gold.

He lifted his hand to shield his eyes from the glare and saw her, his vision, mounted on a white stallion. Blood roared into his head, made him giddy as he stared.

She was smiling, her lashes downcast. And he knew—he *knew* the eyes they hid were gray as smoke. Dimly, he heard her voice, heard her laugh—how well he knew that voice, that laugh—as she offered Owen her hand.

"Servants will see to your horses, my lady . . ."

"I am Aurora, daughter of Ute of the westland. My father sends his regrets for not accompanying me to honor you, Prince Owen. He is unwell."

"He is forgiven for sending such a jewel."

She did her best to work up a flush, and fluttered her lashes. He was handsome, with the look of a young, golden god. Unless you looked in his eyes, as she did. There was the snake. He was his father's son.

"You flatter me, sir, and I thank you. I must beg your indulgence. My horses are precious to me, I fear I fret over them like a hen over chicks. I'd like to see the stables, if you please, and speak with the grooms about their care."

"Of course." He put his hands around her waist. She didn't stiffen as she wished to, but smiled prettily as he lifted her down.

"The city is magnificent." She brushed a hand over her headdress as if to fuss it into place. "A country lass like myself is awed by so much"—she looked back at him now, deliberately provocative—"glamour."

"It dulls before you, Lady Aurora." Then he turned, and she saw his handsome face go hard with temper and those dark eyes gleam with hate.

She followed his glance and felt her world tilt.

She had found her wolf. He was dressed in rags, with the sweat of labor staining them. His dark hair curled madly around a face smudged with stable dirt. And in his hand he carried not a sword but a currycomb.

Their eyes met, and in that single instant she felt the shock of knowledge, and of disbelief.

He took one step toward her, like a man in a trance.

In three strides, Owen stormed to Thane and used the back of his hand to deliver a vicious blow that drew blood. For an instant, only an instant, rage flamed in Thane's eyes. Then he lowered them, as Owen struck again.

"On your knees, worthless cur. You dare cast your eyes on a lady. You'll be whipped for this insult."

Head down, Thane lowered to his knees. "Your pardon, my lord prince."

"If you have time to stand and stare at your betters, you must not have enough to do." Owen pulled out his riding crop, raised it.

To Aurora's disappointment, the wolf of her visions stayed down like a cowed dog.

"Prince Owen." Her knees shook, and her heart thundered. Every instinct had to be denied. She couldn't go to him, speak to him. She must instead play the pampered lady. However it scored her pride, Aurora laid the back of her hand on her brow and pretended to swoon. "I can't bear violence," she said weakly when he rushed back to catch her. "I feel . . . unwell."

"Lady, I'm sorry you had to witness such a . . . display." He looked down on Thane with derision. "This stableboy has some skill with horses, but too often forgets his place."

"Please, don't punish him on my account. I couldn't bear the thought of it." She waved a hand, and after a moment's confusion, Cyra rushed forward with a bottle of salts to hold under Aurora's nose.

"Enough, enough." Aurora nudged her away as the salts made her eyes water. "If you could assist me, my lord, out of the sun?"

"Forgive me, Lady Aurora. Let me take you inside, offer you some refreshment."

"Oh, yes." She leaned against him. "Traveling is so wearing, isn't it?"

She let him lead her away from the stables. Her heart was heavy to find her wolf, at last, and learn he had neither fang nor claw.

Feigning light-headedness, she let herself be led across a courtyard and into the keep. And she noted every detail. The number of guards and their weapons, the richness of the tapestries and tiles, the placement of windows and doors and stairs.

She noted the stone faces and downcast eyes of servants, and the demeanor of the other women, other ladies brought in like broodmares for display.

Some, it seemed to her, were pleased to be considered worthy of Prince Owen's regard. In others, she saw fear lurking in the eyes.

Women were chattel under Lorcan's reign. Property to be

owned by father, husband, brother, or any man with the price. Any suspected of witchcraft were burned.

Women were lesser creatures, Rohan had told her, in Lorcan's world. All the better, she thought. He would hardly suspect that the True One was a woman, and that she bided under his roof until she could slit his throat.

She fluttered and flushed and begged Owen that she be taken to her chambers to rest away the fatigue of the journey.

When she had safely arrived there, she balled her hands into fists. "Simpleton. Bully. Bastard." She took a deep breath and fought for control. "Calling him prince makes my tongue ache."

"He was cruel to that boy," Rhiann murmured.

"It wasn't a boy, but a man. A man without a backbone." With a hiss of rage, she dropped into a chair. The man of her dreams would not grovel in the dirt. She would *not* love a man who would beg pardon of an ass.

So she would forget him. She had to forget him and her woman's heart, and do what came next.

"We're inside," she said to Rhiann. "I'll write a dispatch to Gwayne. See that it's sent today."

4

Aurora dressed with great care in a gown of blue velvet piped with gold. With Cyra's help her heavy hair was tamed into a gold snood. She wore small blue stones at her ears, a delicate pearl cross at her throat. And a dagger strapped to her thigh.

After practicing her smiles and simpers in the glass, she deemed herself ready. She wandered the gallery, knowing that the art and furnishings there had been stolen from her parents or looted from other provinces. She gazed out the windows at the gardens and mazes and lands that had been tended by her fore-bears, then taken by force for another's pride and greed.

And she noted the numbers and locations of guards at every post. She swept down the stairs, meandered into rooms, watched the servants and guests and courtiers.

It pleased her to be able to move freely through the castle, around the gardens. What threat was a woman after all, she thought as she stopped to smell the golden roses and study the rank of guards along the seawall. She was simply a candidate for Owen's hand, sent to offer herself like a ripe fruit for the plucking.

"Where is the music?" she asked Cyra. "Where is the laughter? There are no songs in Lorcan's kingdom, no joy. He rules shadows."

"You will bring back the light."

"I swear that I will." Or die in the attempt, she vowed silently. "There's such beauty here, but it's like beauty trapped behind a locked glass. Imprisoned, waiting. We must shatter the glass."

She rounded a bend in the path and saw a woman seated on a bench with a young girl kneeling at her feet, weeping. The woman wore a small crown atop her golden hair. She looked brittle and thin in her rich robes, and though her face held beauty, it was pale and tired.

"She who calls herself queen." Aurora spoke softly and fought to keep the fury out of her eyes. "Lorcan's wife, who was my mother's woman. There's time before the banquet. We'll see if she can be of use."

Folding her hands at her waist, Aurora stepped forward. She saw the queen start, saw her hand close tight over the girl's shoulder. "Majesty." Aurora dropped into a deep curtsy. "I am Lady Aurora, and beg pardon for disturbing you. May I help?"

The girl had shut off her tears, and though her pretty face was ravaged by them, she got to her feet, bowed. "You are welcome, lady. You will excuse my behavior. It was only a childish trifle that had me seeking my mother's knee. I am Dira, and I welcome you to the City of Stars and our home."

"Highness." Aurora curtsied, then took the hand the queen offered.

"I am Brynn. I hope you have all that you require here."

"Yes, my lady. I thought to walk the gardens before the sun set. They are so lovely, and with summer nearly done, transient."

"It grows cold at twilight." Brynn gathered her cloak at her throat as if she could already feel the oncoming winter. When Brynn rose, Aurora noted that her eyes were strongly blue, and unbearably sad. "Will you accompany us inside? It's nearly time for feasting."

"With pleasure, my lady. We live quiet in the west," she continued. "I look forward to the dancing and feasting, and the time with other women."

"Partridges and peahens," Dira whispered.

"Dira!"

But Aurora laughed over the queen's sharp rebuke, and glanced at the girl with more interest. "So we must seem to you, Highness. Country girls parading in their finery with hopes that Prince Owen will show favor."

"I meant no offense."

"And none was given. It must be wearying to have so much female chattering about day and night. You'll be happy, I'm sure, when the prince has chosen his bride. Then you will have a sister, will you not?"

Dira looked away, toward the seawall. "So it would seem."

A shadow crossed the path, and Aurora would have sworn the world went still.

Lorcan, self-proclaimed king of Twylia, stood before them.

He was tall and strongly built. His hair, nearly copper in color, spilled to the shoulders of his purple cloak. Jewels glinted in his crown, on his fingers. His sharply ridged face had the devil's own beauty, and so cold was the blue of his eyes that Aurora wasn't surprised to feel the queen tremble beside her.

"You dally in the garden while our guests wait? You sit and dream when you are commanded to take your place?"

"Your Majesty." Going with instinct, Aurora lowered herself to one knee at the king's feet, and used a small dash of power to draw his attention and thought to her and away from his wife. "I most humbly beg your pardon for detaining Queen Brynn with my witless chatter. Her Majesty was too kind to send me away and she sought to soothe my foolish nerves. I am to blame for the lateness of her arrival." She looked up and put what she hoped was the slightest light of flirtation in her eyes. "I was nervous, sire, to meet the king."

It was, she realized as his taut mouth relaxed, the right touch. He reached down, lifted her chin. "And who is this dark flower?"

"Sire, I am Aurora, daughter of Ute, and the foolish woman who has earned your displeasure."

"They grow them fair in the west. Rise." He drew her to her feet and studied her face so boldly she didn't have to fake a blush. Though it came more from temper than modesty. "You will sit beside me at tonight's banquet."

Luck or fate had blessed her, Aurora thought, and laid her hand on his. "I am undeserving, and grateful for the honor, sire."

"You will entertain me," he said as he led her inside, without, Aurora noted, another glance at his wife or daughter. "And perhaps show me why my son should consider you for wife."

"The prince should consider me, sire, so that I might continue to entertain you, and serve you as a daughter would, all of your days."

He glanced back at Dira now, with thinly veiled disgust. "And how might a daughter serve me?"

"To do her duty. At the king's pleasure, sire, and at her husband's. To bear strong sons and to present a pleasing face and form. To do their bidding day and . . . night."

He laughed, and when he stepped inside the crowded and brightly lit banquet hall, Aurora was at his side.

*

Thane watched from the spy hole in the secret chamber beside the minstrel's gallery. From there he could look down on the feasting, and the lights and the colors. At the scent of roasted meat his empty belly clutched, but he was used to hunger. Just as he was used to standing in the shadows and looking out on the color and the light.

He could hear women's laughter as the ladies vied for Owen's attention and favor, but there was only one who drew Thane's interest.

She sat beside the king, smiling, sampling the delicacies he piled on her plate, flirting with her eyes over the rim of her goblet.

How could this be the same creature who had come to him in dream and vision the whole of his life? The woman who had offered him such love, such passion, and such shining honesty? This coy miss with her sly smiles and trilling laugh could never make him burn as her light made him burn.

Yet he burned, even now, just watching her.

"Your back needs tending."

Thane didn't turn. Kern appeared when and where he chose, as faeries were wont to do. And was as much bane as blessing.

"I've been whipped before. It'll heal soon enough."

"Your flesh may." Kern waved a hand and the wall between them and the banquet hall shimmered away. "But your heart is another matter. She is very beautiful."

"A fair face is easy beauty. She isn't what I thought she was . . . would be. I don't want her."

Kern smiled. "One doesn't always want destiny."

Thane turned. Kern was old, old as time. His long gray beard covered plump cheeks and spun down to the waist of his bright red robes. But his eyes were merry as a child's, and green as the Lost Forest.

"You show me these things. This woman, this world, and you hint of changes, of restoration." Frustration edged Thane's voice and hardened his face. "You train me for battle, and you heal my hurts when Owen or Lorcan or one of their dogs beats me. But what good does it do me? My mother, my young sister, are no more than prisoners still. And Leia—"

"She is safe. Have I not told you?"

"Safe, at least." Struggling to compose himself, Thane looked back at the feasting, at little Dira. "One sister safe, and lost to me, the other trapped here until she's old enough for me to find sanctuary for her. There will never be one for my mother. She grows so thin."

"She worries for you, for her daughters."

"Leia bides with the women in the Valley of Secrets, at least for now. And Dira is yet too young for the snake to pay her mind—or to plan to marry her off to some slathering lackey. She need not worry for them. She need not think of me at all. I am nothing but a coward who hides his sword."

"It's not cowardice to hide your sword until the time comes to wield it. The time draws near."

"So you always say," Thane replied, and though he knew that Kern's magick kept those who were feasting from seeing him above them, he felt Aurora's gaze as it scanned the gallery. He knew she looked at him, just as he looked at her. "Is she a witch, then, and the visions between us an amusement to her?"

"She is many things."

Thane shook his head. "It doesn't matter. She isn't for me, nor I for her. That was fantasy and foolishness, and is done. It's Dira who concerns me now. Another two years, then Lorcan will seek to marry her off. Then she must be sent away from here, for her own safety. My mother will have no daughter to comfort her, and no son to stand for her."

"You are no good to them dead." Kern's voice went sharp as honed steel. "And no good to any when you wallow in pity."

"Easily said when your time is spent in a raft, and mine in a stable. I gave up my pride, Kern, and have lived without it since my seventh season. Is it so surprising I should be ready to give up my hope?"

"If you do, it will be the end for you."

"There are times I'd welcome the end." But he looked at Dira. She was so young. Innocent and defenseless. He thought of how she had wept to find him beaten and bleeding in the stables. It hurt her, he knew, more than the lash hurt him. Lorcan's blood might have run through her, but she had none of his cruelty.

She was, he thought, his only real pleasure since Leia's escape. So he would hold on to his hope a while longer, for her.

"I don't give up yet," Thane said quietly. "Not yet. But it had best be soon."

"Come, then, let me tend your wounds."

"No." Thane rolled his shoulders, welcomed the pain. "It reminds me. I have work."

"When it's done, meet me. It's time to practice."

★

Fingertip to fingertip, Aurora circled with Owen in a dance. The music was lively, and pleased her a great deal more than her partner. But he couldn't have known of her displeasure as she smiled at him and sent him a laughing glance over her shoulder when the set parted them.

When the music brought them together again, he stroked his thumb over her knuckles. "The king has favored you."

"I am honored. I see much of him in you, my lord."

"When it's my time to rule, I will outreach him." His fingers squeezed hers. "And I will demand much more of my queen than he of his."

"And what does your father demand of his queen?"

"Little more than obedience." He looked over to where Brynn sat, like a statue, with her women. "A comely face, a bowed head, and two pale daughters will not be enough for me."

"Two?"

"Dira is the youngest of Brynn's whelps. There was another, but she was killed by wild beasts in the Black Forest."

"Wild beasts!" Though she couldn't manage a squeal, Aurora clasped a hand to her breast.

"Do not fear, my lady." He smirked. "There are no beasts in the city—none that walk on four legs."

The figures of the dance parted them again, and Aurora executed her turns, her curtsies, and counted the beats impatiently until she faced Owen once more. With her head saucily angled, she stared into his eyes. "And what would be enough for you, my lord, for a queen?"

"Passion. Fire. Sons."

"There must be fire in bed to get sons." She lowered her voice, and spoke with her face close to his. "I would burn to be the mother of kings."

Then she stepped back, dipped low as the dance ended.

"Walk with me."

"With pleasure, sir. But I must have my woman with me, as is proper."

"Do you do only what is proper?"

"A queen would, when eyes are on her."

He lifted a brow in approval. "A brain as well as beauty. Bring her, then."

Aurora put her hand in his and gestured carelessly with the other so Cyra followed them out onto the terrace. "I like the sea," she began, looking out over the cliffs. "The sounds and the smells of it. It's a wall to the back, protection from enemies. But it's also passion, and possibilities. Do you believe there are worlds beyond the world, my lord prince?"

"Tales for children."

"If there were, a king could rule them all, and the sons of such a king would be gods. Even Draco would bow."

"Draco's power is weak, so he sulks in his cave. This"— Owen laid a hand on the hilt of his sword—"this is power."

"A man's power is in his sword and arm, a woman's is in her mind and womb."

"And her heart?" Now he laid a hand on her breast.

Though her skin crawled, she smiled easily. "Not if she gives that heart away." She touched her fingers lightly to his wrist, then eased away. "If I were to do so, my lord, to offer you my heart and my body, my value to you would diminish. A prize easily taken is little prize at all. So I will bid you good night, and hope you consider what I hold to be worth the winning."

"You would leave me with so many choices?" He gestured toward the women in the banquet hall as Aurora moved away.

"So you will see them . . . but think of me." She left him with a laugh, then turned to a mumbled oath when she was certain she was out of earshot.

"Empty-headed, fat-fingered *toad*! He's a man who thinks first with the lance between his legs. Well, there is little warrior in him. I've learned that much at least. Cyra, I need you to talk with the other women, find out all you can about the queen and her daughters. What are they in this puzzle?"

She cut herself off as they walked past guards and began to

talk brightly of the feasting and dancing until she was back in her chambers.

"Rhiann." She let out a huge sigh. "Help me out of this gown. How do women of court bear the weight every day? I need the black tunic."

"You're going out again?"

"Yes. I felt eyes on me when I was at banquet. Eyes from above. Gwayne said there was a spy hole next to the minstrel's gallery. I want a look. Would Lorcan station guards there during a feast? He seems too sure of himself to bother."

No, it had not been guards watching her, Aurora knew. It had been the grass-green eyes of her wolf. She needed to learn why he'd been there.

"And I need to see how the castle is protected during the night." She pulled on her tunic. "I have enough magic to go unnoticed if need be. Did you learn anything of use?" she asked as she strapped on her sword.

"I learned that Owen went back and beat the stable hand after all."

Aurora's mouth tightened. "I'm sorry for it."

"And that the stable hand is Thane, son of Brynn, whom Lorcan took as queen."

Aurora's hands paused in the act of braiding her hair, and her eyes met Rhiann's in the glass. "Brynn's son is cast to the stables? And remains there? His father was a warrior who died in battle beside mine. His mother was my own mother's handmaid. Yet their son grovels at Owen's feet and grooms horses."

"He was not yet four when Lorcan took the throne. Only a child."

"He is not a child today." She swirled on her cloak, drew up the hood. "Stay inside," she ordered.

She slipped out of the chamber, moved silently down the corridors toward the stairs. She drew on her magic to bring smoke into the air, blunt the guards' senses as she hurried by them.

She dashed up to the minstrel's gallery and found the mechanism Gwayne had described for her to open the secret room beside it. Once inside, she approached the spy hole and looked down at the hall.

It was nearly empty now, and servants were beginning to clear the remnants of the feast. The queen had retired, and all but the boldest ladies had followed suit. The laughter had taken on a raucous edge. She saw one of the courtiers slide his hand under the bodice of a woman's gown and fondle her breast.

She hadn't been sheltered from the ways of men and women. The Travelers could be earthy, but there was always a respect and good nature. This, she thought, had neither.

She turned away from it, and focused instead on the essence of what had been in the room before her.

One that was human, she thought, and one that was not. Man and faerie-folk. But what had been their purpose?

To find out, she followed the trail of that essence from the room and out of the castle. Into the night.

There were guards posted on walls, at the gates, but to Aurora's eyes they looked sleepy and dull. Even two hundred good men, she calculated, could take the castle if it was done swiftly and with help from inside. As she worked her way along the wall, she heard the snores of a guard sleeping on duty.

Lorcan, she thought, took much for granted.

She looked toward the south gate. It was there that Gwayne had fled with the queen on the night of the battle. Many brave men had lost their lives so that her mother could escape, so that she could be born.

She would not forget it. And she would take nothing for granted.

Her senses drew her toward the stables. She smelled the horses, heard them shifting in their stalls as she approached. Though she scented man as well—sweat and blood—she knew she wouldn't find him there.

She stopped to stroke her horse's nose, to inspect the stall, and others. Whatever Thane was, he did his job here well. And lived poorly, she noted as she studied the tiny room that held his bedding, the stub of a candle, and a trunk of rough clothes.

Following the diagram in her mind, she searched the floor for the trapdoor that led to the tunnels below the stables. One channel ran to the sea, she remembered, the other to the forest.

It would be a good route to bring in her soldiers, to have them take the castle from the inside. If Lorcan hadn't found it and destroyed it.

But when she opened the door, she felt the air stir. Taking the candle stub, she lit the wick and let its wavery light guide her down the rough steps.

She could hear the roar of the sea, and though she was tempted to take that channel, just to stand by the water, to breathe it in, she turned toward the second path.

She would have Gwayne bring the men through the forest, split into companies. Some to take the walls, others to take the tunnels. Attack the walls first, she calculated, drawing Lorcan's forces there while the second wave came in from under—and behind.

Before he could turn and brace for the second assault, they would run him over. And it would be done.

She prayed that it could be done, and that she would not be sending good men to their deaths for nothing.

She moved slowly through the dark. The low ceiling made it impossible to stand upright, and she could imagine the strain of a man making the same trek in full armor.

And it would be done not after a night of feasting and dancing but after a hard march from the hills, through the forest, with the knowledge that death could wait at the end of the journey.

She was asking this of her people, and asking that they trust the fates that she would be worthy of their sacrifice. That she would be a worthy queen.

She stopped, bracing her back against the wall of stone and dirt as her heart ached. She would wish with every ounce of her blood that it was not so. That she was only an ordinary woman and could leap onto her horse and ride with the Travelers again, as she had always done. She would wish that she could hunt and laugh, love a man and bear his children. Live a life that she understood.

But to wish it was to wish against the fates, to diminish the sacrifices her parents had made, and to turn her back on those who prayed for the True One to come and bring them back into light.

So she lifted her candle again and headed down the tunnel to plot out her strategy.

When she heard the clash of steel, she drew her own sword. Snuffing out the candle, she set it down and moved soft as a cat toward the narrow opening.

She could see them battling in the moonlight, the young man and the old. And neither noticed as she boosted herself out of the tunnel and crouched on the floor of the forest.

5

Here was her wolf, and she thrilled to see him.

He fought with an icy focus and relentless strength that Aurora admired and respected—and envied. The skill, yes, the skill of a warrior was there, but it was enhanced by that cold-blooded, cold-eyed style that told her he would accept death or mete it out with equal dispatch.

The faerie was old, it was true, but a faerie nonetheless. Such creatures were not vanquished easily.

She could see the sweat of effort gleaming on Thane's face, and how it dampened his shirt. And she saw the blood that seeped onto the cloth from the wounds on his back, still fresh from a lashing.

How could a man wield a sword with such great talent and allow himself to be flogged?

And why had he watched the feasting through the spy hole? It was his gaze she had sensed on her. And his essence she had sensed there. His, and that of the old graybeard he battled now.

Even as she puzzled it over, two columns of smoke spiraled on either side of Thane. And became armed warriors. He blocked the sword of the one on his right and spun away from the sword of the one on his left as it whizzed through the air.

Raising her own, Aurora leapt. She cleaved her blade through one of the warriors and vanished it back to smoke. "Foul play, old one." She pivoted, and would have struck Kern down if Thane hadn't crossed swords with her.

"At your back," she snapped out, but the warrior was smoke again with a wave of Kern's hand.

"Lady," the faerie said with an undeniable chuckle, "you mistake us. I only help my young friend with his training." To prove it, Kern lowered his sword and bowed.

"Why am I dreaming?" Thane demanded. He was out of breath as he hadn't been during the bout, and the surging of his blood had nothing to do with swordplay. "What test is this?"

"You are not dreaming," Kern assured him.

"She's not real. I've seen her now, in flesh. And this is the vision, not the woman." Love, lust, longing knotted inside him so that he fought to ice his words with annoyance. "And neither holds interest for me any longer."

"I'm as real as you," Aurora tossed back, then sheathing her sword, she twisted her lips into a sneer. "You fight well. For a groveling stableboy. And your sword would be all that interests me, if I believed you'd gather the courage and wit to use it on something more than smoke."

"So, no vision, then, but the simpering, swooning female." He lifted the cape she'd tossed aside when she leapt to his defense. With a mocking bow, he held it out. "Go back to your feather bed, else you catch a chill."

"I'm chilled enough from you." She knocked his hand aside and turned on Kern. "Why haven't you treated his wounds?"

"He doesn't wish it."

"Ah, he's stupid, then." She inclined her head toward Thane again. "Whether you are stupid or not, I regret you were beaten on my account."

"It's nothing to do with you." Because the beating still shamed him, he rammed his sword back into its sheath. "It's not safe for a woman alone beyond the walls. Kern will show you the way back."

"I found my way out, I can find my way back. I'm not some helpless female," she said impatiently. "You of all men should know—"

"I do not know you," Thane said dully.

She absorbed the blow to her heart. They stood in the dappled moonlight, with only the call of an owl and the rushing of a stream over rocks to break the silence between them.

Even knowing the risk of mediation, Kern stepped up, laying a hand on Thane's shoulder, the other on Aurora's. "Children," he began brightly.

"We're not children any longer. Are we, lady? Not children splashing in rivers, running through the forest." It scored his heart to remember it, to remember the joy and pleasure, the simple comfort of those times with her. To know they were ended forever. "Not children taking innocent pleasure in each other's company."

She shook her head, and thought how she had lain with him, in love, in visions. Him and no other. "I wonder," she said after a moment, "why we need to hurt each other this way. Why we strike out where we once—where we always reached out. And I fear you're right. You don't know me, nor I you. But I know you're the son of a warrior, you have noble blood. Why do you sleep in the stables?"

"Why do you smile at Lorcan, dance with Owen, then wander the night with a sword?"

She only smiled. "It's not safe for a woman alone beyond the walls." There was, for just an instant, a glint of humor in his eyes. "You watched me dance."

He cursed himself for speaking of it. Now she knew of the spy hole as well as the tunnels. And one word to Owen . . . "If you wish to make amends for the beating, you won't speak of seeing me here."

"I have no reason to speak of you at all," she said coolly. "I was told faeries no longer bided near the city."

At her comment Kern shrugged. "We bide where we will, lady, even under Lorcan's reign. Here is my place, and he is my charge."

"I am no one's charge. Are you a witch?" Thane demanded.

"A witch is one of what I am." He looked so angry and frustrated. How she longed to stroke her finger over the lightning-bolt scar above his eye. "Do you fear witchcraft, Thane of the stables?"

Those eyes fired at the insult, as she'd hoped. "I don't fear you."

"Why should an armed man and his faerie guard fear a lone witch?"

"Leave us," Thane demanded of Kern, and his gaze stayed locked on Aurora's face.

"As you wish." Kern bowed deeply, then disappeared.

"Why are you here?"

"Prince Owen needs a wife. Why shouldn't it be me?"

He had to choke down a rage, bubbling black, at the thought of it. "Whatever you are, you're not like the others."

"Why? Because I walk alone at night in the Black Forest, where wild beasts are said to roam?"

"You're not like the others. I know you. I do know you, or what you were once." He had to curl his hand into a fist to keep from touching her. "I've seen you in my dreams. I've tasted your mouth. I'll taste it again."

"In your dreams perhaps you will. But I don't give my kisses to cowards who fight only smoke."

She turned, and was both surprised and aroused when he gripped her arm and dragged her around. "I'll taste it again," he repeated.

Even as he yanked her close, she had the point of her dagger at his throat. "You're slow." She all but purred it. "Release me. I don't wish to slit your throat for so small an offense."

He eased back and, when she lowered the dagger, moved like lightning. He wrested the dagger from her hand, kicked her feet out from under her before she could draw her sword. The force of the fall knocked the wind out of her, and she was pinned under him before she could draw a breath.

"You're rash," he told her, "to trust an enemy."

She had to swallow the joy, and the laugh. They'd wrestled like this before, when there had been only love and innocence between them. Here was her man, after all.

"You're right. The likes of you would have no honor."

With the same cold look in his eyes that she'd seen when he fought, he dragged her arms over her head. She felt the first licks of real fear, but even that she held tight. No groveling stableboy could make her fear. "I will taste you again. I will take something. There has to be something."

She didn't struggle. He'd wanted her to, wanted her to spit and buck and fight him so he wouldn't have to think. For one blessed moment, not to think but only feel. But she went still as stone when he crushed his lips to hers.

Her taste was the same, the same as he'd imagined, remembered, wished. Hot and strong and sweet. So he couldn't think, after all, but simply sank into the blessed relief of her.

And all the aches and misery, the rage and the despair, washed out of him in the flood of her.

She didn't fight him, as she knew she wouldn't win with force. She remained still, knowing that a man wanted response—heat, anger, or acquiescence, but not indifference.

She didn't fight him, but she began to fight herself as his mouth stirred her needs, as the weight of his body on hers brought back wisps of memories.

She'd never really been with a man, but only with him in visions, in dreams. She had wanted no man but him, for the whole of her life. But what she'd found wasn't the wolf she'd known, nor the coward she thought she'd found. It was a bitter and haunted man.

Still, her heart thundered, her skin trembled, and beneath his, her mouth opened and offered. She heard him speak, one word, in the oldest tongue of Twylia. The desperation in his voice, the pain and the longing in it made her heart weep.

The word was "Beloved."

He eased up to look at her. There was a tear on her cheek, and more in her eyes where the moonlight struck them. He closed his own eyes and rolled onto his bloody back.

"I've lived with horses too long, and forget how to be a man."

She was shaken to the bone from her feelings, from her needs, from the loss. "Yes, you forget to be a man." As she had forgotten to be a queen. "But we'll blame this on the night, on the strangeness of it." She got to her feet, walked over to pick up her dagger. "I think perhaps this is some sort of test, for both of us. I've loved you as long as I remember."

He looked at her, into her, and for one moment that was all there was, the love between them. It shimmered, wide and deep as the Sea of Wonders. But in the next moment the heavy hand of duty took over.

"If things were different . . ." Her vision blurred—not with magicks but with a woman's tears. It was the queen who forced them back, and denied herself the comfort. "But they aren't, and this can't be between us, Thane, for there's more at stake. Yet I have such longing for you, as I have always. Whatever's changed, that never will."

"We're not what we were in visions, Aurora. Don't seek me in them, for I won't come to you. We live as we live in the world."

She crouched beside him, brushed the hair from his brow. "Why won't you fight? You have a warrior's skill. You could leave this place, join the rebels and make something of yourself. Why raise a pitchfork in the stables when you can raise a sword against an enemy? I see more in you than what they've made you."

And want more of you, she thought. So much more of you.

"You speak of treason." His voice was colorless in the dark.

"I speak of hope, of right. Have you no beliefs in the world, Thane? None of yourself?"

"I do what I'm fated to do. No more, no less." He moved away from her and sat, staring into the thick shadows. "You should not be here, my lady. Owen would never select a wife bold enough to roam the forest alone, or one who would permit a stable hand to take . . . liberties."

"And if he selects me, what will you do?"

"Do you taunt me?" He sprang to his feet, and she saw what she'd hoped to see in his face. The strength and the fury. "Does it amuse you to find that I could pine for one who would offer herself to another like a sweetmeat on a platter?"

"If you were a man, you would take me—then it would be done." If you would take me, she thought, perhaps things would be different after all.

"Simply said when you have nothing to lose."

"Is your life so precious you won't risk it to take what belongs to you? To stand for yourself and your world?"

He looked at her, the beauty of her face and the purpose that lit it like a hundred candles glowing from within her. "Yes, life is precious. Precious enough that I would debase myself day after day to preserve it. Your place isn't here. Go back before you're missed."

"I'll go, but this isn't done." She reached out, touched his cheek. "You needn't worry. I won't tell Owen or Lorcan about the tunnels or the spy hole. I'll do nothing to take away your small pleasures or to bring you harm. I swear it."

His face went to stone as he stepped back, and he executed a mocking little bow. "Thank you, my lady, for your indulgence."

Her head snapped back as if he'd slapped her. "It's all I can give you." She hurried back to the tunnel and left him alone.

$$*$$

She slept poorly and watched the dawn rise in mists. In that half-light, Aurora took the globe out of its box, held it in the palm of her hand.

"Show me," she ordered, and waited while the sphere shimmered with colors, with shapes.

She saw the ballroom filled with people, heard the music and the gaiety of a masque. Lorcan slithered among the guests, a serpent in royal robes with his son and heir strutting in his wake. The black wolf prowled among them like a tame dog. Though his eyes were green and fierce, he kept his head lowered and kept to heel. Aurora saw the thick and bloody collar that choked his neck.

She saw Brynn chained to the throne with her daughter bound at her feet, and the ghost of another girl weeping behind a wall of glass.

And through the sounds of lutes and harps she heard the calls and cries of the people shut outside the castle. Pleas for mercy, for food, for salvation.

She was robed in regal red. The sword she raised shot hot white light from its killing point. As she whirled toward Lorcan, bent on vengeance, the world erupted. The battle raged—the clash of steel, the screams of the dying. She heard the hawk cry as an arrow pierced its heart. The dragon folded its black wings and sank into a pool of blood.

Flames sprang up at her feet, ate up her body until she was a pillar of fire.

And while she burned, Lorcan smiled, and the black wolf licked his hand.

Failure and death, she thought as the globe went black as pitch in her hand. Had she come all this way to be told her sword would not stand against Lorcan? Her friends would die, the battle would be lost, and she would be burned as a witch while Lorcan continued to rule—with the man she loved as little more than his cowed pet.

She could turn this aside, Aurora thought returning the globe to its box. She could go back to the hills and live as she always had. Free, as the Travelers were free. Content, with only her dreams to plague or stir her.

For life was precious. She rubbed the chill from her arms as she watched the last star wink out over Sorcerer's Mountain. Thane was right, life was precious. But she couldn't, wouldn't, turn away. For more precious than life was hope. And more precious than both was honor.

She woke Cyra and Rhiann to help her garb herself in the robes of a lady. She would wear the mask another day.

★

"Why don't you tell her?" Kern sat on a barrel eating a windfall apple while Thane fed the horses.

"There's nothing to tell."

"Don't you think the lady would be interested in what you are, what you're doing? Or more what you don't?"

"She looks for heroes and warriors, as females do. She won't find one in me."

"She . . ." With a secret little smile, Kern munched his apple. "Does not seem an ordinary female. Don't you wonder?"

Thane dumped oats in a trough. "I can't afford to wonder. I put enough at risk last night because my blood was up. If she chatters about the tunnels, or what passed between us—"

"Does the lady strike you as a chatterbox?"

"No." Thane rested his brow on a mare's neck. "She is glorious. More than my dreams of her. Full of fire and beauty—and more, of truth. She won't speak of it, as she said she wouldn't. I wish I'd never seen her, touched her. Now that I have, every hour of the rest of my life is pain. If Owen chooses her . . ."

He set his teeth against a flood of black rage. "How can I stay and watch them together? How can I go when I'm shackled here?"

"The time will come to break the shackles."

"So you always say." Thane straightened, moved to the next stall. "But the years pass, one the same as the other."

"The True One comes, Thane."

"The True One." With a mirthless laugh, he hauled up buckets of water. "A myth, a shadow, to coat the blisters of Lorcan's rule with false hope. The only truth is the sword, and one day my hand will be free to use it."

"A sword will break your shackles, Thane, but it isn't steel that will free the world. It is the midnight star." Kern hopped off the barrel and laid a hand on Thane's arm. "Take some joy before that day, or you'll never really be free."

"I'll have joy enough when Lorcan's blood is on my sword."

Kern shook his head. "There's a storm coming, and you will ride it. But it will be your choice if you ride it alone."

Kern flicked his wrist, and a glossy red apple appeared in his hand. With a merry grin, he tossed it to Thane, then vanished.

Thane bit into the apple, and the taste that flooded his mouth made him think of Aurora. He offered the rest to a greedy gelding.

Alone, he reminded himself, was best.

6

Wrapped in a purple cloak pinned with a jeweled brooch, Lorcan stood and watched his son practice his swordsmanship. What Owen lacked in style and form he made up for in sheer brutality, and that had his father's approval.

The soldier chosen for the practice had a good arm and a steady eye, and so made the match lively. Still, there were none in the city, or in the whole of Twylia, Lorcan knew, who could best the prince at steel against steel.

None would dare.

He had been given only one son, and that was a bitter disappointment. The wife he had taken in his youth had birthed two stillborn babes before Owen, and had died as she'd lived—without a murmur of complaint or wit—days after his birthing.

He had taken another, a young girl whose robust looks had belied a barren womb. It had been a simple matter to rid himself of her by damning her as a witch. After a month in the dungeons at the hands of his tribunal, she'd been willing enough to confess and face the purifying fires.

So he had taken Brynn. Far cousin of the one who had been queen. He'd wanted the blue of royal blood to run through the veins of his future sons—and had he got them, would have cast his firstborn aside without a qualm.

But Brynn had given him nothing but two daughters. Leia, at least, had possessed beauty, and would have been a rich bargaining chip in a marriage trade. But she'd been willful as well, and had tried to run away when he'd betrothed her.

The wild beasts of the forest had left little more than her torn and bloody cloak.

So he had no child but Dira, a pale, silent girl whose only use would be in the betrothing of her to a lord still loyal enough, still rich enough, to warrant the favor in two or three years' time.

He had planted his seed in Brynn again and again, but she lost the child each time before her term was up, and now was too sickly to breed. Even the maids and servants he took to his bed failed to give him a son.

So it was Owen who would carry his name, and his ambitions turned to the grandsons he would get. A king could not be a god without the continuity of blood.

His son must choose well.

He smiled as he watched Owen draw blood from his opponent, as he beat back his man with vicious strikes until the soldier lost his footing and fell. And Lorcan nodded with approval as Owen stabbed the sword's point into the man's shoulder.

He'd taught his son well. A fallen enemy was, after all, still an enemy.

"Enough." Lorcan's rings flashed in the sunlight as he clapped his hands. "Bear him away, bind him up." He waved off the wounded soldier and threw his arm around Owen's shoulders. "You please me."

"He was hardly worth the effort." Owen studied the stain on

his blade before ramming it home. "It's tedious not to have more of a challenge."

"Come, the envoys have brought the taxes from the four points, and I would speak with you before I deal with them. There are rumbles of rebellion in the north."

"The north is a place of ignorant peasants and hill dwellers who wait for Draco to fly from his mountain." With a glance toward the high peak, Owen snorted in disgust. "A battalion of troops sent up to burn a few huts, put a few of their witches on the pyre should be enough to quiet them."

"The talk that comes down is not of Draco but of the True One."

Owen's mouth twisted as he gripped the hilt of his sword. "Tongues won't flap of what is forbidden once they are cut out. Those who speak of treason must be routed out and reminded there is only one king of Twylia."

"And so they shall be. The envoys brought six rebels, as well as the taxes. They will be tried, and executed, as an example, as part of your betrothal ceremonies. Until then, the tribunal will . . . interrogate them. If these are more than rumbles, we will silence them."

They strode through the gates of the castle and across the great hall. "Meanwhile, preparations for the rest of the ceremonies proceed. You must make your choice within the week."

Inside the throne room, Owen plucked a plum from a bowl and threw himself into a chair. "So many plums." He bit in, smiled. "All so ripe and tasty."

"There's more to your choice than a pleasing face. You may take any who stirs your blood into your bed. You are the prince, and will be king. Your bedmates may slake your lust, but your queen must do that and more. You must have sons."

Lorcan poured wine, and sat by the fire that burned even so

early in the day for his comfort. "Strong sons, Owen. So you must choose a woman who will be more than a pretty vessel. Have any here found your favor?"

"One or two." Owen shrugged. "The latest arrival interests me. She has a bold look in her eye."

"Her dowry would be rich," Lorcan considered. "And her father's lands are valuable. She has beauty enough, and youth. It might do."

"The match would tie the west to us, and as Ute's land runs north along the hills, such positioning would be strategic."

"Yes, yes." Lorcan rested his chin on his fist and considered. "The Realm of Magicks still thrives in pockets of the west, and too many men run tame there who preach of Draco's spell and the True One. It's time to look to the far west and north, and smother any small embers of treason before they flare."

"The Lady Aurora's father, it seems, is unwell." Owen took another bite of his plum. "If we were wed, he might sicken and die—with a bit of help. And so his lands, his fortifications, his wealth would come to me."

"It might do," Lorcan repeated. "I'll take a closer look at this one. If I approve, your betrothal will be announced at week's end at the masque. And you will be pledged the following morning."

Owen raised a brow. "So quickly?"

"With the wedding ceremony to take place at the end of a fortnight—by which time every man in the world must render a token to mark the events—the masque and the wedding. The shepherd must render his finest rams, the farmer one quarter of his crop, the miller a quarter of his grain, and so on, so as to provide their prince and his bride with the stores for their household."

Lorcan stretched his booted feet toward the fire. "If the man has no ram, no crop, no grain, he must render his oldest son or if he has no son, his oldest daughter, to serve the royal couple.

Craftsmen and artisans will bequeath a year of their time so that your home can be built on the western border and furnished as befits your rank."

"Some will not give willingly," Owen pointed out.

"No. And the business of persuading them to do their duty to their king will bury all mutterings of the True One, scatter rebellious forces, and forge our hold on the west. Yes." He lifted his goblet in toast. "I think it may do."

★

Under the guise of serving his mistress, Rohan walked with his head humbly bowed. His heart was full of rage edged in fear. He kept his eyes lowered as he moved past guards and into the sitting room where Aurora gathered with the women to take rose tea and chatter about gowns and the upcoming masque.

"Your pardon, my lady."

Knowing her part, Aurora spared him a single disinterested glance. "I am occupied."

"I beg your pardon, my lady, but the lace you requested has arrived."

"A full day late." She set her cup aside and shook her head at the women who sat closest to her as she rose. "It will probably be inferior, but we'll see what can be done with it. Have it sent to my chambers. I'll come now."

She walked out behind him, careful not to speak to him or to Rhiann, who followed in her wake, until they were behind doors again.

"Lace." She sighed heavily, and poured ale to rid her mouth of the oversweet taste of the rose tea. "How I am lowered."

"Lorcan's envoys returned today with taxes levied against the four points."

Aurora's mouth thinned. "He will not keep them for long."

"They brought also six prisoners."

"Prisoners? What prisoners are these?"

"They say they are rebels, but four are only farmers, and one of them is aged and near crippled, while another is no more than a boy. The other two must have been set upon and taken while scouting. One of them is Eton."

Aurora lowered herself slowly to a chair as Rhiann bit back a cry. "Our Eton? Cyra's betrothed?"

"Eton was wounded, and all are being kept in the dungeons." He curled his hands helplessly into fists. "They're to be questioned by the tribunal."

"Tortured," Aurora whispered.

"It's said they'll be executed for treason within the week. Flogged and branded, then hanged."

"Compose yourself, Rhiann," Aurora ordered when the woman began to weep. "It will not happen. Why were they taken, Rohan? How are they charged with treason?"

"I can't say. There's word among the servants that rebellion is brewing, that the True One is coming."

"So Lorcan strikes before he is struck." She pushed to her feet to pace as she brought the positioning of the dungeons into her mind. "We must get them out, and we will. We have a week."

"You can't leave them there for a week." Rhiann struggled against fresh tears. "To be tortured and starved."

"I have no choice but to leave them until we are ready to attack. If we try to free them now, we could fail, and even if we succeed, such a move would put Lorcan on alert."

"Eton may be dead in a week," Rhiann snapped. "Or worse than dead. Is this how you honor your family?"

"This is how I rule, and it is bitter to me. Eton is like my own brother. Would you have me risk all to spare him?"

"No." Rohan answered before Rhiann could speak. "It

would not honor him if you spared him pain, or even his life, and Lorcan continued to rule."

"Get word to him if you can. Tell him he must hold on until we can find a way. Send a dispatch to Gwayne. It's time. They are to travel in secret. They must not be seen. How long will it take them? Three days?"

"Three—or four."

"It will take three," Aurora said firmly. "I will meet him in the forest, near the tunnel, at midnight when he arrives. I'll know what must be done."

"Cyra." Rhiann grieved for her daughter. "How will we keep this from her?"

"We won't. She has a right to know. I'll tell her. She should hear it from me."

She went out in search of her friend, hoping she would have the right words, and met Owen as she stepped into the courtyard.

"Lady Aurora." He took her hand, bowed over it. "I was about to send word for you."

"I am at your pleasure, my lord prince."

"Then you'll honor me by riding out with me. I've been busy with matters of state all morning, and wish for a brisk gallop and your lovely company."

"I would enjoy nothing more. May I meet you in an hour, my lord, so I might find my maid and change into proper attire?"

"I'll wait. Impatiently."

She curtsied, tipping her face up with a saucy smile before rising and hurrying away. She found Cyra in the kitchens, her eyes bright and round with gossip.

"I require you," Aurora said coolly, then turned away so that Cyra had to rush after her.

"I've learned all about—"

"Not now," Aurora said under her breath. "I'm riding out

with the prince," she said in a clear voice. "I'll want my red riding habit, and be quick about it."

"Yes, my lady."

Only Aurora heard Cyra's muffled giggle as the girl rushed ahead to the bedchamber. And only Aurora hoped she would hear Cyra's laughter again.

"And be quick about it," Cyra mimicked with another giggle as soon as Aurora closed the door behind her. "I had to bite my lip to keep from laughing. Oh, Aurora, I've learned all manner of things. The kitchens are fertile ground."

"Cyra, sit down. I must speak with you."

The tone had Cyra stopping to look at Aurora as she lifted up the red habit. "Do you not ride out with Owen, then?"

"No. Yes, that is—yes." Aurora pushed at her hair. "Yes, within the hour."

"It'll take nearly that long to get this done. A lady of your station would have her hair dressed differently for riding. It has to suit the hat, you know. We'll get started and exchange our news. Oh, Aurora, mine is *so* romantic."

"Cyra." Aurora took the habit and tossed it aside so she could grasp Cyra's hand. "I have word of Eton."

"Eton? What of Eton? He's in the north, scouting for Gwayne." The rosy flush was dying on her cheeks as she spoke, and her fingers trembled in Aurora's. "Is he dead? Is he dead?"

"No. But he's hurt."

"I'll go to him. I have to go to him."

"You can't. Cyra." She pushed her friend into a chair, then crouched at her feet. "Eton and five others were taken by Lorcan's soldiers. He was wounded. I don't know how badly. He was brought here, to the dungeons."

"He's here, in the castle? Now? And he lives?"

"Yes. They will question him. Do you know what that means?"

"They will torture him. Oh." Cyra squeezed her eyes shut. "Oh, my love."

"I can do nothing for him yet. If I try . . . all could be lost, so I can do nothing yet. I'm sorry."

"I need to see him."

"It isn't safe."

"I need to see him. They send food down to the jailers, to the tribunal, and slop to the prisoners. One of the kitchen maids will let me take her place. If he sees me, he'll know there's hope. It will make him stronger. He would never betray you, Aurora, and neither will I. He's proud to serve you, and so am I."

Tears swam into Aurora's eyes, then she pressed her face into Cyra's lap. "It hurts to think of him there."

"Then you must not think of it." She stroked Aurora's hair and knew that she herself would think of little else. "I will pray for him. You'll be a good queen because you can cry for one man when so much depends on you."

Aurora lifted her head. "I'm so afraid. It comes close now, and I'm so afraid that I'll fail. That I'll die. That others will die for me."

"If you weren't afraid, you'd be like Lorcan."

Aurora wiped her eyes. "How?"

"He isn't afraid because he doesn't love. To cause such pain you can't love or fear, but only crave."

"Cyra, my sister." Aurora lifted Cyra's hand and pressed it to her cheek. "You've become wise."

"I believe in you, and it makes me strong. You must change or you'll be late and annoy Owen. You need to keep him happy. It will make his death at your hands all the sweeter."

Aurora's eyes widened. "You talk easily of killing."

"So will you, when I tell you what I've learned. Hurry. This will take some time."

7

"Brynn was one of your mother's women, and her friend," Cyra began.

"I know this. Now she sits as queen. Though not happily, by all appearances." Aurora turned so Cyra could unhook her gown.

"She—Brynn—was widowed in the great battle. Thane was but three. In the year that followed, Lorcan decided to take a new wife. It's said—whispered—that she refused him but that he gave her the choice between giving herself to him and her son's life."

"He would murder a child to win a wife?"

"He wanted Brynn, because she was closest to the queen, in spirit and in blood." Cyra helped Aurora into the riding habit and began to fasten it. "I only know it's said that Brynn wept to another of the handmaidens—the mother of the kitchen girl who spoke to me. She swore her allegiance, and gave herself to Lorcan for his promise to spare her son's life."

Aurora sat at the dressing table, staring at her own face, and asked herself what she would have done. What any woman would have done. "She had no choice."

"Thane was sent to the stables, to work, and was not allowed inside the castle from that day, nor to speak a single word to his mother."

"Hard, hard and cold. He could have taken Brynn by force and killed the boy. He kept him alive, kept Thane alive and within her reach, never to touch or speak. To make them both suffer, to cause pain for the sake of it. Payment," Aurora said aloud as she let herself drift into the nightmare of Lorcan's mind. "Payment for her first refusal of him."

"This is his way," Cyra agreed. "A way of vengeance and retribution. Brynn married Lorcan, and twice miscarried his child before she gave birth to a daughter, who was Leia. Three years after, she bore Dira."

"She had no choice, but Thane . . . he's no longer a child."

"Wait, there's more." Cyra brushed out Aurora's hair and began to braid it. "When Thane was but seven, he ran away—to join the rebels, it's said. He and a young friend. They were caught and brought back. The other boy, the brother of the maid who told me, was hanged."

The horror of it cut through her heart. "By Draco, he hanged a half-grown boy?"

"And forced Thane to watch it done. Thane was beaten and told that if he insulted the king again, another would die in his place. And still he ran away, less than a year later. He was captured, brought back, beaten, and another boy his age was hanged."

"This is beyond evil." Aurora bowed her head. "Beyond madness."

"And more yet. Lorcan took the baby, Dira, his own daughter and half sister to Thane, to the stables where Thane was shackled. She was only days old. And he put his own dagger at the baby's throat. If Thane ran again, if he spoke ill of Lorcan or

Owen, if he disobeyed any law or displeased the king in any way, Dira would die for it, then Leia, then Brynn herself. If he did not submit, any and all who shared his blood would be put to death."

"Could he kill his own?" Struggling to see it, Aurora rubbed a hand over her troubled heart. "Yes, yes, he could do it. She is only a female child, after all," she said bitterly. "And how could a brother, a boy, a man, risk it? He could run, and now he could escape, but he could never forfeit his sisters' lives, risk his mother's."

She thought of what she'd seen in the crystal. The wolf walking like a tame dog, while his mother and sister were chained to the throne. And the ghost of another sister stood trapped behind glass. "No, he could not run, he could not fight. Not even for his own freedom."

"He never did so again," Cyra confirmed as she rolled the braid into a thick knot at the base of Aurora's neck. "He speaks little to others, stays among the horses."

"He makes no friends," Aurora said quietly, "except a girl in a vision and an aged faerie. Because to make friends puts them at risk. So he's always alone."

"It breaks my heart." Cyra dashed a tear from her cheek. "They think he's beaten—Lorcan, Owen, everyone. But I don't believe this is so."

"No." She remembered how he'd looked in the forest with a sword in his hand and the cold fire of battle in his eyes. "It is not so. He has buried his pride and given more than half his life to the waiting, but he is not beaten." She reached back to take Cyra's hand. "Thank you for telling me."

"A man who would humble himself to save another is a great man, greater perhaps than one who fights."

"Stronger. Truer. I misjudged him because I didn't look beyond my own eyes, into my heart. This wolf is not tamed. He stalks. I have fresh hope." She got to her feet, turned. "Go see your man, but take care. Take great care. Tell him, if you can, it won't be long. Three days, no more than four, and we will bring a flood to the City of Stars. I swear on my life, Lorcan will drown in it."

She stepped in front of the looking glass, and her smile was a warrior's smile. "Now we'll go flutter and preen for the son of the devil, and see what use he is to us."

Aurora hurried to the stables, hoping for a moment alone with Thane. Her horse and Owen's were already saddled. Owen's personal guard stood at the riding gelding's head.

She moved to her own mount as if inspecting the horse and the tack.

"You, there." She approached the stables, clapped her hands imperiously. "Stableboy!"

Thane stepped out. He kept his head lowered, but his eyes lifted, and the hot resentment in them blasted her face. "My lady."

For the benefit of the guard, she crooked a finger and moved to her mount's far hind leg. She bent as if to inspect the knee, and as Thane did the same, she whispered. "I must speak with you. Tonight. I'll come to the stables."

"There is nothing more to say, and you put yourself and me at risk."

"It's urgent." Risking a touch, she brushed her fingers over the back of his hand. "Beloved."

She heard the clatter of armor and sword as the guard snapped to attention. Giving her horse a light pat, she straightened and turned to smile at Owen.

"Do you have some trouble with this . . . thing?" Owen demanded, sneering at Thane.

"Indeed, no, my lord. My mount seemed to favor this leg when we rode in. I was complimenting your boy on the care of my horse. I'm very fond of my horse." Deliberately, she reached into her purse and drew out a copper. "For your good work," she said and handed the coin to Thane.

"Thank you, my lady."

"It isn't necessary to give him coin, nor to speak to him."

"I find such small boons ensure good care." She moved, subtly, so that she stood between Thane and Owen, and sent the prince her brightest smile. "As I said, I'm very fond of my horse. Will you help me mount, my lord? I am so looking forward to a gallop."

Owen shoved the mounting block aside and set his hands on Aurora's waist. She laid hers on his shoulders and let out a flirtatious laugh as he vaulted her into the saddle.

"You're very strong, my lord." She gathered her reins. "I also have a fondness for a strong man." With another laugh, she clicked her tongue and sent her horse flying away from the stables.

Owen, she discovered, was a mediocre rider on a superior mount. She reined herself in to keep pace with him. It was good, despite the choice of company, to ride. To feel the freshness of the air on her skin and to be away from the clatter of the castle and the smells of the city.

Her men, she thought, would come from the northwest, using the forest for cover and keeping off the roads. Then the hills would ring with the battle and, when it was done, with victory.

"You look thoughtful, Aurora." Owen studied her as they slowed to a trot at the edge of field and forest.

"Only admiring the beauty of this country, my lord. And wondering how pleasant it is to know that all you see is yours."

"The woman I choose will have part in that."

"If you will it," she said carelessly, and walked her horse

along the forest path. "There is rich land in the west, as well. My father tends what's his with a firm hand and a clear eye. The hills reach high there, and the cattle grow fat on them."

"The name of my bride will be announced at the masque, at week's end."

"So I am told." She slid her gaze toward his, quirked her lips. And slid her power over him like silk. "Do you know it?"

"Perhaps I do." He reached to take her reins and stop her horse, then leapt from his own. While she raised her eyebrows, he circled, then lifted his arms to pluck her from the saddle. "But a prince must take care in selecting a bride. One who will be queen."

She laid her hand on his chest. "So he must—as a woman must take care, my lord, in who takes her favors."

"I want a woman who will stir my blood." He pulled her closer and would have taken her mouth if she hadn't laid her fingers on his lips.

"A man's blood is easily stirred. And if a woman gives him what he desires before a pledge is made, the woman is a fool. What man, what king, wants a foolish wife?"

"If you give me what I desire, and it pleases me, I will make the pledge. Lie with me now, and you will be queen."

"Make me queen." She played her fingers along his jaw. "And I will lie with you. I will give you sons, and great pleasure in the making of them."

"I could take you." He dug his fingers into her hips. "You couldn't stop me." His breath came short as he lifted her to her toes. "You belong to me, as every blade of grass in the field beyond belongs to me. I am your lord. I am your god."

"You have the strength, and the power." And though she had a dagger beneath her skirts, she couldn't afford to use it, not even in defense against rape. "Why take by force today what would be given freely in a few days' time?"

"For excitement."

She only laughed, and tapped his cheek. "To hump like rabbits in the dirt? Hardly befitting you, my lord, or the woman who wishes to sit by your side, and lie by it. The waiting will, I think . . ." She traced her fingertip over his lips. "Hone appetites."

"A sample, then." He circled her throat with his hand, squeezed, then covered her lips with his in a brutal kiss. She tasted his desire, and his delight in force. With all her will she swallowed revulsion and fury, and let him take.

She thought of how he would pay for this, and for the thousands of cruelties to her people, for his part in humiliating Thane. For every lash Eton might suffer.

When his hands pawed at her, when they clamped bruisingly on her breasts, she neither struggled nor winced. For he would pay.

"My lord, I beg you." She hoped the quaver in her voice could be taken for passion rather than the rage she felt. "Indulge me and wait for the rest. You will not be disappointed, I promise."

"Would you rather I nibble some housemaid to sate my appetite?"

"Such a man as you would have great appetites. I will do my best to meet them, at the proper time." She broke free. "Your kisses make me tremble. It will break my heart if you only toy with me."

He grasped her waist and tossed her up to the saddle more roughly than necessary. "You'll know my answer at week's end."

Bastard, she thought as she gathered her reins. But she smiled, with her lashes lowered. "And you, my lord, will know mine."

She wanted to bathe, to rub her lips raw so that there was

nothing left of the taste or feel of him. But she laughed and talked her way through another night of feasting. She lifted her cup to the king in toast. She danced, and pretended only feminine flusters and objections when Owen pulled her into the shadows and touched her body. As if he had the right.

Her mind was too troubled to speak of it to Rhiann as she removed the ball gown and put on her nightdress. She watched the sky, careful not to venture too close to the window, as the world quieted toward sleep.

Then, donning cloak and hood, she slid out into the night, to the stables.

✶

She knew he wasn't there. She understood now that part of her would sense him, would always sense him. So he hadn't waited for her, as she'd asked.

Once again she took a candle and followed after him through the tunnels, and into the forest beyond.

He stood in the moonlight. It showered over his ragged shirt, his unkempt hair, the worn boots.

"I told you not to come."

"I need to speak with you." She blew the candle out, set it down. "To see you. To be with you."

He stepped back. "Are you mad, or simply sent here to ensure I will be?"

"You could have told me when I asked why you stay here."

"It's nothing to do with you."

"Everything you do, everything you are, and think and feel, all of you has to do with all of me."

"You rode with him."

"I do what needs to be done, as you do, Thane." She reached out a hand as she moved to him, but he turned away.

"Will you be wedded to him, and bedded to him? Does that need to be done?"

For the first time in days a smile that came from her heart curved her lips. "You're jealous. I'm small enough to enjoy that. He will never have me as a man has a woman. You already have."

"I haven't. I won't."

"In dreams you have." She moved in, laid her cheek on his back and felt his body go taut as a bowstring. "You've dreamed of me."

Both heart and body strained toward her. "All of my life, it seems, I've dreamed of you."

"You love me."

"All of my life." He spun back, held her at arm's length when she would have embraced him. "You kept me alive, I think, in dreaming of you. The loving of you, and being loved. Now, by the gods, you'll be the death of me."

"No one lives forever." She took off her cloak, spread it on the ground. Then, standing in the moonlight, she drew off her nightdress, let it pool at her feet. "Live now."

He reached out, wound her long, dark hair around his fist. He could walk away from this, still had the strength. Or he could take love, one precious moment of love, and have its comfort and torment with him the rest of his days.

"If hell awaits me, I'll have one night in heaven first."

"We'll have it." She waved a hand and around them cast a circle of protective fire. The light of it shimmered in golds as a thin mist covered the ground in a pure white blanket.

"I've waited for you, Thane." She touched her lips to his, fit her body to his. "Through the light, and through the dark."

"For this one night with you, I would trade a thousand nights alone. Bear a thousand lashes, die a thousand deaths."

"Midnight nears." She smiled as he lowered her to the soft and misted ground. "It's my hour."

"It will be ours. Aurora." He kissed her tenderly, very tenderly. "My light."

Sweet, so sweet, that merging of lips, the brush of fingertips over flesh. She knew his taste, his touch, so warmly familiar, and yet so gloriously new. The feel of his body, the hard muscle, the ridged scars, aroused her, as did the gleam of his eyes in the glow of witch fire.

"Thane. My wolf." With a laugh, she reared up and nipped at his chin. "So much better than a dream."

Their lips met again, a deep search that had her trembling beneath him, and shifting restlessly as needs heated in her blood. Her heart thundered under his palm—the hard callus of his labors, then under his mouth—the hot brand of his need. And her belly began to ache as if with hunger. Her own hands became more demanding, tugging at his worn shirt. The sound of cloth ripping was only another thrill.

He wanted to go slowly, to draw this night into forever. She could vanish, he knew, when the sun struck, and he would be left with more misery than he thought he could bear.

But his need for her was impossible, enormous, and the love that stormed through him stole his breath. The urgency built with every touch, every murmur, until he was half mad.

Whatever he took, she gave, then only demanded more. She cried out his name when he drove her to peak, then clung relentlessly with her mouth like a fever on his.

The empty well of his life flooded full, and he knew for the first time something he would kill to keep.

His hands clamped on her wrists. He looked down at her with eyes fierce and gleaming green. "You'll never belong to him. He'll never touch you like this."

"No." Here was power, she realized. Another kind of female power. "Only you. It is the woman who gives herself to you, and only you." She heard the bells begin to strike the hour. "Mate with me, join with me. Love with me. We'll be more together than either can be alone."

He plunged inside her, watched the power and the pleasure of the moment rush over her face. And felt the rough magic of it whip through him.

Then she was moving under him and with him, and for him. Their fingers locked, their lips met.

Overhead, lightning flashed in the form of a dragon, and the stars flared red as blood.

8

When the witching hour passed, she stayed with him. But she knew the time grew short. If they were as others, she mused, they could remain like this, wrapped warm in her cloak, and sleep until dawn broke.

But they were not as others.

"I have much to tell you," she began.

He only drew her closer to his side. "You're a witch. I know. I'm bewitched. And grateful."

"I've cast no spell on you, Thane."

He smiled and continued to study the stars. "You are the spell."

"We are the spell." She shifted so she could look down at his face. "I'll explain. You are a hero to me."

He looked away from her and started to move.

"A man who would put all he wanted, all he needed, aside to protect others? The greatest of warriors. But that time is ending." She took his hand, brought it to her lips. "Will you stand beside me? Will you pledge me your sword?"

"Aurora, I will pledge you my life. But I won't lift a sword knowing the act will bring another down on my sister. My mother. Or some poor innocent. They hanged my friend, and he was but six seasons. His only crime was in following me."

"I know." She kissed his cheek. "I know." And the other. "No harm will come to your family, or to any in your stead." She reached out, picked up her dagger, and drew it across her palm. "I swear it, on my blood."

He gripped her hand. "Aurora—"

"She is my sister now. She is my mother now. You are my husband now."

Emotion stormed across his face. "You would take me this way? I'm nothing."

"You're the bravest man I know, and you're mine. You are the most honorable, and the most true. Will you take me?"

The world, Thane thought, could change in one magic hour. "I'll get you away to safety. I know how it can be done, with Kern's help—"

"I go nowhere."

"To the Valley of Secrets, through the Realm of Magicks," he continued, ignoring her protest. "My sister is safe there, and so will you be."

"Your sister? Leia lives?"

Fury flashed onto his face. "He would have sold her, like a mare. Bartered her like a whore. She was but sixteen. With Kern's help, she was taken from the castle and away, and her cloak left torn and bloodied deep in the woods. She lives, and I will owe Kern and his kind all of my days. But she is lost to me, and I can't risk getting word of her to my mother, to give her even that much comfort."

Not a ghost, Aurora realized, but a memory. Shielded and safe—and apart. She touched her fingers to his cheeks. "What did it cost you?" she murmured.

"Kern asked for no payment."

"No—what did Lorcan and Owen take from you? What scars do you bear from their anger at the loss of so valuable a possession to them? So many times, when we came to each other in visions, I saw your sadness. But you would never tell me."

"You would always bring me joy. Beloved."

"They whipped you in her stead. Laid the lash on your back because they couldn't lay it on hers. I can see it now, and that you reached through the pain, beyond it, because your sister was saved."

"Don't look." He gripped her hands when her smoky eyes went dark with vision. "There's no pain here now. And there will be none. Kern will help me get you away. You, and my mother and sister, your women. Then I'll find the rebels, and come back to deal with Lorcan and his whelp."

"You won't have to look far for the rebels. They're on their way even now. Your mother and your sister will be safe. I've sworn it. But I stay, and I fight." She laid her hands on his shoulders to stem his protest, and looked deep into his eyes. "A queen does not sit in safety while others win the world."

She got to her feet. "I am Aurora, daughter of Gwynn and Rhys. I am the Lady of the Light. I am the True One, and my time has come. Will you stand with me, Thane the Valiant, and pledge me your sword?"

There was a light around her as she spoke, as gold as sunlight and stronger than the witch fire she'd conjured. For a moment it seemed a crown of stars sat sparkling on her head, and their brilliance was blinding.

He had to struggle to find his voice, but he knelt. "My lady. I never believed in you, and still I knew you from my first breath. All that I have, all that I am is yours. I would die for you."

"No." She dropped to her knees to take his face in her hands.

"You must live for me. And for the child we made tonight." She took his hand and pressed it to her belly.

"You can't know—"

"I do. I do know." Her face, her voice, were radiant. "You gave me a child tonight, and he will be king, and rule this world after us. He will be more than either of us, more still than the sum of us. We must win it back for him, and for our people. We will take from Lorcan, in blood if we must, what he took in blood. But you must live for me, Thane. Swear it."

"I swear it." In all of his memory he'd lived with nothing. Now in one night he was given the world. "A son?"

"For the first. We will make others." With a laugh, she threw her arms around him. "They will be happy, and so well loved. And they will serve, Thane." She drew back. "Serve the world as well as rule it. This can be. I begin to see so much of what can be. I needed you to clear my vision."

"How many come? What are their arms?"

"Now you think like a soldier." Satisfied, she sat on the ground. "I'll know more soon. Here, at midnight the night after next, we meet Gwayne. He is my hawk, and he brings the forces. Two of mine are held now in the dungeon. One is as dear as a brother to me. They must be freed, but not until the night of the masque. I pray they live to see that night, and they are not to be sacrificed."

"I can get them out. I know the tunnels and underground better than any. There are others held there who would stand with you."

"What do you need?"

"One good man and his sword would be enough."

"You shall have him. This must be done, and quietly, in the hour before the masque. The wounded, or those too weak to fight, must be taken through the tunnels and away. Men will die,

Thane. There will be no choice. But I want no man's blood spilled carelessly. Some would swear allegiance if given the opportunity. From what I've seen, not all who serve Lorcan do so with a full heart."

"Some serve only in fear of their lives or the lives of their loved ones." He shrugged when she studied him. "Men often speak their mind around horses. And minions."

"You are no one's minion."

"I've been less than that." His hand curled into a fist. "By the blood, for the first time since childhood I know what it is to want, more than to live, to stretch out of this skin and be. I would have served you," he said quietly. "I have seen you wear the Crown of Stars, and I would have served you in anything you asked, servant to queen. But to have loved you, as a man loves a woman, has changed everything. I can never go back."

"Only for a short time. My wolf will conceal his fangs only for a short time. I must go now. When we move, Thane, we must move quickly." She went willingly into his arms, held close. "We'll have all of our lives for the rest."

And for the rest, he thought, as he let her go, she and the child would be protected at any and all costs.

✱

Hoping to avoid Owen for the day, Aurora made plans to go into the city and there measure the feeling among the people—and the strategy of attack and defense. It was difficult to deny herself a trip to the stables and even a fleeting moment with Thane, but she sent Rohan to order the carriage, as was fitting for a lady of her station.

"Soon there will be no more need for pretense. Or the wait," she added and touched Cyra's shoulder. "The prisoners will be freed, and the wounded among them taken safely into the forest. I promise you."

"He suffers, Aurora. My Eton suffers. I could barely stand to see him so. Many held there don't even know their crime, and some are driven mad by the dark and the starvation."

"It won't be dark much longer. Men held there have fathers or sons or brothers. They'll fight with me. I saw the dragon in the sky last night, and the red stars." She laid a hand on her belly. "I've seen what can be."

She hooked her arm with Cyra's and started across the courtyard. And heard the clash of armor as guards snapped to attention.

The heat of battle flashed in her blood even as she bowed her head and curtsied to the man who called himself king.

"Majesty."

He took her hand to bring her to her feet, and didn't release it. "A pretty light on a gloomy morning."

"You are too kind, sire. But even a dank day in such a place is a joy."

"And do you ride out again today?"

"I go into the city, with your permission, my lord, in hopes to find something appropriate for the masque. I don't wish to dishonor you or the prince by arriving at such a spectacle in my country garb."

"You go unescorted, lady?"

"I have my men, sir, and my women." She fluttered up at him. "Will I not be safe enough?"

He chucked her under the chin and made her spine freeze. "Beauty is never safe enough. Do you not seek the company of the prince?"

"Always, my lord. But . . ." She offered a slow, sidelong

smile. "I fear he may become bored with me if I am too accessible. Do you not think that a man desires a woman more when she is just out of reach?"

"You're a clever one, aren't you?"

"A clever mind is a valuable tool to a woman. As is amiability, so if you prefer I forgo this venture and wait upon Prince Owen's pleasure, I will do so." She glanced over as Rohan brought her carriage into the courtyard. "Shall I send it away again, sire?"

"Go, and enjoy. I look forward to seeing what catches your eye in the shops." He helped her into the carriage, and was obviously pleased when she peeked out the window and sent him one last smile.

"He makes my skin crawl," Aurora said as she flopped back against the seat.

"He would have you for himself if he could." Rhiann nodded wisely. "There's a look in a man's eye when he imagines such things. Having you for his son is his next choice."

"What he'll have is my sword at his throat. And a happy day that will be. How much have we left to spend?" she demanded.

Rhiann carefully counted out the coins in her purse, and had Aurora blowing out a breath.

"I hate to waste it on foolishness, but I have to make a showing. Lorcan will expect it now."

"You can be very particular," Cyra said, and worked up a smile. "Turning up your nose at the offerings, sniffing at materials, waving away baubles."

"I suppose. I'd rather be inside the taverns listening to the talk, but we'll leave that to Rohan." She glanced out the window of the carriage, and her heart ached at the sight of children begging for food. She thought of the taxes levied, all the coins stored inside the palace.

"I have an idea, something that might distract Lorcan and help our army move into the forest unnoticed. Chaos," she declared, "is another kind of weapon."

✳

Furious, Owen stalked into the stables. He'd wanted Aurora, but she was off—with no word to him—to the city. He'd planned another ride, with a picnic by the river. And a seduction.

If he were to choose her, and his mind was nearly made up, he expected her to be available at his whim. It was best she learned that now.

There were others with more beauty, others with more generous attributes. If she refused to come to heel, he would take one of them as queen, and make the intriguing Aurora a consort.

He pushed his way into a stall where Thane was wrapping a foreleg for the mount of one of the soldiers.

"Saddle my horse."

Thane kept his head lowered as he continued to wrap the leg. "Yes, my lord."

"Now, you worthless nit." He struck out, slapping Thane in the face with the back of his hand.

Thane took the blow, and though he knew it was foolish, he checked his grip on the halter so that the frightened horse shied and canted, driving Owen into the wall of the stall.

"You'll pay for that, you ham-handed bastard."

There was enough satisfaction in watching Owen go white as bone and scramble out of the stall to take all the sting out of the next blow. "A thousand pardons, my lord prince."

"I'll deal with you later. Get my horse, and be quick about it."

As Owen strode out of the stables, Thane grinned and wiped the blood from his mouth.

"The mount's wasted on him." Thane turned and saw Kern

leading the already saddled horse from its stall. "A lame one-eyed donkey would be wasted on him."

Thane ran a hand over the gleaming neck of Owen's stallion. "If the gods are with me, and I live, I will have this horse as my own. Thank you for saddling him."

"A simple matter, in a complicated time."

"You knew who she was. Who she is."

"The True One shines."

"She does." Thane rested his brow on the stallion's neck. "I have such love for her. Fierce and frightening love. I'll do what needs to be done, Kern, but I ask you, whatever you've given me over the years, to give it now to my family. I can go into any battle, take any risk, if I know they're protected."

"You've stood as their shield long enough. I'll stand for you when the time comes."

"Then I'll be ready." He led the horse out, and stood meekly at its head while Owen berated him.

"I'll be ready," he repeated and watched Owen spur the mount and ride off.

✶

The sky stayed dim, but no rain fell. Aurora watched the dark clouds and prayed that the storm brewing would hold while her men marched toward the city. She used her time there to study the fortifications, to watch the changing of the guard under the guise of wandering among the shops.

The wares were rich, and the people starving.

"There is talk," Rohan told her as she stood by as if to supervise the loading of her goods into the carriage, "of portents. The dragon flew in the sky last night, and the stars bled."

"And what do the people make of these portents?"

"Some fear it's the end of the world, some hope it's the beginning."

"They're both right."

"But those who dare speak of hope do so in whispers. More were dragged from their homes in the night and charged with treason. There are murmurs, Aurora, that Lorcan will use the masque for some dark purpose, that he plans some sorcery."

"He has no such powers."

"It's said he has sought them." Rohan glanced left, right, to be certain they weren't overheard. "That he has courted the dark. Sacrifices. Human sacrifices to draw power from blood."

"Superstitious mutterings. But we won't ignore them." She climbed into the carriage and rode back to the castle with her mind circling a hundred thoughts.

✳

There was a time for warriors, and a time for witches. When the hour was late, Aurora stirred her power. She called the hawk, and ten of his fellows. Then twenty, then a hundred. And more, until the sky teemed with them. Standing in her window, she raised the wind and, lifting her arms, threw her power into it.

Hawks screamed, circled, dove. Guards and courtiers rushed to the courtyard and the gardens, to the city, to the walls. There were cries of fear, shouts of wonder.

The great birds flew into the castle, through window and door, and sent servants scurrying under chair and bed. The beat of wings, the call of hawk, filled the air as in a golden mass they streaked into the treasury, plucking coins in their talons, streaming out again to drop them like rich rain on the city.

With cries of wonder and delight, men, women, and children rushed out of their homes and hovels to gather the bounty. When the call to arms came, many of the soldiers were as busy as the townspeople stuffing coins into pocket and purse. Before order could be restored, the cry of hawks was an echo, the beat of wings a memory.

The streets of the city glittered with coins.

An early payment, Aurora thought, watching the chaos below her window. The rest would come, very soon.

✷

There was talk of little else the next day. Some blamed the strange raid on faeries, or witchcraft. It was said that the king's rage was black. Soldiers posted proclamations warning that any citizen found with coins would forfeit a hand.

Still, there was not a single coin left on the streets, and for the first time Aurora heard more laughter than woe when she listened to the city.

The confusion had kept her out of Lorcan's and Owen's way through the day, and given her time to have young Rhys slither into the dungeons with food for the prisoners while the guards gossiped.

But the time for giving food and coin to those in need was over, and the time for war was nearly upon her.

Distracted, she hurried toward her chamber to make final preparations for meeting Gwayne, and she didn't see Owen lurking. He had her back to the wall and his hand at her throat. She was already reaching for her dagger before caution had her fisting her hand and struggling to turn the battle light in her eye to fear.

"My lord. You frighten me."

"What game do you play?"

She shivered and turned her lips up in a tremulous smile. "Many, sir, and well. What have I done to displease you?"

"I did not give you leave to fritter off. Two days have passed, and you have not sought my company. I did not give you leave to travel into the city yesterday."

"No, my lord, but your father, the king, did so. I only sought the shops in hope that I might find something to please you for the ball. We have nothing so fine in the west as in the City of Stars. Please, my lord." She touched her hand to his. "You're hurting me."

"I've made it clear that I favor you. If you don't wish me to turn my eye toward another, take care, Aurora."

"Your favor, my lord, is all I could wish, but your passions unnerve me. I'm only a maid."

"I can make you more." He pushed his hand between her legs. "And less."

"Would you treat me so?" She wished for tears, willed them into her eyes as rage spewed through her. "Like a doxy to be fondled in doorways? Do you show your favor by dishonoring me?"

"I take what I wish. When I wish."

"My lady!" Rhiann screamed in shock and rushed down the corridor with Cyra at her heels.

Aurora broke away, to fall sobbing into Rhiann's arms and let herself be carried away into her chamber.

The minute the door was shut and secured, she stood dry-eyed. "Speak of this to no one," she ordered. "No one." She looked at the hand she held close to her side, and the dagger in it. "The prince of pigs has no idea how close he came to being gutted. I will not dine tonight. Send word that Lady Aurora is indisposed."

She sat and picked up a quill. "I have work."

9

She wore a high-necked gown to hide the bruises in a color chosen to blend with the night. There was enough anger left from her encounter with Owen to have her strapping a short sword at her side as well as the dagger on her thigh.

She threw on her cloak, with her mother's brooch pinned inside it.

She carried no lamp or candle, but slipped like a shadow through the castle. At the sound of approaching footsteps, she pressed herself against the wall, and through the veil of witch smoke watched two guards lead a serving girl toward Owen's chambers. The girl's face was pale as the moon, and her eyes dull with fear and resignation.

Aurora's hand clamped on the hilt of her sword, her knuckles white with rage and impotence against the metal. She could not interfere, could do nothing to help the poor girl, for to do so would risk all.

But he would pay. She vowed it. As his father would pay for his treatment of innocence.

She hurried down the steps, easing through doorways, and slipped out of the castle through the kitchen. Drawing up her hood, she made her way to the stables under the cover of darkness.

The instant she was inside, Thane pulled her into his arms. "I worry," he whispered even as his lips sought hers. "Every moment I can't see you, touch you, know you're safe, I worry."

"It's the same for me." She eased back, just to touch his face, and saw the bruises. "Oh, Thane."

"It's nothing. Nothing he won't pay for."

Instinctively she touched the neck of her gown, thought of the marks of Owen's hand hidden under it. "Payment will be made. I swear it. Come, and let's pray that Gwayne and our army await."

He lifted the door to the tunnels, but when he reached for a lamp, Aurora stilled his hand. "No. Tonight, we go by my light. It must be shown," she said as she drew the crystal star from the pocket of her cloak. "To give those who would fight hope, to let them see what they risk their lives for."

The star shimmered, and the light within it grew until it pulsed pure white. It beamed through the dark of the tunnels and became as bright as day.

And she was the light, burning with the power and purity of it. His throat stung, and his heart swelled with a mixture of love and wonder. "My lady. If my heart and my sword, if my life were not already yours, I would lay them before you now."

"Keep your life, beloved, for a thousand stars would never light mine without you. I need my wolf." She took his hand as they moved through the tunnels. "My lord of the stables. You know more of courtly matters than I."

At his quick laugh she shook her head. "You do," she insisted. "I was raised as a Traveler—educated, it's true, by book, by battle, by journeys and song and story, but there will come a time when I must hold court. It plays on my nerves."

"You are every inch a queen. It's a wonder men don't fall to their knees when you pass."

"You love me." And it warmed her to say it. "So it would seem so to you. It won't just be a matter of defeating Lorcan, but of convincing the people of the world that I am true. The work is just beginning."

"I'm used to work."

It was Kern who waited at the end of the tunnel. He wore light armor and his battle sword. "They come, Lady of the Light. But first, I bring you greetings from the Realm of Magicks." He bowed low. "And request to speak as envoy."

"You are welcome, sir." She glanced at Thane in confusion when Kern remained bowed.

Thane grinned, sent her a wink. He hadn't been tutored by a faerie throughout his life without learning the protocol. "You do honor to your queen, Lord of Magicks. Greetings to you from the world of men. You have leave to speak."

"Well done." Kern rose with a twinkle in his eye.

"Meaning no offense, but can we speak freely here?" Aurora gestured with her free hand. "Men and faerie folk share the forest, and the night. I am not queen until I'm crowned, and I have much yet to learn on how to be one. What word do you bring from your realm?"

"I have a lengthy and lyrical speech prepared."

"Lengthy it would be," Thane assured Aurora. "I can't promise the lyrical."

"However"—Kern shot his student a steely stare—"I'll cut it to the bone. The Realm of Magicks is at your command, Lady of the Light. We will fight with you if you'll have us."

"You haven't raised your forces or your powers against Lorcan in all these years. Why do you offer to raise them now?"

"We've raised your wolf, my lady, as it was written. I am for him, and he is for you. The hour to do more had not come."

"Faeries can die at the hand of men—and more, it's said that Lorcan courts magic. Will you and yours risk all that is to come?"

"We have died at the hands of men, hands that follow Lorcan's command. And some of us have turned from truth to embrace the lies. Some from weakness, some from fear, and some from the ambition for greater powers. Our kinds are not so different in such matters, my lady. We will follow the queen into battle. Will the queen trust my word?"

Aurora turned to Thane. "I'll trust yours."

"He's as true as any I know."

"Then thanks to you and your kind, Lord of Magicks. What you've said here tonight, and what you'll do on the morrow, will never be forgotten."

He took the hand she offered, bowed over it. "Your hawks provided fine entertainment in the night, Majesty."

"There is little entertainment in this place. I craved some. And it served to keep Lorcan and his dogs' eyes on the city, and away from the forest."

"Now your white hawk approaches."

She swung around and saw Gwayne step away from the trees, alone. Regal protocol was forgotten in the sheer joy of seeing him. She sprang toward him, threw her arms around him. "I've missed you! There's so much to say, and little time to say it." She drew back, studied his face. "You're tired."

"It was a long journey."

"How many are with you?"

"We're two hundred strong, but many of those are farmers and craftsmen. Boys." He gripped her hands, squeezed. "Some are armed with clubs, pitchforks, or simply stones from the fields, but they come."

"Then they're valued for it, every one."

"They need to see, Aurora, to believe, for they're weary, and some grow frightened. Without a stir of hope, some will scatter by morning."

"They will see, and they will believe." She reached back for Thane's hand. "This is Thane, who is my mate, the wolf of my visions. And Kern of the faeries, who is his teacher and brings us word from his realm of their loyalty to the True One. Take us to the army, Gwayne, so they can see. And pray to the gods I find the words to stir them."

Gwayne led them through the forest, calling a low signal to sentries already posted. The camp was rough, the faces of the men she saw pale with fatigue. Some were old, others much too young, and her heart began to ache with the knowledge of what she would ask of them.

She shook her head before Gwayne could speak. "I must do this myself. If I can't do this, I can't do the rest. They have followed you this far, my hawk. Now they have to follow me."

Gathering herself, she climbed onto a wide stump and stood quietly for a moment while the men shifted and murmured and studied her.

"I am Aurora." She didn't lift her voice, but kept it low so the murmuring stilled as the men strained to hear. "I am the Lady of the Light. I am the queen of Twylia. I am the True One. The woman I am weeps at what has been done to the world, to the people and the magicks of it. My father, the king, was slain through treachery, and my mother, the queen, gave her life for my birth. I am from death, and my heart bleeds knowing that more death will come from me. I am a woman, and have no shame of tears."

She let them fall silently down her face and glimmer in the moonlight filtering through the trees.

"I am Aurora." Her tone strengthened as she loosed her cape and flung it aside. As she drew her sword and raised it to the sky. "I am the Lady of the Light. I am the queen of Twylia. I am the True One. The warrior in me burns at what has been done to the world, to the people and the magicks of it. I will not rest, I will fight unto death to take back what was stolen from me and mine. My sword will sing into battle. I am a warrior, and I have no fear of death when the cause is justice."

Once more she held the crystal star in her palm and drew from it, from herself, the power of light. Men fell back, or dropped to their knees as that light grew and grew until it burned like a thousand candles. Wind whipped through the forest, sent her hair flying as she held both sword and star aloft.

"I am Aurora!" Her voice rang through the night, and the bells began their toll of midnight. "I am the Lady of the Light. I am the queen of Twylia. I am the True One. I am a witch, and my rage for what has been done to the world and my people is cold as ice, is hot as flame, is deep as the sea. My power will light the dark, and it will blind those who stand against me. I am woman and warrior, witch and queen. I will weep and fight and blaze until the world is right again. And all who follow me will be remembered and honored until the end of days."

She threw back her head and punched her power toward the sky. Light carved through the black, and spun in mad circles of golds and reds and silvers. And became a crown of stars.

"None but the True One dares to wear the Crown of Stars. None but the True One can bear its weight and its heat. None but the True One can give the world back to the people and the magicks. When next the moon rises, I will fight for the world and take my crown. Will you follow me?"

They roared for her and cheered. The soldier and the farmer, the old and the young.

She sheathed her sword and passed her hand over the star so that its light slowly dimmed. "Rest now," she called out. "Rest and gather your courage and your might. I go with my hawk, my wolf, and he who serves the dragon to prepare for the battle."

When she would have leapt down, Thane circled her waist with his hands and lifted her to the ground. "A queen shouldn't jump from a tree stump after so stirring a speech."

"I need you to remind me of those small details." Her lips curved at the smile in his eyes. "And to look at me just like that, as often as possible."

"I am at your service."

"And now we need to gather our forces, and our brains. Gwayne? A quiet place where we four can speak?"

"May I serve here, my lady?" Kern asked, and at her nod, he flicked both wrists.

They stood now in a brightly lit chamber with a fire snapping in the hearth. Kern gestured toward a table and the chairs that surrounded it. "This is my rath, and a good private place for plots and plans. Be comfortable. Would you have wine?"

"By the gods, I would," Gwayne said, with feeling. "It's been a dry march."

"And food?" Platters of meat, bread, cheese, and fruit appeared on the table.

"No warrior eats until all eat," Aurora said and earned a proud look from Gwayne.

"Your men will be fed, Majesty. We are pleased to offer our hospitality tonight."

"Then eat." She slapped Gwayne on the back. "While I tell you what I know."

She told him of the masque, of the dungeons, of the threat to

Brynn and Dira, and with Thane's help she drew diagrams of the fortifications and the locations of guards.

"Your father was a good friend," Gwayne said to Thane, "a brave warrior with a true heart. He would be proud to know what you have done, and will do."

"Most of my life I've felt he would be ashamed I hadn't lifted my hand."

"He loved your mother and you above all things. You have each sacrificed self for the life of the other. A man would be proud of such a wife, and such a son."

"I don't want those sacrifices to be in vain," Aurora added. "Brynn and Dira must be protected, and Leia kept safe until the castle and city are back in our hands. Brynn and Dira's presence will be required at the masque. I want at least one man each by their side, to shield them, then to escort them to safety with Rhiann and Cyra."

"There's an anteroom here." Thane pointed to the drawings. "With a passage gained by opening this panel by a mechanism in the hearth. My mother knows of it. Either she or Dira could lead the way from there."

"It must be done quickly, before Lorcan thinks to use them as a bargaining tool. Just as freeing those in the dungeons must be done quickly. And quietly. We strike there first, while the company is gathered in the great hall for the masque. When it's done, we divide our troops. Into the tunnels to strike at the castle from the inside, to the walls—here and here?" She glanced at Thane for approval.

"The weakest points," he agreed. "A breach could be made, and from those three attacks, confining Lorcan and his personal guard between."

She rose as Gwayne and Thane debated battle strategy, and she moved to the fire to study the images she saw in the flames.

She could hear the beat of her own heart, and knew it beat for revenge. There was a lust in her belly for blood—Lorcan's blood.

When she looked down at her hands, they were wet with it, and in her head were the agonized screams of the dying as her sword cut viciously through flesh and bone.

And in the flames she saw the Crown of Stars go black.

"Blood and death," she declared when she sensed Kern behind her. "If I hunger for this, what manner of queen am I?"

"Having hunger and sating appetite are different matters, lady."

"I want this, for myself. His blood on my hands." She held them up, knowing Kern could see as she saw. "But it isn't for the good of the world, is it? To seek to take a life, even such a life as his, this is not light. It is not why I was made. Not why I am here."

"To see that is power, and truth."

"And still, I know there will be blood, there will be death. Of those I love, of those who follow me. I send them into battle and to the grave. This is the weight of power. Tonight, I turned my back on a young girl, knowing she would be ill used. Because if I had intervened, I might have betrayed the greater cause. But is there a greater cause, Kern, than the fate of a single innocent?"

"I don't rule. Such questions are part of a crown."

"Yes, they are. I could do nothing else then. But now . . . It can be done another way. Am I strong enough to trust the crown instead of the sword? I've tested so little of my power to put such matters to it. To call the wind, a flock of birds . . ." She wrapped her arms around herself. "That's a game, not battle."

"And you know what your sword can do."

"Yes. I spoke the truth. I don't fear death in battle, but I fear the lives that will be lost on my account. And I fear what will become of me, and the world, if I take one if there's a choice.

Thane trusts you. So will I." She closed her eyes. "Do you know what is in my mind?"

"I do, my lady."

"And you'll help me."

"I will."

"Then we will plan for battle this way." She glanced back at her teacher, and her lover. "And hope for victory in another."

10

The castle, the city, the countryside made ready for the masque. The prettiest maids were gathered up and brought in to serve and to decorate—and, Aurora noted, to serve *as* decoration. Farmers were ordered to offer their finest crops or livestock to the king in tribute. Wine and ale were hauled in on wagons, and without payment, so that the king and his guests could revel.

Portents were spoken of only in whispers. Lights, such great lights, seen in the forest at midnight. The stars that had circled into a crown in the night sky.

Open talk of such matters could lose a man his tongue.

Lords and ladies from all reaches of Twylia traveled to the City of Stars for the celebrations rather than displease the king who held them under his merciless thumb. Some with eligible daughters sent them to the hills or into caves, or into the Valley of Secrets, risking death or poverty. Others brought the maidens and prayed that the prince would pass their daughters over for others.

There were whispers, too, of rebellion, but the king ignored such foolishness and basked in the glory of the feast to come.

The dark glass showed no man who would claim his crown. And when he drank the blood of a sorcerer to bring visions, he saw only the shape of a wolf and the delicate hand of a woman who held the world in her palm.

He ordered his best hunters into the woods and the hills to track and kill any wolf. And garbed himself in his richest robes.

✱

Time was short, and the risk worth taking. Armed, Thane hurried through the tunnels and chanced the daylight to find Gwayne.

"This isn't your place, or your time," Gwayne told him. "We are moving at sunset and still have much to prepare."

"Lorcan sent six hunters out nearly an hour ago. They'll come this way. If they find you and even one escapes, you'll fight your battle here rather than on your chosen ground."

"Are these men loyal to Lorcan?"

"Loyalty is cheap here."

Gwayne fingered the hilt of his sword. "Then we'd best offer them a dearer coin."

Aurora chose white, the color of truth, for her gown. In her vision she had worn red, the color of blood. So she made this change deliberately, and hopefully. But not foolishly. The long, flowing sleeves hid the dagger she strapped to her wrist. Over Cyra's objections, she left her hair down, falling straight to her waist and unadorned. And in a gesture of pride and defiance, she pinned her mother's brooch to the gown between her breasts.

"He might recognize it," Rhiann objected.

"If he does, it will be too late." She took the globe and the star. "I'll need these." She slipped them into a white velvet purse. Turning from the looking glass, she held out her hands, one to Cyra, one to Rhiann. "You've been mother and sister to me. Whatever changes tonight, nothing changes that. I ask that you see my beloved's mother and sister safe. If the light doesn't shine for the midnight hour, you're to take them to the Valley of Secrets, where Leia bides, and seek sanctuary. Your vow on it."

"Aurora," Rhiann began.

"Your vow on it," Aurora insisted. "I can only do what I must do with a clear heart and mind."

"Then you have it. But the light will shine."

✴

Thane waited until the mounted hunter was directly below the bough, then leapt upon him. The force sent them both tumbling to the ground, and the alarmed horse shied.

Before a breath could be taken, Thane had his sword at the man's throat. "Call out," he said quietly, "and it will be the last sound you make."

"Thane of the stables?" There was as much shock as fear in the tone. "What recklessness is this? I am on king's business."

"It is a new day," Thane said, then hauled the man to his feet. "Take him off with the others." He shoved the hunter toward two of the rebels who waited in the shelter of the trees. "His bow and quiver will be useful. Tell Gwayne I've gone back. I will be listening."

With a sense of purpose in every stride, he hurried back to the stables. Whatever happened, he would not pass another night there, sleeping on the floor like an animal. Tonight his family would be free, and he would live—or die—in the service of his lady.

"You're late," Kern complained the moment Thane climbed through the passage.

"I had business."

"You've had considerable here as well, which I've seen to. Guests are still arriving, and their horses require care. You might have been missed if I hadn't been here to deal with it."

"I'll tend the horses, then I am done will this. I swear if I have any say over what's done, whoever takes my place here will have decent quarters and payment for his labors."

With some reluctance Thane unstrapped his sheath.

"I said I tended the horses. You've no need to labor over them again." Lips pursed, Kern circled Thane. "It will be considerable labor to tend to you."

"What? What's wrong with me?"

Kern pinched one of Thane's ragged sleeves between his fingers. "Nothing a bath and a barber and a tailor of some skill can't fix. But we've no time for all of that. I'll just have to see to it myself."

"I don't need a bloody barber before a battle."

"You need one before a masque. But the bath first. Believe me, you can use one."

Kern snapped his fingers twice and conjured a copper tub full of steaming water.

"I'm not going to the masque, but to the dungeons to help free the prisoners. I don't think they'll care if I smell sweet or not."

"The prisoners are being freed even now."

"Now?" Even as Thane reached for his sword, Kern waved a hand. And Thane was naked.

"For the sake of the gods!"

"You're not needed. My kind are adept at getting into locked places." Kern grinned. "We enjoy it. You'll be needed at the masque, and you won't get past the guards unless you're bathed, groomed, and properly attired. The tub, boy."

"I'll stand with Gwayne, lead—" He found himself in the tub, immersed. He came up sputtering.

"You waste breath arguing. Are you afraid to go to a ball?"

"I'm not going to dance, thundering hell. I'm going to fight."

"And so you may. But if and when, you fight by her side. To get to her side, you need what I'll give you. Wash." Kern circled the tub while Thane sulked and scrubbed.

"Is this the queen's bidding?"

"No. But she will be pleased enough. It is her wish and her will to take the throne with as little blood as possible. The magicks have agreed to aid her in this," he added as Thane's head came up sharply. "We will enchant the guards to sleep, and the walls will be breached without sword. No man will die in the city or outside the keep. But inside, Lorcan's power must be faced and vanquished, or she cannot rule. There is the battle. Dark against light. The pure against the corrupt. And there you must be."

Kern tapped his finger to his lips, considering as Thane hauled himself out of the tub. "Simplicity, I think," he stated and, wagging his finger, garbed Thane in royal blue with tiny flecks of gold. "No, no, not quite."

Thane scowled at the lace spilling over his wrists. "I feel like a fool."

"As long as you don't behave as one, we'll have no problem." He changed the blue to black, the gold to silver, and nodding, drew Thane's hair back in a short queue. "Dress swords only." He snapped and had a jeweled-handled sword in the silver sheath.

Pleased for the first time by the turn of events, Thane drew the sword. "A fine weapon. Good balance."

"It was your father's."

Thane lowered the sword and stared into the eyes of his teacher. "Thank you. I fail, too often, to thank you."

"Meet your destiny, and that is thanks enough. One last touch." Kern waved a hand and covered the top of Thane's face with a black domino.

"Take your place," Kern said quietly. "Stay true to your blood and your heart. The world rests on what passes tonight."

✶

Aurora held herself straight, fixed a flirtatious smile on her face, and stepped into the great hall. Music was playing, and already lines were set for dancing. Tables groaned with platters of food, and hundreds of candles streamed light.

Dress was elaborate, with feathers and furs, high headdresses and flowing trains. She saw Lorcan drinking deeply of wine, with his queen pale and silent beside him.

The first order, she thought, was to separate them so Brynn and Dira could be spirited away to safety. Despite the masks and costumes, she had little trouble in locating Owen and staying out of his line of sight. She walked directly to the king, curtsied.

"Majesty, my humble thanks for the invitation to so lively a celebration."

"The voice is familiar, as is . . . the form." He tapped a finger under his chin, studied her smile and the eyes that looked out of a sparkling silver mask. "What is the name?"

"Sire, the guessing is the game." She trailed a finger down his arm in a daring move. "At least until the hour strikes twelve and we are unmasked. Might I beg for a cup of wine?"

"Asking is enough." He snapped his fingers and a servant hurried over. Deliberately, Aurora shifted to look back at the dancing, and had Lorcan turning his back on his wife. "Would you care to take a turn of the room with me?"

"Delighted and charmed." He offered her his arm. "I believe I have guessed this game, Lady Aurora. You are, I believe, the most daring of the maidens here."

"One expects a king to be wise and clever, and you are, sire." She lifted her glass as they walked, and saw Rhiann nod. The first move would be made.

She chattered, commenting on the costumes, complimenting the music, knowing that she would soon circle toward Owen. But while she did, Brynn and Dira would be safely away. As would her own women.

"Lovely lady." Aurora's heart stopped at the voice when the courtier in black bowed in front of her. "Might I steal you away for a dance?"

Struggling to gather her scattered wits, she inclined her head. "If His Majesty permits."

"Yes, yes, go." He waved her away and held out his cup for more wine.

"Are you mad?" Aurora said under her breath.

"If love is madness, I am so afflicted." Thane led her across the room, and hoped it was far enough away. "But the fact is, I don't dance. Would that I did. You are so beautiful tonight."

"Do something," she hissed.

"I'll feed you." He began to pile a plate with delicacies. "It's something flirtatious courtiers do for ladies at balls—so I've seen when I've spied on them. Sugarplum?" Grinning, he held one up to her lips.

She bit in and laughed. "You are mad. I'm so glad to see you. I want to touch you, and dare not. Your mother and sister are being taken to safety."

"I saw them go. I can never repay you."

"Learn to dance, then one day promise to dance with me."

"On my oath. If I could, I would whisk you out on the terrace, kiss your lips in the light of the rising moon. And there would only be music and moonlight for us." He took her hand, brushed a kiss over it. "I know what you've planned with the magicks. You should have told me."

"I was afraid you and Gwayne would never agree. You wish for blood—both of you, and you've earned it—both of you. I'm denying you your right."

"I would not have agreed." His eyes lifted to hers with a sudden shock of power. "I do not agree. There are bruises on your throat, beloved. You didn't quite cover them."

"Have they any more import than those he put on you?"

"Yes. Oh, yes."

"Find another kitten to stroke." Owen snapped out the order, shoving Thane aside. Even as Thane's hand gripped the hilt of his sword, Aurora stepped between them. "Sir," she said lightly to Owen, "I am no kitten."

"A cat, more like, rubbing herself against any willing leg."

"If you think so of me, I'm surprised you would spend a moment in my company." She started to turn away, resisted when Owen took her arm. With her back to him she mouthed *Not yet* to Thane, then faced Owen once more. "You make a spectacle of us, my lord. The king will not approve."

Owen took her hand, squeezing until her fingers ground bone to bone. He leaned close and spoke in a voice like silk. "I will not choose you. But I will have you. Had you been more agreeable, you would have been queen."

She saw two of the king's personal guards rush into the hall, heard the clamor, and knew the rebels were over the walls and through the tunnels.

She stepped back and, over the shouts, spoke clearly. "I am queen."

11

"You will have nothing," she said. "For nothing is what you have earned. Your time is ended, and mine begins. The hour is about to strike."

"No woman speaks so to me." Owen drew back his hand. And Thane's sword was out and at his throat.

"Touch her, and I will slice your hand off at the wrist." With his free hand Thane pulled off his mask. "Don't interfere," he said to Aurora. "I'm not a man if I don't stand for myself and my lady, at long last."

"Your lady," Owen spat.

"My lady, and my queen." Thane stepped back a pace. "Draw your sword."

Chaos was already reigning as guards battled the rebels who charged into the hall. Lords and courtiers dragged screaming women away from the fray, or simply left them and scrambled for cover themselves. Aurora cast aside her own mask and called out for a sword. She would have no choice now but to fight her way to Lorcan and cut off any chance of escape.

Owen pulled his sword. "Stableboy, I will cut you apart, piece by piece, and feed you to my dogs."

With a thin smile, Thane made a mocking salute with his sword. "Will you fight, you tedious braggart, or simply talk me to death?"

Owen came in fast, striking, thrusting, and Thane felt his blood sing. Their swords crossed, slid hilt to hilt, and he grinned between the lethal vee. "I have dreamed of this."

"You dream your own death."

They broke apart, and steel flashed against steel.

Wielding a sword of her own, Aurora slashed blades aside, shoved a swooning woman into a courtier's arms, then whirled to fight back to back with Gwayne.

"Outside?" she shouted. "The walls, the tunnels."

"It's done. This is all that's left. The faeries hold them fast, and the dungeons are clear."

"Then we end this." She looked toward Lorcan and saw his sword was bright with blood. "We take him."

With Gwayne, she fought her way to the king. They battled through the panicked guests, leaping over the fallen and the fainting to be joined by others as she called them to arms. They pressed the outnumbered guards to the walls, and Aurora locked swords with Lorcan.

"You may take me," she said calmly. "I think you won't, but you may. If you do, these men will cut you down. You will not live through this night unless you lay down your sword."

"You will be hanged." His eyes burned black. There was blood on his hands, she saw. As there was on hers. "You will be drawn, quartered, and hanged."

"Lay down your sword, Lorcan the usurper, or I will end this in death after all."

"There will be death." But he threw down his sword. "It will be yours."

"Tell your guards to lay down their weapons. You're outnumbered here. Tell them to lay down their weapons so you might hear my terms."

"Enough!" He shouted it with Aurora's sword to his throat. "Lay down your swords. Your king commands you."

The sounds of clashing steel dimmed until there was only Thane's blade against Owen's.

"Let him finish," she said to Gwayne. "The hour has not yet struck. This is his time, not mine, and he must live it. Put Lorcan on the throne he values so much, and hold him there."

Across the hall the two men fought like demons. Winded, Owen hacked and cleaved, and cursed when Thane's sword flicked his away. Enraged, he grabbed a candlestand and heaved it, following with vicious sweeps as Thane dodged aside and spun back into attack.

"You are too used to sparring with soldiers who are beaten or banished if they dare best you," Thane taunted. "Now that it's your life—" Thane slashed, and cut neatly through Owen's silk doublet to score the flesh—"You're clumsy."

"You are *nothing*! Coward, whipping boy."

"I carry your scars." Thane sliced the point of his sword down Owen's cheek. "Now you carry mine. And that is enough."

With two quick thrusts, he knocked Owen's sword out of his hand, then pressed his own to his enemy's belly. "I won't kill you, as I wish you many years of life. Years of misery and humiliation. On your knees before your Majesty."

"I will not kneel to you."

"It is not to me you kneel. But to her." He stepped aside, shifting his sword point to the back of Owen's neck so the man could see Aurora standing among the fallen and the frightened.

"You are," she said to Thane, "what I have always wished for.

What I will always prize. In the midst of battle, when vengeance was your right, you chose honor."

"Whore!" Owen shrieked it. "Drab. She lay on her back for me. She—"

Thane shifted his grip on the sword and slammed the hilt into the side of Owen's head. When Owen fell unconscious, Thane booted him carelessly aside. "I'm not perfect," he said with a flashing smile, and Aurora laughed.

"I believe you may be. The hour comes." She could feel the power rising in her. "I almost wish it wouldn't. That we could walk away, and live in a cottage in the woods or ramble across the world in a wagon. I almost wish it, but it comes and I have no choice."

"A cottage, a world, a crown. It's all the same to me, if I'm with you."

"Stand with me, then." She turned and faced Lorcan as he sprawled on the throne under the swords of her men. "Lower your swords, step back. Open the doors, the windows. Let the people in, let them know what happens here at the witching hour, at my hour. Lorcan, stand and face me as you did not face my father or my mother. I am Aurora. I am the Lady of the Light. I am the True One."

She walked toward him as she spoke and flung out her arms. "Are there any here in this company, any here in the City of Stars, in the world, who will not pledge their loyalty to the True One? For they are free to leave this place, and to go in peace. There will not be blood or death."

"You're nothing but a woman, a whore, as my son has said. I am king. The True One is a myth babbled by madmen."

"Behold the dragon!" She pointed toward the window, and the fire that lit the sky in the shape of a dragon.

"A witch's trick." He rose and, pushing out with his hand,

shot a fierce wind through the hall. It blew her hair back, set her gown to billowing. The sharpness of it sliced her hand and drew blood. But she stood against it.

"You would match your power to mine?" She arched her brows. "Here is the world, stained by my blood, and the blood of my people." She drew the crystal globe from her purse, threw it high so it spun near the ceiling and showered light and spilled out voices raised in song. "Take it if you dare. And here is the crown, the Crown of Stars."

She reached in her purse again and flung the star. It flew in dizzying circles and exploded with light.

She stood, draped in billowing white, unarmed, and waited while the bells began to strike midnight. "And this is my hour, the hour of my birth and beginnings. The hour of life and death, of power and portent. The time between time when day meets day and night meets night."

The crown circled, beamed light, and descended toward her head.

Lifting her arms, she accepted her destiny. "And in this hour, the reign of dark is ended and the reign of light begins. I am the True One, and this is my world to protect."

The crown settled on her head, and every man and woman, every soldier and servant, fell to their knees.

Outside, the people who massed could be heard chanting her name like a prayer.

"I am Aurora, descendant of Draco, daughter of Gwynn and Rhys. I am queen of Twylia."

On a roar, Lorcan grabbed the sword from a dazzled rebel and, raising it high, lunged toward Aurora. Murder was in his cry, madness was in his eyes.

And springing like a wolf, Thane leapt forward, spinning to shield her, and ran Lorcan through.

He fell at her feet with his blood splashing the white hem of her gown. With the stars still gleaming on her head, she looked down on him with a pity that was cold as winter.

"So . . . So it ends in death after all. He made his choice. The debt is paid. My father and yours." She turned to Thane, held out her hand. "My mother and yours."

The last bell struck, and the wind died. Her crown sparkled like stars.

"What was taken in blood is restored. In blood. Now let there be peace. Open the larders," she ordered. "Feed the people of the city. No one goes hungry tonight."

"My lady." Gwayne knelt before her. "The people call for you. They call for their queen. Will you go out so they can see you?"

"I will. Only a moment first. A moment," she repeated and turned to Thane. "It will be hard. After the joy, it will be hard. There will be work and sweat and time to restore faith, to bring order, to renew trust. There will be so much to do. I need you beside me."

"I am the queen's man, my lady." He brought her hand to his lips. Then with a laugh born of freedom, he lifted her off her feet, and high above his head. "Beloved. Woman of my visions, mother of my son. My light. My life."

She wrapped her arms around him, tipped her mouth to his for the warmth and power of his kiss as he spun her in circles. "Then there's nothing I can't do. Nothing we can't be."

"We'll be happy."

"Yes. Till the end of days."

With her hand linked with his, she walked out to the cheers of the people of the world.

And they raised her up to be queen, Aurora, the Light.

Winter Rose

For the three roses,
Ruth, Marianne, and Jan,
who've made this so much fun

1

The world was white. And bitter, bitter cold. Exhausted, he drooped in the saddle, unable to do more than trust his horse to continue to trudge forward. Always forward. He knew that to stop, even for moments, in this cruel and keening wind would mean death.

The pain in his side was a freezing burn, and the only thing that kept him from sliding into oblivion.

He was lost in that white globe, blinded by the endless miles of it that covered hill and tree and sky, trapped in the frigid hell of vicious snow gone to icy shards in the whip of the gale. Though even the slow, monotonous movements of his horse brought him agony, he did not yield.

At first the cold had been a relief from the scorching yellow sun. It had, he thought, cooled the fever the wound had sent raging through him. The unblemished stretch of white had numbed his mind so that he'd no longer seen the blood staining the battleground. Or smelled the stench of death.

For a time, when the strength had drained out of him along

with his blood, he'd thought he heard voices in the rising wind. Voices that had murmured his name, had whispered another.

Delirium, he'd told himself. For he didn't believe the air could speak.

He'd lost track of how long he'd been traveling. Hours, days, weeks. His first hope had been to come across a cottage, a village where he could rest and have his wound treated. Now he simply wanted to find a decent place to die.

Perhaps he was dead already and hell was endless winter.

He no longer hungered, though the last time he'd eaten had been before the battle. The battle, he thought dimly, where he'd emerged victorious and unscathed. It had been foolish, carelessly foolish, of him to ride for home alone.

The trio of enemy soldiers had, he was sure, been trying to reach their own homes when they met him on that path in the forest. His first instinct was to let them go. The battle had been won and the invasion crushed. But war and death were still in their eyes, and when they charged him his sword was in his hand.

They would never see home now. Nor, he feared, would he.

As his mount plodded onward, he fought to remain conscious. And now he was in another forest, he thought dully as he struggled to focus. Though how he had come to it, how he had gotten lost when he knew his kingdom as intimately as a man knew a lover's face, was a mystery to him.

He had never traveled here before. The trees looked dead to him, brittle and gray. He heard no bird, no brook, just the steady swish of his horse's hooves in the snow.

Surely this was the land of the dead, or the dying.

When he saw the deer, it took several moments to register. It was the first living thing he'd seen since the flakes had begun to fall, and it watched him without fear.

Why not? he mused with a weak laugh. He hadn't the

strength to notch an arrow. When the stag bounded away, Kylar of Mrydon, prince and warrior, slumped over the neck of his horse.

When he came to again, the forest was at his back, and he faced a white, white sea. Or so it seemed. Just as it seemed, in the center of that sea, a silver island glittered. Through his hazy vision, he made out turrets and towers. On the topmost a flag flew in the wild wind. A red rose blooming full against a field of white.

He prayed for strength. Surely where there was a flag flying there were people. There was warmth. He would have given half a kingdom to spend the last hour of his life by a fire's light and heat.

But his vision began to go dark at the edges and his head swam. Through the waves of fatigue and weakness he thought he saw the rose, red as blood, moving over that white sea toward him. Gritting his teeth, he urged his horse forward. If he couldn't have the fire, he wanted the sweet scent of the rose before he died.

He lacked even the strength to curse fate as he slid once more into unconsciousness and tumbled from the saddle into the snow.

The fall shot pain through him, pushed him back to the surface, where he clung as if under a thin veil of ice. Through it, he saw a face leaning close to his. Lovely long-lidded eyes, green as the moss in the forests of his home, smooth skin of rose and cream. A soft, full mouth. He saw those pretty lips move, but couldn't hear the words she spoke through the buzzing in his head.

The hood of her red cloak covered her hair, and he reached up to touch the cloth. "You're not a flower after all."

"No, my lord. Only a woman."

"Well, it's better to die warmed by a kiss than a fire." He tugged on the hood, felt that soft, full mouth meet his—one sweet taste—before he passed out.

Men, Deirdre thought as she eased back, were such odd creatures. To steal a kiss at such a time was surely beyond folly. Shaking her head, she got to her feet and took in hand the horn that hung from the sash at her waist. She blew the signal for help, then removed her cloak to spread over him. Sitting again, she cradled him as best she could in her arms and waited for stronger hands to carry the unexpected guest into the castle.

✳

The cold had saved his life, but the fever might snatch it back again. On his side of the battle were his youth and his strength. And, Deirdre thought, herself. She would do all in her power to heal him. Twice, he'd regained consciousness during his transport to the bedchamber. And both times he'd struggled, weakly to be sure, but enough to start the blood flowing from his wound again once he was warm.

In her brisk, somewhat ruthless way, she'd ordered two of her men to hold him down while she doused him with a sleeping draught. The cleaning and closing of the wound would be painful for him if he should wake again. Deirdre was a woman who brooked no nonsense, but she disliked seeing anyone in pain.

She gathered her medicines and herbs, pushed up the sleeves of the rough tunic she wore. He lay naked on the bed, in the thin light of the pale gold sun that filtered through the narrow windows. She'd seen unclothed men before, just as she'd seen what a sword could do to flesh.

"He's so handsome." Cordelia, the servant Deirdre had ordered to assist her, nearly sighed.

"What he is, is dying." Deirdre's voice was sharp with command. "Put more pressure on that cloth. I'll not have him bleed to death under my roof."

She selected her medicines and, moving to the bed, concentrated only on the wound in his side. It ranged from an inch under his armpit down to his hip in one long, vicious slice. Sweat dewed on her brow as she focused, putting her mind into his body to search for damage. Her cheeks paled as she worked, but her hands were steady and quick.

So much blood, she thought as her breath came thick and ragged. So much pain. How could he have lived with this? Even with the cold slowing the flow of blood, he should have been long dead.

She paused once to rinse the blood from her hands in a bowl, to dry them. But when she picked up the needle, Cordelia blanched. "My lady . . ."

Absently, Deirdre glanced over. She'd nearly forgotten the girl was there. "You may go. You did well enough."

Cordelia fled the room so quickly, Deirdre might have smiled. The girl never moved so fast when there was work to be done. Deirdre turned back to her patient and began carefully, skillfully, to sew the wound closed.

It would scar, she thought, but he had others. His was a warrior's body, tough and hard and bearing the marks of battle. What was it, she wondered, that made men so eager to fight, to kill? What was it that lived inside them that they could find pride in both?

This one did, she was sure of it. It had taken strength and will, and pride, to keep him mounted and alive all the miles he'd traveled to her island. But how had he come, this dark warrior? And why?

She coated the stitched wound with a balm of her own making and bandaged it with her own hands. Then with the worst tended, she examined his body thoroughly for any lesser wounds.

She found a few nicks and cuts, and one more serious slice on

the back of his shoulder. It had closed on its own and was already scabbed over. Whatever battle he'd fought, she calculated,
had been two days ago, perhaps three.

To survive so long with such grievous hurts, to have traveled
through the Forgotten to reach help, showed a strong will to live.
That was good. He would need it.

When she was satisfied, she took a clean cloth and began to
wash and cool the fever sweat from his skin.

He was handsome. She let herself study him now. He was tall,
leanly muscled. His hair, black as midnight, spilled over the bed
linens, away from a face that might have been carved from stone.
It suited the warrior, she thought, that narrow face with the
sharp jut of cheekbones over hollowed cheeks. His nose was long
and straight, his mouth full and somewhat hard. His beard had
begun to grow in, a shadow of stubble that made him appear
wicked and dangerous even unconscious.

His brows were black slashes. She remembered his eyes were
blue. Even dazed with pain, fever, fatigue, they had been bold
and brilliantly blue.

If the gods willed it, they would open again.

She tucked him up warm, laid another log on the fire. Then
she sat down to watch over him.

*

For two days and two nights the fever raged in him. At times he
was delirious and had to be restrained lest his thrashing break
open his wound again. At times he slept like a man dead, and she
feared he would never rouse. Even her gifts couldn't beat back
the fire that burned in him.

She slept when she could in the chair beside his bed. And
once, when the chills racked him, she crawled under the bed-
clothes with him to soothe him with her own body.

His eyes did open again, but they were blind and wild. The pity she tried to hold back when healing stirred inside her. Once when the night was dark and the cold rattled its bones against the windows, she held his hand and grieved for him.

Life was the most precious gift, and it seemed cruel that he should come so far from home only to lose his.

To busy her mind she sewed or she sang. When she trusted him to be quiet for a time, she left him in the care of one of her women and tended to the business of her home and her people.

On the last night of his fever, despair nearly broke her. Exhausted, she mourned for his wife, for his mother, for those he'd left behind who would never know of his fate. There in the quiet of the bedchamber, she used the last of her strength and her skill. She laid hands on him.

"The first and most vital of rules is not to harm. I have not harmed you. What I do now will end this, one way or another. Kill or cure. If I knew your name"—she brushed a hand gently over his burning brow—"or your mind, or your heart, this would be easier for both of us. Be strong." She climbed onto the bed to kneel beside him. "And fight."

With one hand over the wound that she'd unbandaged, the other over his heart, she let what she was rush through her, race through her blood, her bone. Into him.

He moaned. She ignored it. It would hurt, hurt both of them. His body arched up, and hers back. There was a rush of images that stole her breath. A grand castle, blurring colors, a jeweled crown.

She felt strength—his. And kindness. A light flickered inside her, nearly made her break away. But it drew her in, deeper, and the light grew soft, warm.

For Deirdre, it was the first time, even in healing, that she had looked into another's heart and felt it brush and call her own.

Then she saw, very clearly, a woman's face, her deep-blue eyes full of pride, and perhaps fear.

Come back, my son. Come home safe.

There was music—drumbeats—the laughter and shouts of men. Then a flash that was sun striking off steel, and the smell of blood and battle choked her.

She muffled a cry as she caught a glimpse in her mind. Swords clashing, the stench of sweat and death and fear.

He fought her, thrashing, striking out as she bore down with her mind. Later, she would tend the bruises they gave each other in this final pitched battle for life.

Her muscles trembled, and part of her screamed to pull back, pull away. He was nothing to her. Still, as her muscles trembled, she pit her fire against the fever, just as the enemy sword in his mind slashed against them both.

She felt the bite of it in her side, steel into flesh. The agony ripped a scream from her throat. On its heels, she tasted death.

His heart galloped under her hand, and the wound on his side was like a flame against her palm. But she'd seen into his mind now, and she fought to rise above the pain and use what she'd been given, what she'd taken, to save him.

His eyes were open, glassy with shock in a face white as death.

"Kylar of Mrydon." She spoke clearly, though each breath she took was a misery. "Take what you need. Fire of healing. And live."

The tension went out of his body. His eyes blurred, then fluttered shut. She felt the sigh shudder through him as he slid into sleep.

But the light within her continued to glow. "What is this?" she murmured, rubbing an unsteady hand over her own heart. "No matter. No matter now. I can do no more to help you.

Live," she said again, then leaned down to brush her lips over his brow. "Or die gently."

She started to climb down from the bed, but her head spun. When she fainted, her head came to rest, quite naturally, on his heart.

2

He drifted in and out. There were times when he thought himself back in battle, shouting commands to his men while his horse wheeled under him and his sword hacked through those who would dare invade his lands.

Then he was back in that strange and icy forest, so cold he feared his bones would shatter. Then the cold turned to fire, and the part of him that was still sane prayed to die.

Something cool and sweet would slide down his throat, and somehow he would sleep again.

He dreamed he was home, drifting toward morning with a willing woman in his bed. Soft and warm and smelling of summer roses.

He thought he heard music, harpsong, with a voice, low and smooth, matching pretty words to those plucked notes.

Sometimes he saw a face. Moss-green eyes, a lovely, wide mouth. Hair the color of dark, rich honey that tumbled around a face both unbearably beautiful and unbearably sad. Each time the pain or the heat or the cold would become intolerable, that face, those eyes, would be there.

Once, he dreamed she had called him by name, in a voice that rang with command. And those eyes had been dark and full of pain and power. Her hair had spilled over his chest like silk, and he'd slept once more—deeply, peacefully—with the scent of her surrounding him.

He woke again to that scent, drifted into it as a man might drift into a cool stream on a hot day. There was a velvet canopy of deep purple over his head. He stared at it as he tried to clear his mind. One thought came through.

This was not home.

Then another.

He was alive.

Morning, he decided. The light through the windows was thin and very dull. Not long past dawn. He tried to sit up, and the movement made his side throb. Even as he hissed out a breath, she was there.

"Carefully." Deirdre slid a hand behind his head to lift it gently as she brought a cup to his lips. "Drink now."

She gave him no choice but to swallow before he managed to bring his hand to hers and nudge the cup aside. "What . . ." His voice felt rusty, as if it would scrape his throat. "What is this place?"

"Drink your broth, Prince Kylar. You're very weak."

He would have argued, but to his frustration he was as weak as she said. And she was not. Her hands were strong, hard from labor. He studied her as she urged more broth on him.

That honey hair fell straight as rain to the waist of a simple gray dress. She wore no jewels, no ribbons, and still managed to look beautiful and wonderfully female.

A servant, he assumed, with some skill in healing. He would find a way to repay her, and her master.

"Your name, sweetheart?"

Odd creatures indeed, she thought as she arched a brow. A man would flirt the moment he regained what passed for his senses. "I am Deirdre."

"I'm grateful, Deirdre. Would you help me up?"

"No, my lord. Tomorrow, perhaps." She set the cup aside. "But you could sit up for a time while I tend your wound."

"I dreamed of you." Weak, yes, he thought. But he was feeling considerably better. Well enough to put some effort into flirting with a beautiful housemaid. "Did you sing to me?"

"I sang to pass the time. You've been here three days."

"Three—" He gritted his teeth as she helped him to sit up. "I've no memory of it."

"That's natural. Be still now."

He frowned at her bent head as she removed the bandage. Though a generous man by nature, he wasn't accustomed to taking orders. Certainly not from housemaids. "I would like to thank your master for his hospitality."

"There is no master here. It heals clean," she murmured, and probed gently with her fingers. "And is cool. You'll have a fine scar to add to your collection." With quick competence, she smeared on a balm. "There's pain yet, I know. But if you can tolerate it for now, I'd prefer not to give you another sleeping draught."

"Apparently I've slept enough."

She began to bandage him again, her body moving into his as she wrapped the wound. Fetching little thing, he mused, relieved that he was well enough to feel a tug of interest. He skimmed a hand through her hair as she worked, twined a lock around his finger. "I've never had a prettier physician."

"Save your strength, my lord." Her voice was cool, dismissive, and made him frown again. "I won't see my work undone because you've a yen for a snuggle."

She stepped back, eyeing him calmly. "But if you've that much energy, you may be able to take some more broth, and a bit of bread."

"I'd rather meat."

"I'm sure. But you won't get it. Do you read, Kylar of Mrydon?"

"Yes, of course I . . . You call me by name," he said cautiously. "How do you know it?"

She thought of that dip she'd taken into his mind. What she'd seen. What she'd felt. Neither of them, she was sure, was prepared to discuss it. "You told me a great many things during the fever," she said. And that was true enough. "I'll see you have books. Bed rest is tedious. Reading will help."

She picked up the empty cup of broth and started across the chamber to the door.

"Wait. What is this place?"

She turned back. "This is Rose Castle, on the Isle of Winter in the Sea of Ice."

His heart stuttered in his chest, but he kept his gaze direct on hers. "That's a fairy tale. A myth."

"It's as real as life, and as death. You, my lord Kylar, are the first to pass this way in more than twenty years. When you're rested and well, we'll discuss how you came here."

"Wait." He lifted a hand as she opened the thick carved door. "You're not a servant." He wondered how he could ever have mistaken her for one. The simple dress, the lack of jewels, the undressed hair did nothing to detract from her bearing. Her breeding.

"I serve," she countered. "And have all my life. I am Deirdre, queen of the Sea of Ice."

When she closed the door behind her, he continued to stare. He'd heard of Rose Castle, the legend of it, in boyhood. The palace that stood on an island in what had once been a calm and pretty lake, edged by lush forests and rich fields. Betrayal, jealousy, vengeance, and witchcraft had doomed it all to an eternity of winter.

There was something about a rose trapped in a pillar of ice. He couldn't quite remember how it all went.

Such things were nonsense, of course. Entertaining stories to be told to a child at bedtime.

And yet . . . yet he'd traveled through that world of white and bitter cold. He'd fought and won a battle, in high summer, then somehow had become lost in winter.

Because he, in his delirium, had traveled far north. Perhaps into the Lost Mountains or even beyond them, where the wild tribes hunted giant white bear and dragons still guarded caves.

He'd talked with men who claimed to have been there, who spoke of dark blue water crowded with islands of ice, and of warriors tall as trees.

But none had ever spoken of a castle.

How much had he imagined, or dreamed? Determined to see for himself, he tossed back the bedcovers. Sweat slicked his skin, and his muscles trembled, appalling him—scoring his pride—as the simple task of shifting to sit on the side of the bed sapped his strength. He sat for several moments more, gathering it back.

When he managed to stand, his vision wavered, as if he was looking through water. He felt his knees buckle but managed to grip the bedpost and stay on his feet.

While he waited to steady, he studied the room. It was simply appointed, he noted. Tasteful, certainly, even elegant in its way unless you looked closely enough to see that the fabrics were fraying with age. Still, the chests and the chairs gleamed with polish. While the rug was faded with time, its workmanship was lovely. The candlesticks were gleaming silver, and the fire burned quietly in a hearth carved from lapis.

As creakily, as carefully, as an aged grandfather, he walked across the room to the window.

Through it, as far as he could see, the world was white. The sun was a dim haze behind the white curtain that draped the sky, but it managed to sparkle a bit on the ice that surrounded the castle. In the distance, he saw the shadows of the forest, hints of black and gray smothered in snow. In the north, far north, mountains speared up. White against white.

Closer in, at the feet of the castle, the snow spread in sheets and blankets. He saw no movement, no tracks. No life.

Were they alone here? he wondered. He and the woman who called herself a queen?

Then he saw her, a regal flash of red against the white. She walked with a long, quick stride—as a woman might, he thought, bustle off to the market. As if she sensed him there, she stopped, turned. Looked up at his window.

He couldn't see her expression clearly, but the way her chin angled told him she was displeased with him. Then she turned away again, her fiery cloak swirling, as she continued over that sea toward the forest.

He wanted to go after her, to demand answers, explanations. But he could barely make it back to the bed before he collapsed. Trembling from the effort, he buried himself under the blankets again and slept the day away.

✷

"My lady, he's demanding to see you again."

Deirdre continued to work in the precious dirt under the wide dome. Her back ached, but she didn't mind it. In this, what she called her garden, she grew herbs and vegetables and a few precious flowers in the false spring generated by the sun through the glass.

"I have no time for him, Orna." She hoed a trench. It was a constant cycle, replenishing, tending, harvesting. The garden was life to her world. And one of her few true pleasures. "Between you and Cordelia he's tended well enough."

Orna pursed her lips. She had nursed Deirdre as a babe, had tutored her, tended her, and since the death of Queen Fiona, had stood when she could as mother. She was one of the few in Rose Castle who dared to question the young queen.

"It's been three days since he woke. The man is restless."

Deirdre straightened, rested her weight on the hoe. "Is he in pain?"

Orna's weathered face creased with what might have been impatience. "He says not, but he's a man, after all. He has pain. Despite it, and his weakness, he won't be kept to his chamber much longer. The man is a prince, my lady, and used to being obeyed."

"I rule here." Deirdre scanned her garden. The earlier plantings were satisfactory. She couldn't have the lush, but she could have the necessary. Even, she thought as she looked at her spindly, sun-starved daisies, the occasional indulgence.

"One of the kitchen boys should gather cabbages for dinner," she began. "Have the cook choose two of the hens. Our guest needs meat."

"Why do you refuse to see him?"

"I don't refuse." Annoyed, Deirdre went back to her work. She was avoiding the next meeting, and she knew it. Something had come into her during the healing, something she was unable to identify. It left her uneasy and unsettled.

"I stayed with him three days, three nights," she reminded Orna. "It's put me behind in my duties."

"He's very handsome."

"So is his horse," Deirdre said lightly. "And the horse is of more interest to me."

"And strong," Orna continued, stepping closer. "A prince from outside our world. He could be the one."

"There is no one." Deirdre tossed her head. Hope put no fuel in the fire nor food in the pot. It was a luxury she, above all, could ill afford. "I want no man, Orna. I will depend on no one but myself. It's woman's foolishness, woman's need, and man's deceit that have cursed us."

"Woman's pride as much as foolishness." Orna laid a hand on the staff of the hoe. "Will you let yours stop you from taking a chance for freedom?"

"I will provide for my people. When the time comes I will lie with a man until I conceive. I will make the next ruler, train the child as I was trained."

"Love the child," Orna murmured.

"My heart is so cold." Tired, Deirdre closed her eyes. "I fear there is no love in me. How can I give what isn't mine?"

"You're wrong." Gently Orna touched her cheek. "Your heart isn't cold. It's only trapped, as the rose is trapped in ice."

"Should I free it, Orna, so it could be broken as my mother's was?" She shook her head. "That solves nothing. Food must be put on the table, fuel must be gathered. Go now, tell our guest that I'll visit him in his chambers when time permits."

"This seems like a fine time." So saying, Kylar strode into the dome.

3

He'd never seen anything like the garden before. But then, Kylar had seen a great deal of the unexpected in Rose Castle in a short time. Such as a queen dressed in men's clothing—trousers and a ragged tunic. The result was odd, and strangely alluring. Her hair was tied back, but not with anything so female as a ribbon. She'd knotted it with a thin leather strap, such as he did himself when doing some quick spot of manual labor.

Her face was flushed from her work and as lovely as the flower he'd first taken her for. She did not look pleased to see him. Even as he watched, her eyes chilled.

Behold the ice queen, he thought. A man would risk freezing off important parts of his body should he try to thaw her.

"I see you're feeling better, my lord."

"If you'd spared me five minutes of your time, you'd have seen so before."

"Will you pardon us, Orna." She knelt and began to plant the long eyes of potatoes harvested earlier in the year. It was a distraction, one she needed. Seeing him again stirred her, in dangerous ways. "You'll excuse me, my lord, if I continue with my task."

"Are there no servants to do such things?"

"There are fifty-two of us in Rose Castle. We all have our places and our duties."

He squatted beside her, though it caused his side to weep. Taking her hand, he turned it over and examined the ridge of callus. "Then I would say, my lady, you have too many duties."

"It's not for you to question me."

"You don't give answers, so I must continue to question. You healed me. Why do you resent me?"

"I don't know. But I do know that I require both hands for this task." When he released her, she continued to plant. "I'm unused to strangers," she began. Surely that was it. She had never seen, much less healed, a stranger before. Wouldn't that explain why, after looking into his mind, into his heart, she felt so drawn to him?

And afraid of him.

"Perhaps my manners are unpolished, so I will beg your pardon for any slight."

"They're polished diamond-bright," he corrected. "And stab at a man."

She smiled a little. "Some men, I imagine, are used to softer females. I thought Cordelia would suit your needs."

"She's biddable enough, and pretty enough, which is why you have the dragon guarding her."

Her smile warmed fractionally. "Of course."

"I wonder why I prefer you to either of them."

"I couldn't say." She moved down the row, and when he started to move with her, he gasped. She cursed. "Stubborn." She rose, reached down, and to his surprise, wrapped her arms around him. "Hold on to me. I'll help you inside."

He simply buried his face in her hair. "Your scent," he told her. "It haunts me."

"Stop it."

"I can't get your face out of my head, even when I sleep."

Her stomach fluttered, alarming her. "Sir, I will not be trifled with."

"I'm too damn weak to trifle with you." Hating the unsteadiness, he leaned heavily against her. "But you're beautiful, and I'm not dead." When he caught his breath, he eased away. "I should be. I've had time to think that through." He stared hard into her eyes. "I've seen enough battle to know when a wound is mortal. Mine was. How did I cheat death, Deirdre? Are you a witch?"

"Some would say." Because his color concerned her, she unbent enough to put an arm around his waist. "You need to sit before you fall. Come back inside."

"Not to bed. I'll go mad."

She'd tended enough of the sick and injured to know the truth of that. "To a chair. We'll have tea."

"God spare me. Brandy?"

She supposed he was entitled. She led him through a doorway, down a dim corridor away from the kitchen. She skirted the main hallway and moved down yet another corridor. The room where she took him was small, chilly, and lined floor to ceiling with books.

She eased him into a chair in front of the cold fireplace, then went over to open the shutters and let in the light.

"The days are still long," she said conversationally as she walked to the fireplace. This one was framed in smooth green marble. "Planting needs to be finished while the sun can warm the seeds."

She crouched in front of the fire, set the logs to light. "Is there grass in your world? Fields of it?"

"Yes."

She closed her eyes a moment. "And trees that go green in spring?"

He felt a wrench in his gut. For home—and for her. "Yes."

"It must be like a miracle." Then she stood, and her voice was brisk again. "I must wash, and see to your brandy. You'll be warm by the fire. I won't be long."

"My lady, have you never seen a field of grass?"

"In books. In dreams." She opened her mouth again, nearly asked him to tell her what it smelled like. But she wasn't sure she could bear to know. "I won't keep you waiting long, my lord."

She was true to her word. In ten minutes she was back, her hair loose again over the shoulders of a dark green dress. She carried the brandy herself.

"Our wine cellars were well stocked once. My grandfather, I'm told, was shrewd in that area. And in this one," she added, gesturing toward the books. "He enjoyed a glass of good wine and a good book."

"And you?"

"The books often, the wine rarely."

When she glanced toward the door, he saw her smile, fully, warmly, for the first time. He could only stare at her as his throat went dry and his heart shuddered.

"Thank you, Magda. I would have come for it."

"You've enough to do, my lady, without carting trays." The woman seemed ancient to Kylar. Her face as withered as a winter apple, her body bowed as if she carried bricks on her back. But she set the tea tray on the sideboard and curtseyed with some grace. "Should I pour for you, my lady?"

"I'll see to it. How are your hands?"

"They don't trouble me overmuch."

Deirdre took them in her own. They were knotted and swollen at the joints. "You're using the ointment I gave you?"

"Yes, my lady, twice daily. It helps considerable."

Keeping her eyes on Magda's, Deirdre rubbed her thumbs rhythmically over the gnarled knuckles. "I have a tea that will help. I'll show you how to make it, and you'll drink a cup three times a day."

"Thank you, my lady." Magda curtseyed again before she left the room.

Kylar saw Deirdre rub her own hands as if to ease a pain before she reached for the teapot. "I'll answer your questions, Prince Kylar, and hope that you'll answer some of mine in turn." She brought him a small tray of cheese and biscuits, then settled into a chair with her tea.

"How do you survive?"

To the point, she thought. "We have the garden. Some chickens and goats for eggs and milk, and meat when meat is needed. There's the forest for fuel and, if we're lucky, for game. The young are trained in necessary skills. We live simply," she said, sipping her tea. "And well enough."

"Why do you stay?"

"Because this is my home. You risked your life in battle to protect yours."

"How do you know I didn't risk it to take what belonged to someone else?"

She watched him over the rim of her cup. Yes, he was handsome. His looks were only more striking now that he'd regained some of his strength. One of the servants had shaved him, and without the stubble of beard he looked younger. But little less dangerous. "Did you?"

"You know I didn't." His gaze narrowed on her face. "You know. How is that, Deirdre of the Ice?" He reached out, clamped a hand on her arm. "What did you do to me during the fever?"

"Healed you."

"With witchcraft?"

"I have a gift for healing," she said evenly. "Should I have used it, or let you die? There was no dark in it, and you are not bound to me for payment."

"Then why do I feel bound to you?"

Her pulse jumped. His hand wasn't gripping her arm now. It caressed. "I did nothing to tie you. I have neither desire nor the skill for it." Cautiously, she moved out of reach. "You have my word. When you're well enough to travel, you're free to go."

"How?" It was bitter. "Where?"

Pity stirred in her, swam into her eyes. She remembered the face of the woman in his mind, the love she'd felt flow between them. His mother, she thought. Even now watching for his return home.

"It won't be simple, nor without risk. But you have a horse, and we'll give you provisions. One of my men will travel with you as far as possible. I can do no more than that."

He put it aside for now. When the time came, he would find his way home. "Tell me how this came to be. This place. I've heard stories—betrayal and witchcraft and cold spells over a land that was once fruitful and at peace."

"So I am told." She rose again to stir the fire. "When my grandfather was king, there were farms and fields. The land was green and rich, the lake blue and thick with fish. Have you ever seen blue water?"

"I have, yes."

"How can it be blue?" she asked as she turned. There was puzzlement on her face, and more, he thought. An eagerness he hadn't seen before. It made her look very young.

"I haven't thought about it," he admitted. "It seems to be blue, or green, or gray. It changes, as the sky changes."

"My sky never changes." The eagerness vanished as she walked to the window. "Well," she said, and straightened her shoulders. "Well. My grandfather had two daughters, twin-born. His wife died giving them life, and it's said he grieved for her the rest of his days. The babes were named Ernia, who was my aunt, and Fiona, who was my mother, and on them he doted. Most parents dote on their children, don't they, my lord?"

"Most," he agreed.

"So he did. Like their mother, they were beautiful, and like their mother, they were gifted. Ernia could call the sun, the rain, the wind. Fiona could speak to the beasts and the birds. They were, I'm told, competitive, each vying for their father's favor though he loved them both. Do you have siblings, my lord?"

"A brother and a sister, both younger."

She glanced back. He had his mother's eyes, she thought. But her hair had been light. Perhaps his father had that ink-black hair that looked so silky.

"Do you love them, your brother and your sister?"

"Very much."

"That is as it should be. But Ernia and Fiona could not love each other. Perhaps it was because they shared the same face, and each wanted her own. Who can say? They grew from girl to woman, and my grandfather grew old and ill. He wanted them married and settled before his death. Ernia he betrothed to a king in a land beyond the Elf Hills, and my mother he promised to a king whose lands marched with ours to the east. Rose Castle was to be my mother's, and the Palace of Sighs, on the border of the Elf Hills, my aunt's. In this way he divided his wealth and lands equally between them, for he was, I'm told, a wise and fair ruler and a loving father."

She came back to sit and sip at tea gone cold. "In the weeks before the weddings, a traveler came and was welcome here as all were in those days. He was handsome and clever, quick of tongue and smooth with charm. A minstrel by trade, it's said he sang like an angel. But fair looks are no mirror of the heart, are they?"

"A pleasant face is only a face." Kylar lifted a shoulder. "Deeds make a man."

"Or woman," she added. "So I have always believed, and so, in this case, it was. In secret, this handsome man courted and seduced both twins, and both fell blindly in love with him. He came to my mother's bed, and to her sister's, bearing a single red rose and promises never meant to be kept. Why do men lie when women love?"

The question took him aback. "My lady . . . not all men are deceivers."

"Perhaps not." Though she was far from convinced. "But he was. One evening the sisters, of the same mind, wandered to the rose garden. Each wanted to pluck a red rose for her lover. It was there the lies were discovered. Instead of comforting each other, instead of raging against the man who had deceived them both, they fought over him. She-wolves over an unworthy badger. Ernia's temper called the wind and the hail, and Fiona's had the beasts stalking out of the forest to snarl and howl."

"Jealousy is both a flawed and a lethal weapon."

She angled her head. Nodded. "Well said. My grandfather heard the clamor and roused himself from his sickbed. Neither marriage could take place now, as both his daughters were disgraced. The minstrel, who had not slipped away quickly enough, was locked in the dungeon until his punishment could be decided. There was weeping and wailing from the sisters, as that punishment would surely be banishment, if not death. But he was spared when it came to be known that my mother was with child. His child, for she had lain with no other."

"You were the child."

"Yes. So, by becoming, I saved my father's life. The grief of this, the shame of this, ended my grandfather's. Before he died, he ordered Ernia to the Palace of Sighs. Because of the child, he decreed that my mother would marry the minstrel. It was this that drove Ernia mad, and on the day the marriage took place, the day her own father died in despair, she cast her spell.

"Winter, endless years of it. A sea of ice to lock Rose Castle away from the world. The rosebush where flowers had been plucked from lies would not bear bud. The child her sister carried would never feel the warmth of summer sun on her face, or walk in a meadow or see a tree bear fruit. One faithless man, three selfish hearts, destroyed a world. And so became the Isle of Winter in the Sea of Ice."

"My lady." He laid a hand on hers. Her life, he thought, the whole of it had been spent without the simple comfort of sunlight. "A spell cast can be broken. You have power."

"My gift is of healing. I cannot heal the land." Because she wanted to turn her hand over in his, link fingers, feel that connection, she drew away. "My father left my mother before I was born. Escaped. Later, as she watched her people starve, my mother sent messengers to the Palace of Sighs to ask for a truce. To beg for one. But they never came back. Perhaps they died, or lost their way. Or simply rode on into the warmth and the sun. No one who has left here has ever come back. Why would they?"

"Ernia the Witch-Queen is dead."

"Dead?" Deirdre stared into the fire. "You're sure of this?"

"She was feared, and loathed. There was great celebration

when she died. It was on the Winter Solstice, and I remember it well. She's been dead for nearly ten years."

Deirdre closed her eyes. "As her sister has. So they died together. How odd, and how apt." She rose again to walk to the window. "Ten years dead, and her spell holds like a clenched fist. How bitter her heart must have been."

And the faint and secret hope she'd kept flickering inside that upon her aunt's death the spell would break, winked out. She drew herself up. "What we can't change, we learn to be content with." She stared out at the endless world of white. "There is beauty here."

"Yes." It was Deirdre that Kylar watched. "Yes. There is beauty here."

4

He wanted to help her. More, Kylar thought, he wanted to save her. If there had been something tangible to fight—a man, a beast, an army—he would have drawn his sword and plunged into battle for her.

She moved him, attracted him, fascinated him. Her steady composure in the face of her fate stirred in him both admiration and frustration. This was not a woman to weep on a man's shoulder. It annoyed him to find himself wishing that she would, as long as the shoulder was his.

She was an extraordinary creature. He wanted to fight for her. But how did a man wage war on magic?

He'd never had any real experience with it. He was a soldier, and though he believed in luck, even in fate, he believed more in wile and skill and muscle.

He was a prince, would one day be a king. He believed in justice, in ruling with a firm touch on one hand and a merciful one on the other.

There was no justice here, where a woman who had done no wrong should be imprisoned for the crimes and follies and wickedness of those who had come before.

She was too beautiful to be shut away from the rest of the world. Too small, he mused, too fragile to work her hands raw. She should be draped in silks and ermine rather than homespun.

Already after less than a week on the Isle of Winter, he felt a restlessness, a need for color and heat. How had she stayed sane never knowing a single summer?

He wanted to bring her the sun.

She should laugh. It troubled him that he had not once heard her laugh. A smile, surprisingly warm when it was real enough to reach her eyes. That he had seen. He would find a way to see it again.

He waded through the snow across what he supposed had once been a courtyard. Though his wound had troubled him on waking, he was feeling stronger now. He needed to be doing, to find some work or activity to keep his blood moving and his mind sharp. Surely there was some task, some bit of work he could undertake for her here. It would repay her in some small way, and serve to keep his mind and hands busy while his body healed.

He recalled the stag he'd seen in the forest. He would hunt, then, and bring her meat. The wind that had thrashed ceaselessly for days had finally quieted. Though the utter stillness that followed it played havoc with the nerves, it would make tracking through the forest possible.

He moved through a wide archway on the other side of the courtyard. And stopped to stare.

This, he realized with wonder, had been the rose garden. Gnarled and blackened stalks tangled out of the snow. Once, he imagined, it would have been magnificent, full of color and scent and humming bees.

Now it was a great field of snow cased in ice.

Bisecting that field were graceful paths of silver stone, and someone kept them clear. There were hundreds of bushes, all brittle with death, the stalks spearing out of their cold graves like blackened bones.

Benches, these, too, cleared of snow and ice, stood in graceful curves of deep jewel colors. Ruby, sapphire, emerald, they gleamed in the midst of the stark and merciless white. There was a small pond in the shape of an open rose, and its flower held a rippled sheet of ice. Dead branches with vicious thorns strangled iron arbors. More spindly corpses climbed up the silver stone of the walls as if they'd sought to escape before winter murdered them.

In the center, where all paths led, was a towering column of ice. Under the glassy sheen, he could see the arch of blackened branches studded with thorns, and hundreds of withered flowers trapped forever in their moment of death.

The rosebush, he thought, where the flowers of lies had been plucked. No, he corrected as he moved toward it. More a tree, for it was taller than he was and spread wider than the span of both his arms. He ran his fingertips over the ice, found it smooth. Experimentally, he took the dagger from his belt, dragged its tip over the ice. It left no mark.

"It cannot be reached with force."

Kylar turned and saw Orna standing in the archway. "What of the rest? Why haven't the dead branches been cleared and used for fire?" he asked her.

"To do so would be to give up hope." She had hope still, and more when she looked into Kylar's eyes.

She saw what she needed there. Truth, strength, and courage. "She walks here."

"Why would she punish herself in such a way?" he demanded.

"It reminds her, I think, of what was. And what is." But not, Orna feared, of what might be. "Once, when my lady was but eight, and the last of the dogs died, breaking her heart, she took her grandfather's sword. In her grief and temper, she tried to hack through that ice into the bush. For nearly an hour she stabbed and sliced and beat at it, and could not so much as scratch the surface. In the end, she went to her knees there where you stand now and wept as if she'd die from it. Something in her did die that day, along with the last of the dogs. I have not heard her weep since. I wish she would."

"Why do you wish for your lady's tears?"

"For then she would know her heart is not dead but, like the rose, only waiting."

He sheathed his dagger. "If force can't reach it, what can?"

She smiled, for she knew he spoke of the heart as much as the rose. "You will make a good king in your time, Kylar of Mrydon, for you listen to what isn't said. What can't be vanquished with sword or might can be won with truth, with love, with selflessness. She is in the stables, what is left of them. She wouldn't ask for your company, but would enjoy it."

★

The stables lined three sides of another courtyard, but this one was crisscrossed with crooked paths dug through or trampled into the snow. Kylar saw the reason for it in the small troop of children waging a lively snow battle at the far end. Even in such a world, he thought, children found a way to be children.

As he drew closer to the stables, he heard the low cackle of hens. There were men on the roof, working on a chimney. They tipped their caps to him as he passed under the eaves and into the stables.

It was warmer, thanks to carefully banked fires, and clean as a parlor. The queen, he thought, tended her goats and chickens well. Iron kettles heated over the fires. Water for the stock, he concluded, made from melted snow. He noted barrows of manure. For use in her garden, he decided. A wise and practical woman, Queen Deirdre.

Then he saw the wise and practical woman, with her red hood tossed back, her gold hair raining down as she cooed up at his warhorse.

When the horse shook its great head and blew, she laughed. The rich female sound warmed his blood more thoroughly than the fires.

"His name is Cathmor."

Startled, embarrassed, Deirdre dropped the hands she'd lifted to stroke the horse's muzzle. She knew she shouldn't have lingered, that he would come check on his horse as it had been reported he did twice daily. But she'd so wanted to see the creature herself.

"You have a light step."

"You were distracted." He walked up beside her, and to her surprise and delight, the horse bumped his shoulder in greeting.

"Does that mean he's glad to see you?"

"It means he's hoping I have an apple."

Deirdre fingered the small carrot from her garden she'd tucked in her pocket. "Perhaps this will do." She pulled it out, started to offer it to Kylar.

"He would enjoy being fed by a lady. No, not like that." He took her hand and, opening it, laid the carrot on her palm. "Have you never fed a horse?"

"I've never seen one." She caught her breath as Cathmor dipped his head and nibbled the carrot out of her palm. "He's bigger than I imagined, and more handsome. And softer." Unable to resist, she stroked her hand down the horse's nose. "Some of the children have been keeping him company. They'd make a pet of him if they could."

"Would you like to ride him?"

"Ride?"

"He needs the exercise, and so do I. I thought I would hunt this morning. Come with me."

To ride a horse? Just the idea of it was thrilling. "I have duties."

"I might get lost alone." He brought her hand back up, ran it under his along Cathmor's silky neck. "I don't know your forest. And I'm still a bit weak."

Her lips twitched. "Your wits are strong enough. I could send a man with you."

"I prefer your company."

To ride a horse, she thought again. How could she resist? Why should she? She was no fluttery girl who would fall into stutters and blushes by being alone with a man. Even this man.

"All right. What do I do first?"

"You wait until I saddle him."

She shook her head. "No, show me how to do it."

When it was done, she sent one of the boys scurrying off to tell Orna she was riding out with the prince. She needn't have bothered, for as they walked the horse out of the stables, her people began to gather at the windows, in the courtyard.

When he vaulted into the saddle, they cheered him like a hero.

"It's been a long time since they've seen anyone ride," she explained as Cathmor pranced in place. "Some of them, like me, never have." She let out a breath. "It's a long way up."

"Give me your hand." He reached down to her. "Trust me."

She would have to if she wanted this amazing treat. She offered her hand, then yelped in shock when he simply hauled her up in the saddle in front of him.

"You might have warned me you intended to drag me up like a sack of turnips. If you've opened your wound again—"

"Quiet," he whispered, entirely too close to her ear for comfort, and with her people cheering, he kicked Cathmor into a trot.

"Oh." Her eyes popped wide as her bottom bounced. "It's not what I expected." And hardly dignified.

With shouts and whoops, children raced after them as they trotted out of the castle.

"Match the rhythm of your body to the gait of the horse," he told her.

"Yes, I'm trying. Must you be so close?"

He grinned. "Yes. And I'm enjoying it. You shouldn't be uneasy with a man, Deirdre, when you've seen him naked."

"Seeing you naked hardly gives me cause to relax around you," she shot back.

With a rolling laugh, he urged the horse to a gallop.

Her breath caught, but with delight rather than fear. Wind rushed by her cheeks, and snow flew up into the air like tattered lace. She closed her eyes for an instant to absorb the sensation, and the wild thrill made her dizzy.

So fast, she thought. So strong. When they charged up a hill she wanted to throw her arms in the air and shout for the sheer joy of it.

Her heart raced along with the horse, continued to pound even when they slowed at the verge of the forest that had been known as the Forgotten for the whole of her lifetime.

"It's like flying," she mused. "Oh, thank you." She leaned down to press her cheek to the horse's neck. "I'll never forget it. He's a grand horse, isn't he?"

Flushed with pleasure, she turned. His face was too close, so close she felt the warmth of his breath on her cheek. Close enough that she saw a kind of heat kindling in his eyes.

"No." He caught her chin with his hand before she could turn away again. "Don't. I kissed you before, when I thought I was dying." His lips hovered a breath from hers. "I lived."

He had to taste her again; it seemed his sanity depended on it. But because he saw her fear, he took her mouth gently, skimming his lips over ones that trembled. Soothing as well as seducing. He watched her eyes go soft before her lashes fluttered down.

"Kiss me back, Deirdre." His hand slid down until his arm could band her waist and draw her closer. "This time kiss me back."

"I don't know how." But she already was.

Her limbs went weak, wonderfully weak, even as her pulse danced madly. Warmth enveloped her, reaching places inside that had never known its comfort.

The light that had sparked inside her when their hearts had brushed in healing spread.

On the Isle of Winter in the snowy rose garden, beneath a shield of ice, a tiny bud—tender green—formed on a blackened branch.

He nibbled at her lips until she parted them. And when he deepened the kiss she felt, for the first time in her life, a true lance of heat in her belly.

Yearning for more, she eased back, then indulged herself by letting her head rest briefly on his shoulder. "So it's this," she whispered. "It's this that makes the women sing in the kitchen in the morning."

He stroked her hair, rubbed his cheek against it. "It's a bit more than that." Sweet, he thought. Strong. She was everything a man could want. Everything, he realized, that he wanted.

"Yes, of course." She sighed once. "More than that, but it starts like this. It can't for me."

"It has." He held her close when she would have drawn away. "It did, the minute I saw you."

"If I could love, it would be you. Though I'm not sure why, it would be you. If I were free, I would choose you." She turned away again. "We came to hunt. My people need meat."

He fought the urge to yank her around, to plunder that lovely mouth until she yielded. Force wasn't the answer. So he'd been told. There were better ways to win a woman.

5

She spotted the tracks first. They moved soundlessly through the trees, and she was grateful for the need for silence.

How could she explain or ask him to understand, when she couldn't understand herself? Her heart was frozen, chilled to death by pride and duty, and the fear that she might do her people more harm.

Her father had made her in lies, then had run away from his obligation. Her mother had done her duty, and she had been kind. But her heart had been broken into so many pieces there had been none left for her child.

And what sort of child was it who could grieve more truly for a dead dog than for her own dead mother?

She had nothing emotionally to give a man, and wanted nothing from one. In that way she would survive, and keep her people alive.

Life, she reminded herself, mattered most. And what she felt for him was surely no more than a churning in the blood.

But how could she have known what it was like to be held by

him? To feel his heart beat so strong and fast against hers? None of the books she'd read had captured with their clever words the true thrill of lips meeting.

Now that she understood, it would be just another precious memory, like a ride on horseback, to tuck away for the endless lonely nights.

She would decide later, she thought, if the nights were longer, lonelier, with the memory than they were without it.

But today she couldn't allow herself to think like a woman softened by a man's touch. She must think like a queen with people to provide for.

She caught the scent of the stag even before the horse did, and held up a hand. "We should walk from here," she said under her breath.

He didn't question her, but dismounted, then reached up to lift her down. Then his arms were around her again, her hands on his shoulders, and her face tilted up to his. Even as she shook her head, he brushed his lips over her brow.

"Deirdre the fair," he said softly. "Such a pretty armful."

The male scent of him blurred the scent of the stag. "This is not the time."

Because the catch in her voice was enough to satisfy him, for now, he reached over for his bow and quiver. But when she held out her hands for them, he lifted his eyebrows.

"The bow is too heavy a draw for you." When she continued to stare, hands outstretched, he shrugged and gave them to her.

So, he thought, he would indulge her. They'd make do with more cabbage tonight.

Then he was left blinking as she tossed aside her cloak and streaked through the trees in her men's clothes like a wraith—soundless and swift. Before he could tether his horse, she'd vanished and he could do no more than follow in her tracks.

He stopped when he caught sight of her. She stood in the gloomy light, nearly hip-deep in snow. With a gesture smooth and polished as a warrior, she notched the arrow, drew back the heavy bow. The sharp *ping* of the arrow flying free echoed. Then she lowered the bow, and her head.

"Everyone misses sometimes," he said as he started toward her.

Her head came up, her face cold and set. "I did not miss. I find no pleasure in the kill. My people need meat."

She handed the bow and quiver back to him, then trudged through the snow to where the stag lay.

Kylar saw she'd taken it down, fast, mercifully fast, with a single shot.

"Deirdre," he called out. "Do you ask yourself how game, even so sparse, come to be here where there is no food for them?"

She continued walking. "My mother did what she could, leaving a call that would draw them to the forest. She hoped to teach me to do the same, but it's not my gift."

"You have more than one," he said. "I'll get the horse."

★

Once the deer was strapped onto the horse, Kylar cupped his hands to help Deirdre mount. "Put your right foot in my hands, swing your left leg over the saddle."

"There isn't room for both of us now. You ride, I'll walk."

"No, I'll walk."

"It's too far when you've yet to fully recover. Mount your horse." She started to move past him, but he blocked her path. Her shoulders straightened like an iron bar. "I said, mount. I am a queen, and you merely a prince. You will do as I bid."

"I'm a man, and you merely a woman." He shocked her speechless by picking her up and tossing her into the saddle. "You'll do what you're told."

However much she labored side by side with her people, no one had ever disobeyed a command. And no man had ever laid hands on her. "You . . . *dare*."

"I'm not one of your people." He gathered the reins and began to walk the horse through the forest. "Whatever our ranks, I'm as royal as you. Though that doesn't mean a damn at the moment. It's difficult to think of you as a queen when you're garbed like a man and I've seen you handle a bow that my own squire can barely manage. It's difficult to think of you as a queen, Deirdre," he added with a glance back at her furious face, "when I've held you in my arms."

"Then you'd best remember what that felt like, for you won't be allowed to do so again."

He stopped, and turning, ran his hand deliberately up her leg. When she kicked out at him, he caught her boot and laughed. "Ah, so there's a temper in there after all. Good. I prefer bedding a woman with fire in her."

Quick as a snake the dagger was out of her belt and in her hand. And its killing point at his throat. "Remove your hand."

He never flinched, but realized to his own shock that this wasn't merely a woman he could want. It was a woman he could love. "Would you do it, I wonder? I think you might while the temper's on you, but then you'd regret it." He brought his hand up slowly, gripped her knife hand by the wrist. "We'd both regret it. I tell you I want to bed you. I give you the truth. Do you want lies?"

"You can bed Cordelia, if she's willing."

"I don't want Cordelia, willing or not." He took the knife from her hand, then brushed a kiss over her palm. "But I want you, Deirdre. And I want you willing." He handed her back the dagger, hilt first. "Can you handle a sword as well as you do a dagger?"

"I can."

"You're a woman of marvels, Deirdre the fair." He began to walk again. "I understand developing skill with the bow, but what need have you for sword or dagger?"

"Ignoring training in defense is careless and lazy. The training itself is good for the body and the mind. If my people are expected to learn how to handle a blade, then so should I be."

"Agreed."

When he paused a second time, her eyes narrowed in warning. "I'm going to shorten the stirrups so you can ride properly. What happened to your horses?"

"Those who left the first year took them." She ordered herself to relax and pleased herself by stroking Cathmor's neck again. "There were cattle, too, and sheep. Those that didn't die of the cold were used as food. There were cottages and farmhouses, but people came to the castle for shelter, for food. Or wandered off hoping to find spring. Now they're under the snow and ice. Why do you want to bed me?"

"Because you're beautiful."

She frowned down at him. "Are men so simple, really?"

He laughed, shook his head, and her fingers itched to tangle in his silky black mane rather than the horse's. "Simple enough about certain matters. But I hadn't finished the answer. Your beauty would be enough to make me want you for a night. Try this now, heels down. That's fine."

He gave her foot a friendly pat, then walked back to the horse's head. "Your strength and your courage add layers to beauty. They appeal to me. Your mind's sharp and cleaves clean. That's a challenge. And a woman who can plant potatoes like a farmwife and draw a dagger like an assassin is a fascinating creature."

"I thought when a man wanted to pleasure himself with a

woman, he softened her with pretty words and poetry and long looks full of pain and longing."

What a woman, Kylar mused. He'd never seen the like of her. "Would you like that?"

She considered it, and was relaxed again. It was easier to discuss the whole business as a practical matter. "I don't know."

"You wouldn't trust them."

She smiled before she could stop it. "I wouldn't, no. Have you bedded many women?"

He cleared his throat and began to walk a bit faster. "That, sweetheart, isn't a question I'm comfortable answering."

"Why not?"

"Because it's . . . it's a delicate matter," he decided.

"Would you be more comfortable telling me if you've killed many men?"

"I don't kill for sport, or for pleasure," he said, and his voice turned as frigid as the air. "Taking a man's life is no triumph, my lady. Battle is an ugly business."

"I wondered. I meant no offense."

"I would have let them go." He spoke so softly that she had to lean forward to hear clearly.

"Who?"

"The three who set upon me after the battle had been won. When I was for home. I would have let them pass in peace. What purpose was there in more blood?"

She'd already seen this inside him, and knew it for truth. He had not killed in hate nor in some fever of dark excitement. He had killed to live. "They wouldn't let you pass in peace."

"They were tired, and one already wounded. If I'd had an escort as I should, they would have surrendered. In the end, it was their own fear and my carelessness that killed them. I'm sorry for it."

More for the waste of their lives, she realized, than for his own wounds. Understanding this, she felt something sigh inside her. "Kylar."

It was the first time she'd spoken his name, as she might to a friend. And she leaned down to touch his cheek with her fingertips, as she might touch a lover's.

"You'll rule well."

✳

She invited him to sup with her that night. Another first. He dressed in the fresh doublet Cordelia brought him, one of soft linen that smelled lightly of lavender and rosemary. He wondered from what chest it had been unearthed for his use, but as it fit well enough, he had no cause to complain.

But when he followed the servant into the dining hall, he wished for his court clothes.

She wore green again, but no simple dress of homespun. The velvet gown poured down her body, dipping low at the creamy rise of her breasts and sweeping out from her waist in soft, deep folds. Her hair was long and loose, but over it sparkled a crown glinting with jewels. More draped in shimmering ropes around her throat.

She stood in the glow of candlelight, beautiful as a vision, and every inch a queen.

When she offered a hand, he crossed to her, bowed deeply before touching his lips to her knuckles. "Your Majesty."

"Your Highness. The room," she said with a gesture she hoped hid the nerves and pleasure she felt upon seeing the open approval on his face, "is overlarge for two. I hope you'll be comfortable."

"I see nothing but you."

She titled her head. Curious, this flirting, she decided. And entertaining. "Are these the pretty words and poetry?"

"They're the truth."

"They fall pleasantly on the ear. It's an indulgence to have a fire in here," she began as she let him escort her to the table. "But tonight there is wine, and venison, and a welcome guest."

At the head of the long table were two settings. Silver and crystal and linen white as the snow outside the windows. Behind them, the mammoth fire roared.

Servants slipped in to serve wine and the soup course. If he'd been able to tear his gaze away from Deirdre, he might have seen the glint in their eyes, the exchanged winks and quick grins.

She missed them as well, as she concentrated on the experience of her first formal meal with someone from outside her world. "The fare is simple," she began.

"As good as a bounty. And the company feeds me."

She studied him thoughtfully. "I do think I like pretty words, but I have no skill in holding a conversation with them."

He took her hand. "Why don't we practice?"

Her laugh bubbled out, but she shook her head. "Tell me of your home, your family. Your sister," she remembered. "Is she lovely?"

"She is. Her name is Gwenyth. She married two years ago."

"Is there love?"

"Yes. He was friend and neighbor, and they had a sweetness for each other since childhood. When I last saw her she was great with her second babe." The faintest cloud passed over his face. "I'd hoped to make my way home for the birthing."

"And your brother?"

"Riddock is young, headstrong. He can ride like the devil."

"You're proud of him."

"I am. He'd give you poetry." Kylar lifted his goblet. "He has a knack for it, and loves nothing more than luring pretty maids out to the garden in the moonlight."

She asked questions casually so he would talk. She was unsure of her conversational skills in this arena, and it was such a pleasure to just sit and listen to him speak so easily of things that were, to her, a miracle.

Summer and gardens, swimming in a pond, riding through a village where people went to market. Carts of glossy red apples—what would they taste like? Baskets of flowers whose scent she could only dream of.

She had a picture of his home now, as she had pictures in books.

She had a picture of him, and it was more than anything she'd ever found in a book.

Willing to pay whatever it cost her later, she lost herself in him, in the way his voice rose and fell, in his laugh. She thought she could sit this way for days, to talk like this with no purpose in it, no niggling worries. Just to be with him by the warmth of the fire, with wine sweet on her tongue and his eyes so intimately on hers.

She didn't object when he took her hand, when his fingers toyed with hers. If this was flirtation, it was such a lovely way to pass the time.

They spoke of faraway lands and cultures. Of paintings and of plays.

"You've put your library to good use," he commented. "I've known few scholars as well read."

"I can see the world through books, and lives through the stories. Once a year, on Midsummer, we put on a pageant. We have music and games. I choose a story, and everyone takes a part as if it were a play. Surviving isn't enough. There must be life and color."

There were times, secretly, when she pined near weeping for true color.

"All the children are taught to read," she continued, "and to do sums. If you have only a window on the world, you must look out of it. One of my men—well, he's just a boy really—he makes stories. They're quite wonderful."

She caught herself, surprised at the sound of her own voice rambling. "I've kept you long enough."

"No." His hand tightened on hers. He was beginning to realize it would never be long enough. "Tell me more. You play music, don't you? A harp. I heard you playing, singing. It was like a dream."

"You were feverish. I play a little. Some skill inherited from my father, I suppose."

"I'd like to hear you play again. Will you play for me, Deirdre?"

"If you like."

But as she started to rise, one of the men who'd helped serve rushed in. "My lady, my lady, it's young Phelan!"

"What's happened?"

"He was playing with some of the boys on the stairs, and fell. We can't wake him. My lady, we fear he's dying."

6

Afraid to move him, they'd left the boy covered with a blanket at the base of the stairs. At first glance, Kylar thought the child, for he was hardly more, was already dead. He'd seen enough of death to recognize its face.

He judged the boy to be about ten, with fair hair and cheeks still round with youth. But those cheeks were gray, and the hair was matted with blood.

Those who circled and knelt around the boy made way when Deirdre hurried through.

"Get back now," she ordered. "Give him room."

Before Deirdre could kneel, a weeping woman broke free to fall at her feet and clutch at her skirts with bloodstained hands. "My baby. Oh, please, my lady! Help my little boy."

"I will, Ailish. Of course I will." Knowing that time was precious, Deirdre bent down and firmly loosened the terrified woman's hold on her. "You must be strong for him, and trust. Let me see to him now."

"He slipped, my lady." Another youth came forward with a

jerky step. His eyes were dry, but huge, and there were tracks of tears still drying on his cheeks. "We were playing horse and rider on the stairs, and he slipped."

"All right." Too much grief, she thought, feeling waves of it pressing over her. Too much fear. "It's all right now. I'll tend to him."

"Deirdre." Kylar kept his voice low, so only she could hear over the mother's weeping. "There's nothing you can do here. I can smell death on him."

As could she, and so she knew she had little time. "What is the smell of death but the smell of fear?" She ran her hands gently over the crumpled body, feeling the hurts, finding so much broken in the little boy that her heart ached from it. Medicines would do no good here, but still her face was composed as she looked up.

"Cordelia, fetch my healing bag. Make haste. The rest, please, leave us now. Leave me with him. Ailish, go now."

"Oh, no, please, my lady. Please, I must stay with my boy."

"Do you trust me?"

"My lady." She gripped Deirdre's hand, wept on it. "I do."

"Then do as I bid you. Go now and pray."

"His neck," Kylar began, then broke off when Deirdre whipped her head around and stared at him.

"Be silent! Help me or go, but don't question me."

When Ailish was all but carried away, and the two of them were alone with the bleeding boy, Deirdre closed her eyes. "This will hurt him. I'm sorry for it. Hold him down, hold him as still as you can, and do nothing to interfere. Nothing, do you understand?"

"No." But Kylar shifted until he could clamp the boy's arms.

"Block thoughts of death from your mind," she ordered.

"And fear, and doubt. Block them out as you would in battle. There's too much dark here already. Can you do this?"

"I can." And because she asked it of him, Kylar let the cold come into him, the cold that steeled the mind to face combat.

"Phelan," she said. "Young Phelan, the bard." Her voice was soft, almost a crooning as she traced her hands over him again. "Be strong for me."

She knew him already, had watched him grow and learn and be. She knew the sound of his voice, the quick flash of his grin, the lively turn of his mind. He had been hers, as all in Rose Castle were hers, from the moment of his first breath.

And so she merged easily with him.

While her hands worked, stroking, kneading, she slid into his mind. She felt his laughter inside her as he pranced and raced with his friends up and down the narrow stone steps. Felt his heart leap inside her own as his feet slipped. Then the fear, oh, the terror, an instant only before the horrible pain.

The snap of bone made her cry out softly, had her head rearing back. Something inside her crushed like thin clay under a stone hammer, and the sensation was beyond torment.

Her eyes were open now, Kylar saw. A deep and too brilliant green. Her breath came fast and hard, sweat pearled on her brow. And the boy screamed thinly, straining under his grip.

Both made a sound of agony as she slid a hand under the boy to cup his neck, laid her other on his heart. Both shuddered. Both went pale as death.

Kylar started to call out to her, to reach for her as she swayed. But he felt the heat, a ferocious fist of it that seemed to pump out of her, into the boy until the arms he held were like sticks of fire.

And the boy's eyes opened, stared up blindly.

"Take, young Phelan." Her voice was thick now, echoed richly off the stone. "Take what you need. Fire of healing." She leaned down, laid her lips gently on his. "Live. Stay with us. Your mother needs you."

As Kylar watched, thunderstruck, color seeped back into the boy's face. He would have sworn he felt death skitter back into the shadows.

"My lady," the boy said, almost dreamily. "I fell."

"Yes, I know. Sleep now." She brushed her hand over his eyes, and they closed on a sigh. "And heal. Let his mother in, if you will," she said to Kylar. "And Cordelia."

"Deirdre—"

"Please." The weakness threatened to drag her under, and she wanted to be away, in her own chamber, before she lost herself to it. "Let them in so I can tell them what must be done for him."

She stayed kneeling when Kylar rose. The sounds of her people were like the dull roar of the ocean in her head. Even as Ailish collapsed next to her son, to gather him close to kiss Deirdre's now trembling hand, Deirdre gave clear, careful instructions for his care.

"Enough!" Alarmed by her pallor, Kylar swept her off the floor and into his arms. "Tend the boy."

"I'm not finished," Deirdre managed.

"Yes, by the blood, you are." The single glance he swept over those gathered challenged any to contradict him. "Where is your chamber?"

"This way, my lord prince." Orna led him through a doorway, down a corridor to another set of stairs. "I know what to do for her, my lord."

"Then you'll do it." He glanced down at Deirdre as he carried her up the stairs. She had swooned after all, he noted. Her skin was like glass, her eyes closed. The boy's blood was on her hands. "What did she risk by snatching the boy from death?"

"I cannot say, my lord." She opened a door, hurried across a chamber to the bed. "I will care for her now."

"I stay."

Orna pressed her lips together as he laid Deirdre on the bed. "I must undress her. Wash her."

Struggling with temper, he turned to stalk to the window. "Then do so. Is this what she did for me?"

"I cannot say." Orna met his eyes directly when he turned back. "She did not speak of it to me. She does not speak of it with anyone. Prince Kylar, I will ask you to turn your back until my lady is suitably attired in her night garb."

"Woman, her modesty is not an issue with me." But he turned, stared out the window.

He had heard of those who could heal with the mind. But he had not believed it, not truly believed, before tonight. Nor had he considered what price the healer paid to heal.

"She will sleep," Orna said some time later.

"I won't disturb her." He came to the bed now, gazed down. There was still no color in her cheeks, but it seemed to him her breathing was steadier. "Nor will I leave her."

"My lady is strong, as valiant as ten warriors."

"If I had ten as valiant, there would never be another battle to fight."

Pleased with his response, Orna inclined her head. "And my lady has, despite what she believes, a tender heart." Orna set a bottle and goblet on the table near the bed. "See that you don't bruise it. When she wakes, give her some of this tonic. I will not be far, should you need me."

Alone, Kylar drew a chair near the bed and watched Deirdre

sleep. For an hour, and then two. She was motionless and pale as marble in the firelight, and he feared she would never wake but would sleep like the beauty in another legend, for a hundred years.

Even days before he would have deemed such things foolishness, stories for children. But now, after what he'd seen, what he'd felt, anything seemed possible.

Still, side by side with the worry inside him, anger bloomed. She had risked her life. He had seen death slide its cold fingers over her. She had bargained her life for the child's.

And, he was sure now, for his own.

When she stirred, just the slightest flutter of her lashes, he poured the tonic Orna had left into the cup.

"Drink this." He lifted her head from the pillow. "Don't speak. Just drink now."

She sipped, and sighed. The hand she lifted to his wrist slid limply away again. "Phelan?" she whispered.

"I don't know." He brought the cup to her lips a second time. "Drink more."

She obeyed, then turned her head. "Ask. Ask how young Phelan fares. Please. I must be sure."

"Drink first. Drink it all."

She did as he bade, and kept her eyes open and on his now. If she'd had the strength, she would have gone to find out herself. But the weakness was still dragging at her, and she could only trust Kylar to the task. "Please. I won't be easy until I know his condition."

Kylar set the empty cup aside, then crossed the chamber to the door. Orna sat on a chair in the corridor, sewing by candlelight. She glanced up when she saw him. "Tell my lady not to fret. Young Phelan is resting. Healing." She got to her feet. "If you would like to retire, my lord, I will sit with my lady."

"Go to your bed," he said shortly. "I stay with her tonight."

Orna bowed her head and hid a smile. "As you wish."

He stepped back inside, closed the door. And turning saw that Deirdre was sitting up in bed, with her hair spilling like honey over the white lawn of her nightdress.

"Your boy is resting, and well."

At his words, he saw color return to her face, watched the dullness clear from her eyes. He came to the foot of the bed, which was draped in deep red velvet. "You recover quickly, madam."

"The tonic is potent." Indeed she now felt clear of mind, and even the echoes of pain were fading from her body. "Thank you for your help. His mother and father would have been too distraught to assist. Their worry could have distracted me. More, fear feeds death."

She glanced around the room, a little warily. Orna hadn't laid out her nightrobe. "If you'd excuse me now, I'll go see for myself."

"Not tonight."

To her shock he sat on the side of the bed near her. Only pride kept her from shifting over, or tugging up the blankets.

"I have questions."

"I've answered several of your questions already."

He lifted his brows. "Now I have more. The boy was dying. His skull crushed, his neck damaged if not broken. His left arm was shattered."

"Yes," she said calmly. "And inside his body, more was harmed. He bled inside himself. So much blood for such a little boy. But he has a strong heart, our Phelan. He is particularly precious to me."

"He would have been dead in minutes."

"He is not dead."

"Why?"

"I can't answer." Restlessly, she pushed at her hair. "I can't explain it to you."

"Won't."

"Can't."

When she would have turned her face away, he caught her chin, held it firmly. "Try."

"You overstep," she said stiffly. "Continually."

"Then you should be growing accustomed to it. I held the boy," he reminded her. "I watched, and I felt life come back into him. Tell me what you did."

She wanted to dismiss him, but he had helped her when she'd needed his help. So she would try. "It's a kind of search, and a merging. An opening of both." She lifted a hand, let it fall. "It is a kind of faith, if you will."

"It caused you pain."

"Do you think fighting death is painless? You know better. To heal, I must feel what he feels, and bring him up. . . ." She shook her head, frustrated with words. "Take him back to the pain. Then we ride it together, so that I see, feel, know."

"You rode more than pain. You rode death. I saw you."

"We were stronger."

"And if you hadn't been?"

"Then death would have won," she said simply. "And a mother would be grieving her firstborn tonight."

"And you? Deirdre of the Ice, would your people be grieving you?"

"There is a risk. Do you turn from battle, Kylar? Or do you face it knowing your life might be the price paid at end of day? Would you not stand for any one of your people if they had need? Would you expect me to do less for one of mine?"

"I was not one of yours." He took her hand before she could

look away. "You rode death with me, Deirdre. I remember. I thought it a dream, but I remember. The pain, as if the sword cut into me fresh. That same pain mirrored in your eyes as you looked down at me. The heat of your body, the heat of your life pouring into me. I was nothing to you."

"You were a man. You were hurt." She reached out now, laying her hand on his cheek. "Why are you angry? Should I have let you die because my medicines weren't enough to save you? Should I have stepped back from you and my own gift because it would cause me a moment's pain to save you? Does your pride bleed now because a woman fought for your life?"

"Perhaps it does." He closed his hand over her wrist. "When I carried you in here I thought you would die, and I was helpless."

"You stayed with me. That was kind."

He made some sound, then pushed himself off the bed to pace. "When a man goes into battle, Deirdre, it's sword to sword, lance to lance, fist to fist. These are tangible things. What you've done, magic or miracle, is so much more. And you were right. I can't understand it."

"It changes how you think of me."

"Yes."

She lowered her lashes, hid the fresh pain. "There is no shame in it. Most men would not have stayed to help, certainly not have stayed to speak with me. I'm grateful. Now if you'd excuse me, I'd like to be alone."

Slowly, he turned back to her. "You misunderstand me. Before I thought of you as a woman—beautiful, strong, intelligent. Sad. Now I think of you as all of that, and so much more. You humble me. You expect me to step away from you, because of all you are. I can't. I want to be with you, and I have no right."

With her heart unsteady, she looked at him again. "Is it gratitude that draws you to me?"

"I am grateful. I owe you for every breath I take. But it isn't gratitude I feel when I look at you."

She slid out of bed to stand on her own feet. "Is it desire?"

"I desire you."

"I've never had a man's arms around me in love. I want them to be yours."

"What right do I have when I can't stay with you? I should already be gone. Both my family and my people wait."

"You give me truth, and truth means more than pretty words and empty promises. I wondered about this, and now I know. When I healed you I felt something I've never felt before. Mixed with the pain and the cold that comes into me so bitter there was . . . light."

Watching him, she spread her hands. "I said I did nothing to bind you to me, and that is truth. But something happened in me when I was part of you. It angered me, and it frightened me. But now, just now . . ." She drew a breath and spoke without a blush. "It excites me. I've been so cold. Give me one night of warmth. You said you wanted me willing." She reached up, tugged the ribbons loose from the bodice of the nightdress. "And I am," she said as the white gown slid down to pool at her feet.

7

She was a vision. More than he could have dreamed. Slim and small, she stood in the glow of candle and firelight.

"Will you give me a night?" she asked him.

"Deirdre. My love. I would give you a lifetime."

"I want no pledges that can't be kept, no words but truth. Only give me what can be, and it will be enough," she replied somberly.

"My lady." He felt, somehow, that the step toward her was the most momentous of his life. And when he took her hands, that he was taking the world. "It is the truth. Why or how I don't know. But never have I spoken cleaner truth."

She believed he meant it, in this time. In this place. "Kylar, lifetimes are for those who are free."

So she would be, he promised himself. Whatever had to be done. But now wasn't for plans and battles. "If you won't accept that pledge, let me pledge this. That I have loved no other as I love you tonight."

"I can give that vow back to you. I thought it would be for duty." She lifted her hands to his face, traced the shape of it with

her fingers. "And I thought the first time, it would be with fear."
She laughed a little. "My heart jumps. Can you feel it?"

He laid a hand on her breast, felt the shiver. Felt the leap. "I
won't hurt you."

"Oh, no." She laid a hand on his heart in turn. They had
brushed once before, she thought. Heart to heart. Nothing had
been the same for her since. Nothing would be the same for her
ever again. "You won't hurt me. Warm me, Kylar, as a man
warms his woman."

He drew her into his arms. Gently, gently. Laid his lips on
hers. Tenderly. There once more, she thought. There. That miracle of mouth against mouth. Sighing out his name, she let herself
melt into the kiss.

"The first time you kissed me, I thought you were foolish."

His lips curved on hers. "Did you?"

"Half frozen and bleeding, and you would waste your last
breath flirting with a woman. Such is a man."

"Not a waste," he corrected. "But I can do better now." With
a flourish that pleased them both, he swept her into his arms.
"Come to bed, my lady."

As she had once longed to do, she toyed with his silky black
hair. "You must teach me what to do."

His muscles tightened, nerves and thrills, at the thought of her
innocence. Tonight she would give him what she had given no
other. In the candle glow he saw her face, saw that she gave him
this treasure without fear, without shame.

No, he would not hurt her, but would do all in his power to
bring her joy.

He laid her on the bed, rubbed his cheek against hers. "It will
be my pleasure to instruct you."

"I've seen the goats mate."

His burst of laughter was muffled in her hair. "This, I can

promise, will be somewhat different than the mating of goats. So pay attention," he said, grinning now as he lifted his head, "while I give you your first lesson."

He was a patient teacher, and surely, she thought as her skin began to shiver and sing under his hands, a skilled one. His mouth drank from hers, deep, then deeper until it was how she imagined it might be to slide bonelessly into a warm river.

Surrounded, floating, then submerged.

His hands roamed over her breasts, then cupped them as if he could hold her heartbeat in his palms. The sensation of those strong, hard hands on her flesh shimmered straight down to her belly. His mouth skimmed the side of her throat, nibbling.

"How lovely." She murmured it, arching a little to invite more. "How clever for breasts to give pleasure as well as milk."

"Indeed." His thumbs brushed over her nipples, and made her gasp. "I've often thought the same."

"Oh . . . but what do I . . ." Her words, her thoughts trailed off into a rainbow when that nibbling mouth found her breast.

She made a sound in her throat, half cry, half moan. It thrilled him, that sound of shocked pleasure, the sudden shudder of her body, the quick jolt of her heart under his lips. As she arched again, her fingers combed through his hair, gripped there and pressed him closer. The sweet taste of her filled him like warmed wine.

He rose over her to tug his doublet aside, but before he could satisfy himself with that glorious slide of his flesh to her flesh, she lifted her hands, ran them experimentally over his chest.

"Wait." She needed to catch her breath. It was all running through her so quickly that it nearly blurred. She wanted everything, but clearly, so that she might remember each stroke, each taste, each moment.

"I touched you when you were hurt. But this is different. I

looked at your body, but didn't see it as I do now." Carefully she traced her finger along the scar running up his side. "Does this trouble you?"

He felt the line of heat, took her hand quickly. "No." Even now, he thought, she would try to heal. "There will be no pain tonight, for either of us."

He lowered to her, took her mouth again. There was a hint of urgency now, a taste of need. So much to feel, she mused dreamily. So much to know. And with the warmth of him coursing through her, she enfolded him. There was a freedom here, she discovered, in being about to touch him, stroke, explore, with no purpose other than pleasure. The hard muscles, the pucker in his smooth skin that was a scar of battle.

The strength of him excited her, challenged her own so that her hands, her mouth, her movements under him became more demanding.

This was fire, she realized. The first true licks of flame that brought nothing but delight and a bright, blinding need for more.

"I'm not fragile." Indeed she felt alive with power, nearly frantic with a kind of raging hunger. "Show me more. Show me all."

No matter how his blood swam, he would be careful with her. But he could show her more. His hands roamed down her body, over her thighs. As if she knew what they both needed, she opened to him. Her breath came short, shivering out with quick little moans. Her nails bit into his back as she began to writhe under him.

He lifted his head and watched her fly over that first peak of pleasure.

Heat, such heat. She had never known such fire outside of healing magic. And this, somehow, this went deeper, spread wider. Her body was like a single wild flame. She cried out, the wanton sound of her own voice another shock to her system. Beyond control, beyond reason, she gripped his hips and called out his name.

When he plunged into her, the glory of it was like a shaft of lightning, bright and brilliant. There was a storm of those glorious and violent shocks as he thrust inside her. She locked herself around him, her face pressed against his neck and repeated his name as that miraculous heat consumed her.

✱

"Sweetheart." When he could speak again, he did so lazily, with his head nuzzled between her breasts. "You are the most clever of students."

She felt golden, beautiful, and for the first time in her memory, more woman than queen. For one night, she told herself, one miraculous night, she would be a woman.

"I'm sure I could do better, my lord, with a few more lessons."

She was flushed, all but glowing, and her hair was a tangle of honeyed ropes over the white linen. "I believe you're right." He grinned and nibbled his way up her throat, lingered over her lips, then shifted so that she lay curled beside him.

"I'm so warm," she told him. "I never knew what it was like to be so warm. Tell me, Kylar, what's it like to have the sun on your face, full and bright?"

"It can burn."

"Truly?"

"Truly." He began to toy with her hair. "And the skin reddens or browns from it." He ran a fingertip down her arm. Pale as milk, soft as satin. "It can dazzle the eyes." He turned so he could look down at her. "You dazzle mine."

"There was an old man who was my tutor when I was a child. He'd been all over the world. He told me of great tombs in a desert where the sun beat like fury, of green hills where flowers bloomed wild and the rain came warm. Of wide oceans where great fish swam that could swallow a boat whole and dragons with silver wings flew. He taught me so many marvelous things, but he never taught me the wonders that you have tonight."

"There's never been another. Not like you. Not like this."

Because she read the truth in his eyes, she drew him closer. "Show me more."

As they loved, inside a case of ice, the first green bud on a blackened stalk unfurled to a single tender leaf. And a second began to form.

✴

When he woke, she was gone. At first he was baffled, for he slept like a soldier, and a soldier slept light as a cat. But he could see she had stirred the fire for him and had left his clothes folded neatly on the chest at the foot of the bed.

It occurred to him that he'd slept only an hour or two, but obviously like the dead. The woman was tireless—bless her—and had demanded a heroic number of lessons through the night.

A pity, he mused, she hadn't lingered in bed a bit longer that morning. He believed he might have managed another.

He rose to draw back the hangings on the windows. He judged it to be well into the morning, as her people were about their chores. He couldn't tell the time by the light here, for it varied so little from dawn to dusk. It was always soft and dull, with that veil of white over sky and sun. Even now a thin snow was falling.

How did she bear it? Day after day of cold and gloom. How did she stay sane, and more—content? Why should so good and loving a queen be cursed to live her life without warmth?

He turned, studied the chamber. He'd paid little attention to it the night before. He'd seen only her. Now he noted that she lived simply. The fabrics were rich indeed, but old and growing thin.

There had been silver and crystal in the dining hall, he recalled, but here her candlestands were of simple metal, the bowl for her washing a crude clay. The bed, the chest, the wardrobe were all beautifully worked with carved roses. But there was only a single chair and table.

He saw no pretty bottles, no silks, no trinket boxes.

She'd seen to it that the appointments in his guest chamber were suited to his rank, but for herself, she lived nearly as spartanly as a peasant.

His mother's ladies had more fuss and fancy in their chambers than this queen. Then he glanced at the fire and with a clutching in his belly realized she would have used much of the furniture for fuel, and fabric for clothes for her people.

She'd worn jewels when they dined. Even now he could see how they gleamed and sparkled over her. But what good were diamonds and pearls to her? They couldn't be sold or bartered, they put no food on the table.

A diamond's fire brought no warmth to chilled bones.

He washed in the bowl of water she'd left for him, and dressed.

There on the wall he saw the single tapestry, faded with age. Her rose garden, in full bloom, and as magnificent in silk thread as he'd imagined it. Alive with color and shape, it was a lush paradise caught in a lush moment of summer.

There was a figure of a woman seated on the jeweled bench beneath the spreading branches of the great bush that bloomed wild and free. And a man knelt at her feet, offering a single red rose.

He trailed his fingers over the threads and thought he would give his life and more to be able to offer her one red rose.

✱

He was directed by a servant to Phelan's room, where the young bard had his quarters with a gaggle of other boys. The other boys gone, Phelan was sitting up in the bed with Deirdre for company. The chamber was small, Kylar noted, simple, but warmer by far than the queen's own.

She was urging a bowl of broth on Phelan and laughing in delight at the faces he made.

"A toad!"

"No, my lady. A monkey. Like the one in the book you lent me." He bared his teeth and made her laugh again.

"Even a monkey must eat."

"They eat the long yellow fruit."

"Then you'll pretend this is the long yellow fruit." She snuck a spoonful in his mouth.

He grimaced. "I don't like the taste."

"I know, the medicine spoils it a bit. But my favorite monkey needs to regain his strength. Eat it for me, won't you?"

"For you, my lady." On a heavy sigh, the boy took the bowl and spoon himself. "Then can I get up and play?"

"Tomorrow, you may get up for a short while."

"My lady." There was a wealth of horror and grief in the tone. Kylar could only sympathize. He'd once been a small boy and knew the tedium of being forced to stay idle in bed.

"A wounded soldier must recover to fight another day," Kylar said as he crossed to the bed. "Were you not a soldier when you rode the horse on the stairs?"

Phelan nodded, staring up at Kylar as if fascinated. To him the prince was as magnificent and foreign as every hero in every story he'd ever heard or read. "I was, my lord."

"Well, then. Do you know your lady kept me abed three full days when I came to her wounded?" He sat on the edge of the bed, leaned over, and sniffed at the bowl. "And forced the same broth on me. It's a cruelty, but a soldier bears such hardships."

"Phelan will not be a soldier," Deirdre said firmly. "He is a bard."

"Ah." Kylar inclined his head in a bow. "There is no man of more import than a bard."

"More than a soldier?" Phelan asked, with eyes wide.

"A bard tells the tales and sings the songs. Without him, we would know nothing."

"I'm making a story about you, my lord." Excited now, Phelan spooned up his broth. "About how you came from beyond, traveled the Forgotten wounded and near death, and how my lady healed you."

"I'd like to hear the story when you've finished it."

"You can make the story while you rest and recover." Pleased that the bowl was empty, Deirdre took it as she stood, then leaned over to kiss Phelan's brow.

"Will you come back, my lady?"

"I will. But now you rest, and dream your story. Later, I'll bring you a new book."

"Be well, young bard." Kylar took Deirdre's hand to lead her out.

"You rose early," he commented.

"There's much to be done."

"I find myself jealous of a ten-year-old boy."

"Nearly twelve is Phelan. He's small for his age."

"Regardless, you didn't sit and feed me broth or kiss my brow when I was well enough to sit up on my own."

"You were not so sweet-natured a patient."

"I would be now." He kissed her, surprised that she didn't flush and flutter as females were wont to do. Instead she answered his lips with a reckless passion that stirred his appetite. "Put me to bed, and I'll show you."

She laughed and nudged him back. "That will have to wait. I have duties."

"I'll help you."

Her face softened. "You have helped me already. But come. I'll give you work."

8

There was no lack of work. The prince of Mrydon found himself tending goats and chickens. Shoveling manure, hauling endless buckets of snow to a low fire, carting precious wood to a communal pile.

The first day he labored he tired so quickly that it scored his pride. On the second, muscles that had gone unused during his recovery ached continually.

But the discomfort had the benefit of Deirdre rubbing him everywhere with one of her balms. And made the ensuing loving both merry and slippery.

She was a joy in bed, and he saw none of the sadness in her eyes there. Her laughter, the sound he'd longed to hear, came often.

He grew to know her people and was surprised and impressed by the lack of bitterness in them. He thought them more like a family, and though some were lazy, some grim, they shouldered together. They knew, he realized, that the survival of the whole depended on each.

That, he thought, was another of Deirdre's gifts. Her people held the will to go on, day after day, because their lady did. He couldn't imagine his own soldiers bearing the hardships and the tedium with half as much courage.

He came upon her in her garden. Though the planting and maintenance there was divided, as all chores were in Rose Castle, he knew she often chose to work or walk there alone.

She did so now, carefully watering her plantings with snowmelt.

"Your goat herd has increased by one." He glanced down at his stained tunic. "It's the first such birthing I've attended."

Deirdre straightened, eased her back. "The kid and the she-goat are well?"

"Well and fine, yes."

"Why wasn't I called?"

"There was no need. Here, let me." He took the spouted bucket from her. "Your people work hard, Deirdre, but none as hard as their queen."

"The garden is a pleasure to me."

"So I've seen." He glanced up at the wide dome. "A clever device."

"My grandfather's doing." Since he was watering, she knelt and began to harvest turnips. "He inherited a love for gardening from his mother, I'm told. It was she who designed and planted the rose garden. I'm named for her. When he was a young man, he traveled, and he studied with engineers and scientists and learned much. I think he was a great man."

"I've heard of him, though I thought it all legend." Kylar looked back at her as she placed turnips in a sack. "It's said he was a sorcerer."

Her lips curved a little. "Perhaps. Magic may come through the blood. I don't know. I do know he gathered many of the books in the library, and built this dome for his mother when she was very old. Here she could start seedlings before the planting time and grow the flowers she loved, even in the cold. It must have given her great pleasure to work here when her roses and other flowers were dormant with winter."

She sat back on her heels, looked over her rows and beyond to the sad and spindly daisies she prized like rubies. "I wonder if somehow he knew that his gift to his mother would one day save his people from starvation."

"You run low on fuel."

"Yes. The men will cut another tree in a few days." It always pained her to order it. For each tree cut meant one fewer left. Though the forest was thick and vast, without new growth there would someday be no more.

"Deirdre, how long can you go on this way?"

"As long as we must."

"It's not enough." Temper that he hadn't realized was building inside him burst out. He cast the bucket aside and grabbed her hands.

She'd been waiting for this. Through the joy, through the sweetness, she'd known the storm would come. The storm that would end the time out of time. He was healed now, and a warrior prince, so healed, could not abide monotony.

"It's enough," she said calmly, "because it's what we have."

"For how much longer?" he demanded. "Ten years? Fifty?"

"For as long as there is."

Though she tried to pull away, he turned her hands over. "You work them raw, haul buckets like a milkmaid."

"Should I sit on my throne with soft white hands folded and let my people work?"

"There are other choices."

"Not for me."

"Come with me." He gripped her arms now, tight, firm, as if he held his own life.

Oh, she'd dreamed of it, in her most secret heart. Riding off with him, flying through the forest and away to beyond. Toward the sun, the green, the flowers.

Into summer.

"I can't. You know I can't."

"We'll find the way out. When we're home, I'll gather men, horses, provisions. I'll come back for your people. I swear it to you."

"You'll find the way out." She laid her hands on his chest, over the thunder of his heart. "I believe it. If I didn't I would have you chained before I'd allow you to leave. I won't risk your death. But the way back . . ." She shook her head, turned away from him when his grip relaxed.

"You don't believe I'll come back."

She closed her eyes because she didn't believe it, not fully. How could he turn his back on the sun and risk everything to travel here again for what he'd known for only a few weeks? "Even if you tried, there's no certainty you'd find us again. Your coming was a miracle. Your safe passage home will be another. I don't ask for three in one lifetime."

She drew herself up. "I won't ask for your life, nor will I accept it. I will send a man with you—my best, my strongest—if you will take him. If you will give him good horses, and provisions, I will send others if the gods show him the way back again."

"But you won't leave."

"I'm bound to stay, as you are bound to go." She turned back, and though tears stung her throat, her eyes were dry. "It's said that if I leave here while winter holds this place, Rose Castle will vanish from sight, and all within will be trapped for eternity."

"That's nonsense."

"Can you say that?" She gestured to the white sky above the dome. "Can you be sure of it? I am queen of this world, and I am prisoner."

"Then bid me stay. You've only to ask it of me."

"I won't. And you can't. First, you're destined to be king. It is your fate, and I have seen the crown you'll wear inside your own mind and heart. And more, your family would grieve and your people mourn. With that on your conscience, the gift we found together would be forever tainted. One day you would go in any case."

"So little faith in me. I ask you this: Do you love me?"

Her eyes filled, sheened, but the tears did not fall. "I care for you. You brought light inside me."

" 'Care' is a weak word. Do you love me?"

"My heart is frozen. I have no love to give."

"That is the first lie you've told me. I've seen you cuddle a fretful babe in your arms, risk your life to save a small boy."

"That is a different matter."

"I've been inside you." Frustrated fury ran over his face. "I've seen your eyes as you opened to me."

She began to tremble. "Passion is not love. Surely my father had passion for my mother, for her sister. But love he had for neither. I care for you. I desire you. That is all I have to give. The gift of a heart, woman to man, has doomed me."

"So because your father was feckless, your mother foolish, and your aunt vindictive, you close yourself off from the only true warmth there is?"

"I can't give what I don't have."

"Then take this, Deirdre of the Sea of Ice. I love you, and I will never love another. I leave tomorrow. I ask you again, come with me."

"I can't. I can't," she repeated, taking his arm. "I beg you. Our time is so short, let us not have this chill between us. I've given you more than ever I gave a man. I pledge to you now there will never be another. Let it be enough."

"It isn't enough. If you loved, you'd know that." One hand gripped the hilt of his sword as if he would draw it and fight what stood between them. Instead, he stepped back from her. "You make your own prison, my lady," he said, and left her.

Alone, Deirdre nearly sank to her knees. But despair, she thought, would solve no more than Kylar's bright sword would. So she picked up the pail.

"Why didn't you tell him?"

Deirdre jolted, nearly splashing water over the rim. "You have no right to listen to private words, Orna."

Ignoring the stiff tone, Orna came forward to heft the bag of turnips. "Hasn't he the right to know what may break the spell?"

"No." She said it fiercely. "His choices, his actions must be his own. He is entitled to that. He won't be influenced by a sense of honor, for his honor runs through him like his blood. I am no damsel who needs rescuing by a man."

"You are a woman who is loved by one."

"Men love many women."

"By the blood, child! Will you let those who made you ruin you?"

"Should I give my heart, take his, at the risk of sacrificing all who depend on me?"

"It doesn't have to be that way. The curse—"

"I don't know love." When she whirled around, her face was

bright with temper. "How can I trust what I don't know? She who bore me couldn't love me. He who made me never even looked on my face. I know duty, and I know the tenderness I feel for you and my people. I know joy and sadness. And I know fear."

"It's fear that traps you."

"Haven't I the right to fear?" Deirdre demanded. "When I hold lives in my hands, day and night? I cannot leave here."

"No, you cannot leave here." The undeniable truth of that broke Orna's heart. "But you can love."

"And loving, risk trapping him in this place. This cold place. Harsh payment for what he's given me. No, he leaves on the morrow, and what will be will be."

"And if you're with child?"

"I pray I am, for it is my duty." Her shoulders slumped. "I fear I am, for then I will have imprisoned his child, our child, here." She pressed a hand to her stomach. "I dreamed of a child, Orna, nursing at my breast and watching me with my lover's eyes, and what moved through me was so fierce and strong. The woman I am would ride away with him to save what grows inside me. The queen cannot. You will not speak of this to him, or anyone."

"No, my lady."

Deirdre nodded. "Send Dilys to me, and see that provisions are set aside for two men. They will have a long and difficult journey. I await Dilys in the parlor."

She set the bucket aside and walked quickly away.

Before going inside, Orna hurried through the archway and into the rose garden.

When she saw that the tiny leaf she'd watched unfurl from a single green bud was withering, she wept.

9

Even pride couldn't stop her from going to him. When time was so short there was no room for pride in her world. She brought him gifts she hoped he would accept.

And she brought him herself.

"Kylar." She waited at his chamber door until he turned from the window where he stared out at the dark night. So handsome, she thought, her dark prince. "Would you speak with me?"

"I'm trying to understand you."

That alone, that he would try, lightened her heart. "I wish you could." She came forward and laid what she carried on the chest by his bed. "I've brought you a cloak, since yours was ruined. It was my grandfather's, and with its lining of fur is warmer than what you had. It befits a prince. And this brooch that was his. Will you take it?"

He crossed to her, picked up the gold brooch with its carved rose. "Why do you give it to me?"

"Because I treasure it." She lifted a hand, closed it over his on the brooch. "You think I don't cherish what you've given me, what you've been to me. I can't let you leave believing that. I can't bear the thought of you going when there's anger and hard words between us."

There was a storm in his eyes as they met hers. "I could take you from here, whether you're willing or not. No one could stop me."

"I would not allow it, nor would my people."

He stepped closer, and circled her throat with his hand with just enough force that the pulse against his palm fluttered with fear. "No one could stop me." His free hand clamped over hers before she could draw her dagger. "Not even you."

"I would never forgive you for it. Nor lie willingly with you again. Anger makes you think of using force as an answer. You know it's not."

"How can you be so calm, and so sure, Deirdre?"

"I'm sure of nothing. And I am not calm. I want to go with you. I want to run and never look back, to live with you in the sunlight. To once smell the grass, to breathe the summer. Once," she said in a fierce whisper. "And what would that make me?"

"My wife."

The hand under his trembled, then steadied before she drew it away. "You honor me, but I will never marry."

"Because of who made you, how you were made?" He took her by the shoulders now so that their gazes locked. "Can you be so wise, so warm, Deirdre, and at the same time so cold and closed?"

"I will never marry because my most sacred trust is to do no harm. If I were to take a husband, he would be king. I would share the welfare of all my people with him. This is a heavy burden."

"Do you think I would shirk it?"

"I don't, no. I've been inside your mind and heart. You keep your promises, Kylar, even if they harm you."

"So you spurn me to save me?"

"Spurn you? I have lain with you. I have shared with you my body, my mind, as I have never shared with another. Will never share again in my lifetime. If I take your vow and keep you here, if you keep your vow and stay, how many will be harmed? What destinies would we alter if you did not take your place as king in your own land? And if I went with you, my people would lose hope. They would have no one to look to for guidance. No one to heal them. There is no one here to take my place."

She thought of the child she knew grew inside her.

"I accept that you must go, and honor you for it," she said. "Why can't you accept that I must stay?"

"You see only black and white."

"I *know* only black and white." Her voice turned desperate now, with a pleading he'd never heard from her. "My life, the whole of it, has been here. And one single purpose was taught to me. To keep my people alive and well. I've done this as best I can."

"No one could have done better."

"But it isn't finished. You want to understand me?" Now she moved to the window, pulled the hangings over the black glass to shut out the dark and the cold. "When I was a babe, my mother gave me to Orna. I never remember my mother's arms around me. She was kind, but she couldn't love me. I have my father's eyes, and looking at me caused her pain. I felt that pain."

She pressed her hands to her heart. "I felt it inside me, the hurt and the longing and the despair. So I closed myself off from it. Hadn't I the right?"

There was no room for anger in him now. "She had no right to turn from you."

"She did turn from me, and that can't be changed. I was

tended well, and taught. I had duties, and I had playmates. And once, when I was very young there were dogs. They died off, one by one. When the last . . . his name was Griffen—a foolish name for a dog, I suppose. He was very old, and I couldn't heal him. When he died, it broke something in me. That's foolish, too, isn't it, to be shattered by the death of a dog."

"No. You loved him."

"Oh, I did." She sat now, with a weary sigh. "So much love I had for that old hound. And so much fury when I lost him. I was mad with grief and tried to destroy the ice rose. I thought if I could chop it down, hack it to bits, all this would end. Somehow it would end, for even death could never be so bleak. But a sword is nothing against magic. My mother sent for me. There would be loss, she told me. I had to accept it. I had duties, and the most vital was to care for my people. To put their well-being above my own. She was right."

"As a queen," Kylar agreed. "But not as a mother."

"How could she give what she didn't have? I realize now, with her bond with the animals, she must have felt grief as I did for the loss. She *was* grief, my mother. I watched her pine and yearn for the man who'd ruined her. Even as she died, she wept for him. His deceit, his selfishness stole the color and warmth from her life, and doomed her and her people to eternal winter. Yet she died loving him, and I vowed that nothing and no one would ever rule my heart. It is trapped inside me, as frozen as the rose in the tower of ice outside this window. If it were free, Kylar, I would give it to you."

"You trap yourself. It's not a sword that will cut through the ice. It's love."

"What I have is yours. I wish it could be more. If I were not queen, I would go with you on the morrow. I would trust you to take me to beyond, or would die fighting to get there with you. But I can't go, and you can't stay. Kylar, I saw your mother's face."

"My mother?"

"In your mind, your heart, when I healed you. I would have given anything, anything, to have seen such love and pride for me in the eyes of the one who bore me. You can't let her grieve for a son who still lives."

Guilt clawed at him. "She would want me happy."

"I believe she would. But if you stay, she will never know what became of you. Whatever you want for yourself, you have too much inside you for her to leave her not knowing. And too much honor to turn away from your duties to your family and your own land."

His fists clenched. She had, with the skill of a soldier, outflanked him. "Does it always come to duty?"

"We're born what we're born, Kylar. Neither you nor I could live well or happy if we cast off our duty."

"I would rather face a battle without sword or shield than leave you."

"We've been given these weeks. If I ask you for one more night, will you turn me away?"

"No." He reached for her hand. "I won't turn you away."

✳

He loved her tenderly, then fiercely. And at last, when dawn trembled to life, he loved her desperately. When the night was over, she didn't cling, nor did she weep. A part of him wished she would do both. But the woman he loved was strong, and helped him prepare for his journey without tears.

"There are rations for two weeks." She prayed it would be

enough. "Take whatever you need from the forest." As he cinched the saddle on his horse, Deirdre slipped a hand under his cloak, laid it on his side.

And he moved away. "No." More than once during the night, she'd tried to explore his healing wound. "If I have pain, it's mine. I won't have it be yours. Not again."

"You're stubborn."

"I bow before you, my lady. The queen of willful."

She managed a smile and laid a hand on the arm of the man she'd chosen to guide the prince. "Dilys. You are Prince Kylar's man now."

He was young, tall as a tree and broad of shoulder. "My lady, I am the queen's man."

This time she touched his face. They had grown up together, and once had romped as children. "Your queen asks that you pledge now your loyalty, your fealty, and your life to Prince Kylar."

He knelt in the deep and crusted snow. "If it is your wish, my queen, I so pledge."

She drew a ring from her finger, pressed it into his hand. "Live." She bent to kiss both his cheeks. "And if you cannot return—"

"My lady."

"If you cannot," she continued, lifting his head so their gazes met, "know you have my blessing, and my wish for your happiness. Keep the prince safe," she whispered. "Do not leave him until he's safe. It is the last I will ever ask of you."

She stepped back. "Kylar, prince of Mrydon, we wish you safe journey."

He took the hand she offered. "Deirdre, queen of the Sea of Ice, my thanks for your hospitality, and my good wishes to you and your people." But he didn't release her hand. Instead, he took a ring of his own and slid it onto her finger. "I pledge to you my heart."

"Kylar—"

"I pledge to you my life." And before the people gathered in the courtyard, he pulled her into his arms and kissed her, long and deep. "Ask me now, one thing. Anything."

"I will ask you this. When you're safe again, when you find summer, pluck the first rose you see. And think of me. I will know, and be content."

Even now, he thought, she would not ask him to come back for her. He touched a hand to the brooch pinned to his cloak. "Every rose I see is you." He vaulted onto his horse. "I will come back."

He spurred his horse toward the archway with Dilys trotting beside him. The crowd rushed after them, calling, cheering. Unable to resist, Deirdre climbed to the battlements, stood in the slow drift of snow and watched him ride away from her.

His mount's hooves rang on the ice, and his black cloak snapped in the frigid wind. Then he whirled his horse, and reared high.

"I will come back!" he shouted.

When his voice echoed back to her, over her, she nearly believed it. She stood, her red cloak drawn tight, until he disappeared into the forest.

Alone, her legs trembling, she made her way down to the rose garden. There was a burning inside her chest, and an ache deep, deep within her belly. When her vision blurred, she stopped to catch her breath. With a kind of dull surprise she reached up to touch her cheeks and found them wet.

Tears, she thought. After so many years. The burning inside her chest became a throbbing. So. She closed her eyes and stumbled forward. So, the frozen chamber that trapped her heart could melt after all. And, melting, bring tears.

Bring a pain that was like what came with healing.

She collapsed at the foot of the great ice rose, buried her face in her hands.

"I love." She sobbed now, rocking herself for comfort. "I love him with all I am or will ever be. And it hurts. How cruel to show me this, to bring me this. How bitter your heart must have been to drape cold over what should be warmth. But you did not love. I know that now."

Steadying as best she could, she turned her face up to the dull sky. "Even my mother did not love, for she willed him back with every breath. I love, and I wish the one who has my heart safe, and whole, and warm. For I would not wish this barren life on him. I'll know when he feels the sun and plucks the rose. And I will be content."

She laid a hand on her heart, on her belly. "Your cold magic can't touch what's inside me now."

And drawing herself up, turning away, she didn't see the delicate leaf struggling to live on a tiny green bud.

★

The world was wild, and the air itself roared like wolves. The storm sprang up like a demon, hurling ice and snow like frozen arrows. Night fell so fast that there was barely time to gather branches for fuel.

Wrapped in his cloak, Kylar brooded into the fire. The trees were thick here, tall as giants, dead as stones. They had gone beyond where Deirdre harvested trees and into what was called the Forgotten.

"When the storm passes, can you find your way back from

here?" Kylar demanded. Though they sat close to warm each other, he was forced to shout to be heard over the screaming storm.

Dilys's eyes, all that showed beneath the cloak and hood, blinked once. "Yes, my lord."

"Then when travel is possible again, you'll go back to Rose Castle."

"No, my lord."

It took Kylar a moment. "You will do as I bid. You have pledged your obedience to me."

"My queen charged me to see you safe. It was the last she said to me. I will see you safe, my lord."

"I'll travel more quickly without you."

"I don't think this is so," Dilys said in his slow and thoughtful way. "I will see you home, my lord. You cannot go back to her until you have reached home. My lady needs you to come back to her."

"She doesn't believe I will. Why do you?"

"Because you are meant to. You must sleep now. The road ahead is longer than the road behind."

The storm raged for hours. It was still dark, still brutal when Kylar awoke. Snow covered him, turning his hair and cloak white, and even the fur did little to fight the canny cold.

He moved silently to his horse. It would take, he knew, minutes only to move far enough from camp that his trail would be lost. In such a hellish world, you could stand all but shoulder to shoulder with another and not see him beside you.

The man Dilys would have no choice but to return home when he woke and found himself alone.

But though he walked his horse soundlessly through the deep snow, he'd gone no more than fifty yards when Dilys was once more trudging beside him.

Brave of heart and loyal to the bone, Kylar thought. Deirdre had chosen her man well.

"You have ears like a bat," Kylar said, resigned now.

Dilys grinned. "I do."

Kylar stopped, jumped down from the horse. "Mount," he ordered. "If we're traveling through hell together, we'll take turns riding." When Dilys only stood and stared, Kylar swore. "Will you argue with me over everything or do as your lady commanded and I now bid?"

"I would not argue, my lord. But I don't know how to mount the horse."

Kylar stood in the swirling snow, cold to the marrow of his bones, and laughed until he thought he would burst from it.

10

On the fourth day of the journey, the wind rose so fierce that they walked in blindness. Hoods, cloaks, even Cathmor's dark hide were white now. Snow coated Dilys's eyebrows and the stubble of his beard, making him look like an old man rather than a youth not yet twenty.

Color, Kylar thought, was a stranger to this terrible world. Warmth was only a dim memory in the Forgotten.

When Dilys rode, Kylar waded through snow that reached his waist. At times he wondered if it would soon simply bury them both.

Fatigue stole through him and with it a driving urge just to lie down, to sleep his way to a quiet death. But each time he stumbled, he pulled himself upright again.

He had given her a pledge, and he would keep it. She had willed him to live, through pain and through magic. So he would live. And he would go back to her.

Walking or riding, he slipped into dreams. In dreams he sat

with Deirdre on a jeweled bench in a garden alive with roses, brilliant with sunlight.

Her hands were warm in his.

So they traveled a full week, step by painful step, through ice and wind, through cold and dark.

"Do you have a sweetheart, Dilys?"

"Sir?"

"A sweetheart?" Taking his turn in the saddle, Kylar rode on a tiring Cathmor with his chin on his chest. "A girl you love."

"I do. Her name is Wynne. She works in the kitchens. We'll wed when I return."

Kylar smiled, drifted. The man never lost hope, he thought, nor wavered in his steady faith. "I will give you a hundred gold coins as a marriage gift."

"My thanks, my lord. What is gold coins?"

Kylar managed a weak chuckle. "As useless just now as a bull with teats. And what is a bull, you'd ask," Kylar continued, anticipating his man. "For surely you've seen a teat in your day."

"I have, my lord, and a wonder of nature they are to a man. A bull I have heard of. It is a beast, is it not? I read a story once—" Dilys broke off, raising his head sharply at the sound overhead. With a shout, he snagged the horse's reins, dragged at them roughly. Cathmor screamed and stumbled. Only instinct and a spurt of will kept Kylar in the saddle as the great tree fell inches from Cathmor's rearing hooves.

"Ears like a bat," Kylar said a second time while his heart thundered in his ears. The tree was fully six feet across, more than a hundred in length. One more step in its path and they would have been crushed.

"It is a sign."

The shock roused Kylar enough to clear his mind. "It is a dead tree broken by the weight of snow and ice."

"It is a sign," Dilys said stubbornly. "Its branches point there." He gestured, and still holding the reins, he began to lead the horse to the left.

"You would follow the branches of a dead tree?" Kylar shook his head, shrugged. "Very well, then. How could it matter?"

He dozed and dreamed for an hour. Walked blind and stiff for another. But when they stopped for midday rations from their dwindling supply, Dilys held up a hand.

"What is that sound?"

"The bloody wind. Is it never silent?"

"No, my lord. Beneath the wind. Listen." He closed his eyes. "It is like . . . music."

"I hear nothing, and certainly no music."

"There."

When Dilys went off at a stumbling run, Kylar shouted after him. Furious that the man would lose himself without food or horse, he mounted as quickly as he could manage and hurried after.

He found Dilys standing knee-deep in snow, one hand lifted, and trembling. "What is it? My lord, what is this thing?"

"It's only a stream." Concerned that the man's mind had snapped, Kylar leaped down from the horse. "It's just a . . . a stream," he whispered as the import raced through him. "Running water. Not ice, but running water. The snow." He turned a quick circle. "It's not so deep here. And the air. Is it warmer?"

"It's beautiful." Dilys was hypnotized by the clear water rushing and bubbling over rock. "It sings."

"Yes, by the blood, it is, and it does. Come. Quick now. We follow the stream."

The wind still blew, but the snow was thinning. He could see clearly now, the shape of the trees, and tracks from game. He had only to find the strength to draw his bow, and they would have meat.

There was life here.

Rocks, stumps, brambles began to show themselves beneath the snow. The first call of a bird had Dilys falling to his knees in shock.

Snow had melted from their hair, their cloaks, but now it was Dilys's face that was white as ice.

"It's a magpie," Kylar told him, both amused and touched when his stalwart man trembled at the sound. "A song of summer. Rise now. We've left winter behind us."

Soon Cathmor's hooves hit ground, solid and springy, and a single beam of light streamed through trees that were thick with leaves.

"What magic is this?"

"Sun." Kylar closed his hand over the rose brooch. "We found the sun." He dismounted and on legs weak and weary walked slowly to a brilliant splash of color. Here, at the edge of the Forgotten, grew wild roses, red as blood.

He plucked one, breathed in its sweet scent, and said: "Deirdre."

And she, carrying a bucket of melted snow to her garden, swayed. She pressed a hand to her heart as it leaped with joy. "He is home."

* * *

✳

She moved through her days now with an easy contentment. Her lover was safe, and the child they'd made warm inside her. The child would be loved, would be cherished. Her heart would never be cold again.

If there was yearning in her, it was natural. But she would rather yearn than have him trapped in her world.

On the night she knew he was safe, she gave a celebration with wine and music and dancing. The story would be told, she decreed, of Kylar of Mrydon. Kylar the brave. And of the faithful Dilys. And all of her people, all who came after, would know of it.

On a silver chain around her neck, she wore his ring.

She hummed as she cleared the paths in her rose garden.

"You sent men out to scout for Dilys," Orna said.

"It is probably too early. But I know he'll start for home as soon as he's able."

"And Prince Kylar. You don't look for him?"

"He doesn't belong here. He has family in his world, and one day a throne. I found love with him, and it blooms in me—heart and womb. So I wish for him health and happiness. And one day, when these memories have faded from his mind, a woman who loves him as I do."

Orna glanced toward the ice rose, but said nothing of it. "Do you doubt his love for you?"

"No." Her smile was warm and sweet as she said it. "But I've learned, Orna. I believe he was sent to me to teach me what I never knew. Love can't come from cold. If it does, it's selfish, and is not love but simply desire. It gives me such joy to think of him in the sunlight. I don't wish for him as my mother wished for my father, or curse him as my aunt cursed us all. I no longer see my life here as prison or duty. Without it, I would never have known him."

"You're wiser than those who made you."

"I'm luckier," Deirdre corrected, then leaned on her shovel as Phelan rushed into the garden.

"My lady, I've finished my story. Will you hear it?"

"I will. Fetch that shovel by the wall. You can tell me while we work."

"It's a grand story." He ran for the shovel and began heaving snow with great enthusiasm. "The best I've done. And it begins like this: Once, a brave and handsome prince from a far-off land fought a great battle against men who would plunder his kingdom and kill his people. His name was Kylar, and his land was Mrydon."

"It is a good beginning, Phelan the bard."

"Yes, my lady. But it gets better. Kylar the brave defeated the invaders, but, sorely wounded, became lost in the great forest known as the Forgotten."

Deirdre continued to work, smiling as the boy's words brought her memories back so clearly. She remembered her first glimpse of those bold blue eyes, that first foolish brush of lips.

She would give Phelan precious paper and ink to scribe the story. She would bind it herself in leather tanned from deer hide. In this way, she thought with pride, her love would live forever.

One day, their child would read the story, and know what a man his father was.

She cleared the path past jeweled benches, toward the great frozen rose, while the boy told his tale and labored tirelessly beside her.

"And the beautiful queen gave him a rose carved on a brooch that he wore pinned over his heart. For days and nights, with his faithful horse, Cathmor, and the valiant and true Dilys, he fought the wild storms, crossed the iced shadows of the Forgotten. It was his lady's love that sustained him."

"You have a romantic heart, young bard."

"It is a *true* story, my lady. I saw it in my head." He continued on, entertaining and delighting her with words of Dilys's stubborn loyalty, of black nights and white days, of a giant tree crashing and leading them toward a stream where water ran over rock like music.

"Sunlight struck the water and made it sparkle like diamonds."

A bit surprised by the description, she glanced toward him. "Do you think sun on water makes diamonds?"

"It makes tiny bright lights, my lady. It dazzles the eye."

Something inside her heart trembled. "Dazzles the eye," she repeated on a whisper. "Yes, I have heard of this."

"And at the edge of the Forgotten grew wild roses, fire-red. The handsome prince plucked one, as he had promised, and when its sweetness surrounded him, he said his lady's name."

"It's a lovely story."

"It is not the end." He all but danced with excitement.

"Tell me the rest, then." She started to smile, to rest on her shovel. Then there came the sound of wild cheering and shouts from without the garden.

"This is the end!" The boy threw his shovel carelessly aside and raced to the archway. "He is come!"

"Who?" she began, but couldn't hear her own voice over the shouts, over the pounding of her blood.

Suddenly the light went brilliant, searing into her eyes so that with a little cry of shock, she threw a hand up to shield them. Wild wind turned to breeze soft as silk. And she heard her name spoken.

Her hand trembled as she lowered it, and her eyes blinked against a light she'd never known. She saw him in the archway of the garden, surrounded by a kind of shimmering halo that gleamed like melted gold.

"Kylar." Her heart, every chamber filled with joy, bounded in her breast. Her shovel clattered on the path as she ran to him.

He caught her up, spinning her in circles as she clung to him.

"Oh, my love, my heart. How can this be?" Her tears fell on his neck, her kisses on his face. "You should not be here. You should never have come back. How can I let you go again?"

"Look at me. Sweetheart, look at me." He tipped up her chin. "So there are tears now. I'd hoped there would be. I ask you again. Do you love me, Deirdre?"

"So much I could live on nothing else my whole life. I would not have had to risk yours to come back." She laid her palms on his cheeks. Then her lips trembled open, her fingers shook. "You came back," she whispered.

"I would have crossed hell for you. Perhaps I did."

She closed her eyes. "That light. What is that light?"

"It is the sun. Unveiled. Here, take off your cloak. Feel the sun, Deirdre."

"I'm not cold."

"You'll never be cold again. Open your eyes, my love, and look. Winter is over."

Gripping his hand, she turned to watch the snow melting away, vanishing before her staring eyes. Blackened stalks began to crackle, break out green, and at their feet soft, tender blades of grass spread in a shimmering carpet.

"The sky." Dazed, she reached up as if she could touch it. "It's blue. Like your eyes. Feel it, feel the sun." She held her hands out to cup the warmth.

On a cry of wonder, she knelt, ran her hands over the soft grass, brought her hands to her face to breathe in the scent. Though tears continued to fall, she laughed and held those hands out to him. "Is it grass?"

"It is."

"Oh." She covered her face with her hands again, as if she could drink it. "Such perfume."

He knelt with her, and would remember, he knew, the rapture on her face the first time she touched a simple blade of grass. "Your roses are blooming, my lady."

Speechless, she watched buds spear, blooms unfold. Yellows, pinks, reds, whites in petals that flowed from bud to flower, and flowers so heavy they bent the graceful green branches. The fragrance all but made her drunk.

"Roses." Her voice quivered as she reached out to touch, felt the silky texture. "Flowers." And buried her face in blooms.

She squealed like a girl when a butterfly fluttered by her face and landed on a tender bud to drink.

"Oh!" There was so much, almost too much, and she was dizzy from it. "See how it moves! It's so beautiful."

In turn, she tipped her face back and drank in the sunlight.

"What is that across the blue of the sky? That curve of colors?"

"It's a rainbow." Watching her was like watching something be born. And once again, he thought, she humbled him. "Your first rainbow, my love."

"It's lovelier than in the books. In them it seemed false and impossible. But it's soft and it's real."

"I brought you a gift."

"You brought me summer," she murmured.

"And this." He snapped his fingers, and through the arch, down the path raced a fat brown puppy. Barking cheerfully, it leaped into Deirdre's lap. "His name is Griffen."

Drowned in emotion, she cradled the pup as she might a child, pressed her face into its warm fur. She felt its heartbeat, and the quick, wet lash of its tongue on her cheek.

"I'm sorry," she managed, and broke down and sobbed.

"Weep, then." Kylar bent to touch his lips to her hair. "As long as it's for joy."

"How can this be? How can you bring me so much? I turned you away, without love."

"No, you let me go, with love. It took me time to understand that—and you. To understand what it cost you. There would have been no summer if I hadn't left you, and returned."

He lifted her damp face now, and the puppy wiggled free and began to race joyfully through the garden. "Is that not so?"

"It is so. Only the greatest and truest love, freely given, could break the spell and turn away winter."

"I knew. When I plucked the rose, I understood. I watched summer bloom. It came with me through the forest. As I rode, the trees behind me went into leaf, brooks and streams sprang free of ice. With every mile I put behind me, every mile I came closer to you, the world awoke. Others will come tomorrow. I couldn't wait."

"But how? How did you come back so quickly?"

"My land is only a day's journey from here. It was magic that kept you hidden. It's love that frees you."

"It's more." Phelan wiggled his way through the crowd of people who gathered in the archway. He gave a cry of delight as the pup leaped at him. "It is truth," he began, "and sacrifice and honor. All these tied by love are stronger than a shield of ice and break the spell of the winter rose. When summer comes to Rose Castle, the Isle of Winter becomes the Isle of Flowers and the Sea of Ice becomes the Sea of Hope. And here, the good queen gives hand and heart to her valiant prince."

"It is a good ending," Kylar commented. "But perhaps you would wait until I ask the good queen for her hand and her heart."

She dashed tears from her cheeks. Her people, her love, would not see her weep at such a time. "You have my heart already."

"Then give me your hand. Be my wife."

She put her hand in his, but because she must be a queen, turned first to her people. "You are witness. I pledge myself in love and in marriage, for a lifetime, to Kylar, prince of Mrydon. He will be your king, and to him you will give your service, your respect, and your loyalty. From this day, his people will be your brothers and your sisters. In time, our lands will be one land."

She let them cheer, let his name ring out along with hers into the wondrous blue bowl of sky. And her hand was warm in Kylar's.

"Prepare a feast of celebration and thanks, and make ourselves ready to welcome the guests that come on the morrow. Leave us now, for I need a moment with my betrothed. Take the pup to the kitchen, Phelan, and see that he is well fed. Keep him for me."

"Yes, my lady."

"His name is Griffen." Her gaze met Orna's, and smiled as her people left her alone with her prince. "There is one last thing to be done."

She walked with him down the path to where the reddest roses bloomed on the tallest bush under thinning ice. Without a thought, she plunged her hand through it, and the shield shattered like glass. She picked the first rose of her life, offered it to him.

"I've accepted you as queen. That is duty. Now I give myself to you as a woman. This is for love. You brought light to my world. You freed my heart. Now and forever, that heart is yours."

She started to kneel, and he stopped her. "You won't kneel to me."

Her brows lifted, and command once again cloaked her. "I am queen of this place. I do as I wish." She knelt. "I am yours, queen and woman. From this hour, this day will be known and celebrated as Prince Kylar's Return."

With a gleam in his eye, he knelt as well, and made her lips twitch. "You will be a willful wife."

"This is truth."

"I would not have it otherwise. Kiss me, Deirdre the fair."

She put a hand on his chest. "First, I have a gift for you."

"It can wait. I lived on dreams of your kisses for days in the cold."

"This gift can't wait. Kylar, I have your child in me. A child made from love and warmth."

The hand that had touched her face slid bonelessly to her shoulder. "A child?"

"We've made life between us. A miracle, beyond magic."

"Our child." His palm spread over her belly, rested there as his lips took hers.

"It pleases you?"

For an answer he leaped up, hoisted her high until her laughter rang out. She threw her arms toward the sky, toward the sun, the sky, the rainbow.

And the roses grew and bloomed until branches and flowers reached over the garden wall, tumbled down, and filled the air with the promise of summer.

A World Apart

1

In the sweltering jungle, under the bloodred sun, Kadra hunted. Her steps were silent, her eyes—green as the trio of stones that encrusted the hilt of her sword—were alert, watchful, merciless.

For four days and four nights she had tracked her prey, over the Stone Mountains, beyond the Singing River, and into the verdant heat of the Land of Tulle.

What she stalked rarely ventured to these borders, and she herself had never traveled so far in the south of A'Dair.

There were villages here, small enclaves of lesser hunters, settlements of farmers and weavers with their young and their animals. The young were as much food to what she hunted as the cattle and mounts were.

She trod on the mad red flowers that were strewn on the path, ignored the sly silver slide of a snake down the trunk of a tree. She saw, sensed, scented both, but they were of no interest to her.

The Bok demons were her only interest now, and destroying them her only goal.

It was what she had been born for.

Other scents came to her—the beasts, large and small, that inhabited the jungle, and the thick, wet fragrance of vine and blossom. The blood—no longer fresh—of one that had been caught and consumed by what she hunted.

She passed a great fall of water that raged over the cliffs to pound its drumbeat into the river below. Though she had never walked upon this ground, this she knew by its light and music as a sacred place. One that no demon could enter. So she stopped to drink of its purifying waters, to fill her water bag for the journey yet to come.

And poured drops from her hand to the ground in thanks to the powers of life.

Beyond the falls, the busier scents of people—sweat, flesh, cooking, springwater from a village well—reached her keen senses.

It was her duty to protect them, and her fate that none among them could ever be her companion, her friend, her lifemate. These were truths she had never questioned.

At last she caught the overripe stench that was Bok.

The sword streaked out of its sheath, a bright battle sound as she pivoted on the heels of her soft leather boots. The dagger, its point a diamond in the sun, flipped from its wrist mount to her hand.

The dark blue claws of the Bok that had leaped from a branch overhead whizzed past her face, missing their mark. She set into a fighting stance and waited for his next charge.

It looked oddly normal. Other than those lethal retractable claws, the scent, the needle-sharp fangs that snapped out when the lips were peeled back for battle, the Bok looked no different from the people they devoured at every opportunity.

This one was small for his species, no more than six feet, which put him on a level with her. He was naked but for the thin skin of his traveling armor. Except for claws and teeth, he was unarmed. The vicious gouges across his chest and arms were stained from his pale green blood. And told her he had run afoul of his companions and had been forced out of the pack.

A distraction for her, she imagined, and didn't intend to spend much time dispatching him.

"They sacrificed you," she said as she circled. "What was your crime?"

He only hissed, flicking his long tongue through those sharp teeth. She taunted him with a happy grin, muscles ready. Above all else, she lived for combat.

When he leaped, she spun her sword up, down, and severed his head with one smooth stroke. Though the ease of the job was a bit of a disappointment, she grunted in satisfaction as the green blood sizzled and smoked. And the body of the Bok melted away to nothing but an ugly smear on the ground.

"Not much of a challenge," she muttered and sheathed her sword. "Still, the day is young, so there is hope for better."

Her hand was still on the hilt when she heard the scream.

She ran, her dark hair flying behind her, the band of her rank that encircled her head glinting like vengeance. When she burst into the small clearing with its tidy line of huts, she saw that the single Bok had been but a brief distraction, delaying her just long enough.

Bodies of animals and a few men who had tried to defend their homes lay torn and bleeding on the ground. Others were running in panic, some holding their young clutched to them as they scattered. And she knew they would be hunted down and rent to pieces if a single demon escaped her duty.

Sorrow for the dead and the thrill of upcoming battle warred inside her.

Three of the Bok were crouched in the dirt, still feeding. Their eyes glowed red, their vicious teeth snapped as she charged. They sprang, mad enough with blood to choose fight over flight.

She cleaved the arm from one, leaped into a flying kick to knock another out of her way as she plunged her ready dagger into the heart of the third.

"I am Kadra," she shouted, "Slayer of Demons. Guardian of the red sun."

"You are too late," the remaining Bok hissed at her. "You are outnumbered. Our king will tear out your heart, and we will share in the feast."

"Today you go hungry."

He was faster than the others, and fueled by his grisly meal. This, she knew, would be an opponent more worthy of her skill.

He chose not his claws but the long hooked blade he drew from the sheath at his side.

Steel rang to steel as the screams and the stench rose around her. She knew there were at least three others and she knew now that the demon king, the one called Sorak, was among them.

His death was her life's work.

The Bok fought well with his sickle sword, and swiped out with those blue claws. She felt the pain, an absent annoyance, as they dug furrows over her bare shoulder. Instead of retreating, she pushed into the attack, into the flashing blue and silver to run him through with a fierce thrust.

"I am Kadra," she murmured as the Bok smoked to the ground. "I am your death."

She wheeled to aim her weapon and her gaze on the demon king and the three warriors that flanked him outside the open doorway of a hut.

At last, she thought. Praise the powers of life, at last.

"I am your death, Sorak," she said. "As I was death for

Clud, your father. On this day, in this hour, I will rid my world of you."

"Keep your world." The king of demons, regal in his red tunic and bands of gold, lifted a small, clear globe. "I go to another. There I will conquer and feed. There I will rule."

His handsome face was sheened with sweat and blood. His dark hair coiled, sleek and twisted, like snakes over his elegant shoulders. Then he bared his teeth, and the illusion of rough beauty vanished into horror.

"Where I go, the food is plentiful. There, I will be a god. Keep your world, Kadra, Demon Slayer. Or come with me." He beckoned with a voice seductive as a caress. "I will give you the Demon Kiss. I will make you my queen and plant my young inside you. We will rule this new world together."

"You want to kiss me? To join with me?"

"You have shed the blood of my sire. I have drunk the blood of a slayer. We are well matched. Together we will have power beyond all imagining."

His three warriors were armed. And a demon king's strength knew no equal among his kind. Four against one, Kadra thought with a leap of her heart. It would be her greatest battle.

"Come, then." She all but purred it. "Come embrace me."

She pursed her own lips, then charged.

To her shock, the demon swirled his cloak, and with his warriors, vanished in a sudden flash of light.

"Where . . . how?" She spun in a circle, sword raised, dagger ready, and her blood still singing a war song. She could smell them, a lingering stench. It was all that was left of them.

Women were weeping. Children wailing. And she had failed. Three Bok, and their hellborn king, had escaped her. Their eyes had met, and yet Sorak had defeated her without landing a blow.

"You have not lost them yet."

Kadra looked toward the hut where a woman stood in the doorway. She was pale and beautiful, her hair a midnight rain, her face like something carved from delicate glass. But her eyes, green as Kadra's own, were ancient, and in them it seemed worlds could live.

In them, Kadra saw pain.

"Lady," she said respectfully as she stepped toward her. "You are injured."

"I will heal. I know my fate, and it is not time for me to pass."

"Call the healer," Kadra told her. "I must hunt."

"Yes, you must hunt. Come inside, I will show you how."

Now Kadra's eyebrows raised. The woman was beautiful, true, and there was an air of magic about her. But she was still only a female.

"I'm a demon slayer. Hunting is what I know."

"In this world," the woman agreed. "But not in the one where you must go. The demon king has stolen one of the keys. But there are others."

She swayed, and Kadra leaped forward, cursing, to catch her. Frail bones, she thought. Such delicate bones would shatter easily.

"Why did they let you live?" Kadra demanded as she helped the woman inside.

"It is not in their power to destroy me. To harm, but not to vanquish. I did not know they were coming." She shook her head as she lowered herself into a chair by a hearth left cold in the heat of day. "My own complacency blinded me to them. But not to you." She smiled then, and those eyes were brilliant. "Not to you, Kadra, Slayer of Demons. I've waited for you."

"Why?"

"You call me lady, and once I was. Once I was a young girl of rank who took a brave warrior into her heart, and gave him her body in love. He was killed in the Battle of the Singing River.

"It was a great battle against the Bok and the demon tribes who joined them." Impressed, Kadra tilted her head. She had been weaned on battle stories, and this was the greatest of all. "Many were destroyed on all sides. Many brave warriors perished, as did three slayers. The numbers of Bok were halved, but still Clud escaped and since increased those numbers again to plague our world.

"I watched the battle in my fire, and in the moment my love was struck down, in that moment of grief, I bore a girl child. She who was born to take up a sword as her father had done. She who would be more than those who made her. You are she. You are my blood and flesh and bone. I am she who bore you. I am your mother."

Kadra retreated one step. Where there had been pity was now anger. "I have no mother."

"You know I speak true. You have vision enough to see."

She felt the truth like a burn in the heart, but wanted only to deny it. "Humans who are not slayers keep their young. They tend and guard and protect them even at the risk of death."

"So it should be." The woman's voice thickened with regret. "I could not keep you with me. My duty was here, holding the keys, and yours was your training. I could not give you a mother's comfort, a mother's care, or a father's pride. Parting with you was another death for me."

"I need no mother," Kadra said flatly. "Nor father. I am a slayer."

"Yes. This is your fate, and even I could not turn your life's wheel away from it. As I cannot turn it now from where you must go, from what you must do."

"I must hunt."

"And you will. Our world and another are at stake. I could not keep you then," she stated. "I cannot keep you now. Though I have never let you go."

Kadra shook her head. She was accustomed to physical pain, but not to this hurt inside the heart. "The one who bore me was a warrior, as I am. She died at demon claws when I was but a child."

"Your foster mother. A good and brave warrior. At her side you learned what you needed to learn. When she was taken from you, you learned more. Now, you will learn the rest. I am Rhee."

"Rhee." Kadra, fearless in battle, went pale. "Rhee is a legend, a sorceress of unspeakable power. She is closed in a crystal mountain, of her own making, and will free herself when the world has need."

"Stories and tales, with only some truths." For the first time, Rhee's lips curved in a smile lovely in humor. "The green of Tulle is my home. No mountain of glass. You have my magic in you, and it is you who must free herself. There is great need. In this world, and the other."

"What other?" Kadra snapped. "This *is* the world. The only world."

"There are more, countless others. The world from which the demons sprang. Worlds of fire, worlds of ice. And a world not so different from this—yet so different. Sorak has gone to this world, through the portal opened by the glass key. He has gone to plunder and kill, to gather power until he is immortal. He wants your blood, wants your death to avenge his father. More, even more, he wants the power he believes he will gain by making you his mate."

"He will not have me, in this world or any. He would have slain his own father in time if I had not destroyed Clud before him."

"You see the truth. This is vision."

"This is sense."

"Whatever you choose to name it," Rhee said with a wave of her hand. "But a king cannot rule without vanquishing his most feared foe. Or changing her. He will not rest until you are destroyed by death or by his kiss. He goes through the portal to begin his own hunt. With every death from demon hands in that place, another here will die. This is the balance. This is the price."

"You speak in riddles. I will fetch the healer before I hunt."

"If you turn away," Rhee said as Kadra got to her feet, "if you choose the wrong path, all is lost. The world you know, the one you need to know. There is more than one key." Rhee breathed raggedly as her pain grew, took another clear globe from the folds of her skirt. "And more than one mirror."

She waved a hand toward the empty hearth. Fire, bright as gold, leaped into the cold shadow.

In it, Kadra saw another jungle. One of silver and black. Mountains . . . No, structures of great height—surely they could not be huts—rivers of black and white that had no current. Over them great armies of people marched. Over them battalions of animals on four round legs raced.

"What is this place?"

"A great village. They call it a city. A place where people live and work, where they eat and sleep. Where they live and die. This is called New York, and it is there you'll find them. The demons you must stop, and the man who will help you."

Though fascinated, and just a bit frightened of the images in the flames, Kadra smirked. "I need no man in battle."

"So you have been taught," Rhee said with a smile. "Perhaps you needed to believe you needed no one, no man, to become what you have become. Now you will become more. To do so, you will need this man. He is called Doyle, Harper Doyle."

"What good is a harper to a warrior?" Kadra demanded. "A fine warrior he'll make with his song and story as sword and shield."

"He is what you need. You will fail without him. Even with him there is great risk."

"Why should I believe any of this? Any witch might conjure pictures in a fire. Any woman might spin a tale as easily as thread."

"The stone in your crown of rank, those in your sword, I gave to you. For strength, for clear vision, for valor, and last, for love. They were my tears when I gave you to your fate. In my eyes you see your own. In your heart, you see the truth. Now we must prepare."

Kadra set her hand on the hilt of her sword. "I am prepared."

With a heavy sigh, Rhee got to her feet. She walked to a wooden cupboard, took out a metal box. "Take this." She offered a bag of stones. "Where you go," she explained, "they have great value."

Kadra looked into the bag of shining stones. "Then where I go is a very foolish place."

"In some ways. In others, fantastic." Rhee's expression was soft. "You have much to see. I will give you what knowledge I can, but there are limits. Even for me." She held out her hands, gripped Kadra's before Kadra could draw back.

"The rest," she said, and glinting tears scored down her cheeks, "is up to you, and the man called Doyle."

A great roar, like rushing water over cliffs, filled Kadra's head. In it were words, a hundred thousand words, spoken in countless tongues. A pressure, as a boulder laid on her heart, filled her chest.

The light was blinding.

"Valor and strength you have, my child. Use them on this

journey wild. But open yourself to vision, to love, before it's too late. Gather them close and face your fate. Would I could keep you safe with me," she murmured, and her lips brushed a kiss over Kadra's. "But once again I set you free."

The world whirled and spun. The air sucked her in, tumbled her, then spat her rudely out.

2

Sprawled in bed, plagued by the mother of all hangovers, the man called Doyle let out a surprised and pained grunt when a half-naked woman dropped on top of him.

He saw eyes of intense and burning green. Eyes, he thought blearily, that he'd been dreaming of moments before he'd awakened with a head the size of Nebraska.

There was an instant of recognition, a strange and intimate knowledge, and with it a bone-deep longing. Then there was nothing but shock.

He had time to blink, a split second to admire what he was certain was a very creative hallucination, before the very sharp and very real point of a dagger pressed against his carotid artery.

"I am Kadra," the mostly naked and well-armed hallucination stated in a throaty voice as oddly familiar as her eyes. "Slayer of Demons."

"Okay, that's really interesting." If he'd been drunk and stupid enough the night before to bring a crazy woman back to his apartment, and couldn't even remember heating up the sheets with her, he deserved to get his throat cut.

But it really wasn't the way he wanted to start the day.

"Would you mind getting that pig-sticker away from my jugular? You're spoiling a perfectly good hangover."

Frowning, she sniffed at him, then used her free hand to pull up his top lip and study his teeth. Satisfied, she drew back the dagger, slid it handily into its wrist sheath.

"You are not a demon. You may live."

"Appreciate it." Going with instinct rather than sanity, Harper shoved her, snatched at the dagger. The next thing he knew, she'd executed a neat back flip off the bed, landed on her feet beside it. With a very big sword raised over her head.

"You win." He tossed the dagger aside, held up both hands.

"You yield?"

"Damn right. Why don't you put that thing down before somebody—especially me—gets hurt? Then we can go call the nice people at the asylum. They'll come pick you up and take you for a little ride."

Disgusted that she'd landed on a coward, she shook her head. But she lowered the sword. "Are you the harper called Doyle?"

"I'm Harper Doyle."

"We have to hunt."

"Sure, no problem." Smiling at her, he eased toward the far side of the bed. Whatever that feeling had been when he'd first looked into her eyes, he was sure now he hadn't been drunk enough, hadn't been stupid enough to bring her home with him. "Just let me get my hunting gear and we'll be off."

Using his body to block her view, he slid open the drawer in the nightstand and drew out his Glock. "Now, put that goddamn sword down, Xena."

234 Nora Roberts

"I am Kadra," she corrected and studied the object in his
hand. "This is a gun." The name, the purpose of it were floating
in her head, in the maze of knowledge Rhee had given her. The
fascination for it, this new weapon, made her yearn. "I would
like to have one."

She looked at him, studying his face for the first time, and
found herself shocked that it brought her another kind of
yearning.

"I was sent to you," she told him.

"Fine, we'll get to that. But right now, put the sword down," he
repeated. "I'd really hate to spoil my record and shoot a woman."

It was more comfortable to study the gun, and her feelings for
an interesting weapon. "The missile goes through flesh and
bone. It can be very efficient." She nodded, sent her sword home.
"Perhaps you are a warrior. We will talk."

"Oh, yeah," Harper agreed. "We're going to have a very nice
chat."

His head felt as if someone had spent the night attempting a
lobotomy with a dull, rusty blade. He could accept that. In a be-
mused celebration of his thirtieth birthday—how could he be
thirty when he'd been eighteen two minutes ago—he'd consumed a tanker truck of alcohol. He'd been entitled to get plastered with a couple of pals. He was entitled to the hangover.

Having a woman—a gorgeous green-eyed Amazon who filled
out her black leather bikini in a way that gratified every young
boy's comic-book fantasies—leap on him out of nowhere was a
really nice plus. Just the sort of happy birthday surprise a man
who'd reached the point of no return on the path to adulthood
could appreciate.

But having that erotic armful hold a knife to his throat wasn't
part of the acceptable package.

And where the hell *had* she come from? he wondered as she

stood there eyeing his gun. There was nothing but simple curiosity and avid interest on that sharp-boned siren's face.

Had he been so drunk he'd forgotten to lock his door? It was
a possibility—a remote one, but a possibility. But she'd called
him by name. No way she was from the neighborhood. He was a
trained observer, and even if he'd been a myopic accountant
rather than a private investigator he would have noticed a six-
foot brunette with legs that went to eternity.

"Jake." The solution trickled through his suffering brain.
Though he relaxed a little, he held the gun steady. "Jake put you
up to this, didn't he? Some weird-ass birthday surprise. Jake's
who sent you."

"I am sent by Rhee, the sorceress. How is it that a harper has
such a weapon? Have you killed many demons?"

"Look, it's too early in the morning for Dungeons and Dragons. Show's over, sister."

"I am not your sister," she began as he eased out of bed. Then
her eyebrows shot up. He was naked, but that neither surprised
nor shocked her. Her instant and elemental attraction did.

He was taller than she by nearly a full hand, broader in the
chest and shoulders, with fine, sleek muscles.

Reevaluating, she pursed her lips. His hair was the deep
brown of oak bark, and though unkempt by sleep, it created a
good frame for a strong face. His eyes were the bold blue of the
marsh bells, his nose slightly crooked, which told her it had
weathered a break. His mouth was firm, as was his jaw. Though
his skin was pale, like a scholar's who closeted himself with
scrolls, she began to see possibilities.

"You have a fine build for a harper," she told him.

"Yeah?" Amused now, though still cautious, he reached for
the jeans he'd peeled off the night before. "How much did Jake
pay you for the gig?"

"I know no Jake. I do not take payment for slaying. It is my destiny. Do you require payment?"

"Depends." How the hell was he going to get into his jeans and hold the gun at the same time?

"The knowledge was given me that these have value in your world." She tugged the bag of stones from her belt, tossed them on the bed. "Take what you need, then dress. We must begin the hunt."

"Look, I appreciate a joke as much as the next guy. But I'm naked and hungover, and it irritates me to wake up with a knife to my throat. I want coffee, a barrel of aspirin, and a shower."

"Very well. If you will not hunt, show me how to use your weapon."

"You're a piece of work." He gestured toward the bedroom door with the Glock. "Out. Back to Central Casting, or Amazons R Us, or wherever the hell—"

She moved so fast that all he saw was a blur of limbs and leather and flying hair. She leaped, executed a handspring off the bed, and some part of her—boot, elbow, fist—connected with his jaw.

An entire galaxy of stars exploded in his head. By the time they novaed and died, he was flat on his back, with her standing astride him turning the Glock over in her hands.

"It has good weight," she said conversationally. "How is the missile . . ." She trailed off when with a twitch of her finger she fired. Her eyes widened with something like lust when through the open bathroom door, she saw the corner of his vanity sheared off.

"It is faster than an arrow," she commented, very pleased.

Not Jake, he corrected. Jake might have a weird sense of the ridiculous, but his old college friend wouldn't have sent him a lunatic who liked to play with guns. "Who the hell are you?"

"I am Kadra." She nearly sighed with the repetition—perhaps the harper was loose in the brains. With some sympathy she offered a hand to help him up. "Slayer of Demons. I have come to hunt, to fulfill my destiny. Though it does not please either of us, you are obliged to assist."

"Give me the gun, Kadra."

"It is a good weapon."

"Yeah, it's a good weapon. It belongs to me."

Her lips moved into a pout, then her face brightened again. "I will fight you for it."

"I'm at a disadvantage at the moment." He got to his feet, very slowly, kept his voice mild and easy. "You know, naked, hungover."

"Hung over what?"

"Maybe we could fight later, after we clear up a few points."

"Very well. I will give you the weapon, and you will give me your word that you will help me hunt the Bok."

"Helping people's what I do." Maybe she was in trouble, he thought. Not that he intended to get involved, but he could at least listen before he called the guys in the white coats. "Is that why you're here?" Gently, he nudged her gun hand aside so he wouldn't end up with a bullet in the belly. "You need help?"

"I am a stranger here, and require a guide." She reached out, squeezed his biceps. "You are strong. But slow." With no little regret, she returned the Glock. "Can you make more of the gun?"

"Maybe." She'd threatened him with a knife, with a sword. She'd knocked him on his ass and disarmed him.

Damn if he didn't respect her for it.

In any case, she'd made his first morning as a thirty-year-old man interesting. He hadn't become a PI because he liked the boring.

Added to that, there was something . . . something about her that pulled at him. Her looks were enough to knock a man flat. But it wasn't that—or not only that. You couldn't find the answers, he reminded himself, unless you asked the questions.

"I'm going to put my pants on," he told her. "I want you to step back and keep your hands away from that sword."

She stepped back. "I have no wish to harm you, or any of your people. You have my word as a slayer."

"Good to know." When she was at a safe distance, he tugged on his jeans, then snugged the gun in the waistband. "Now, I'm going to make coffee, and we'll talk about all this."

"Coffee. This is a stimulant consumed in liquid form."

"There you go. In the kitchen," he added, gesturing toward the door.

She strode out ahead of him. Whatever shape he might have been in, Harper thought, however baffled he might be, a man who didn't admire and appreciate that view was a sorry specimen.

Still, he glanced at the front door of his apartment as he passed. It was locked, bolted, chained.

So she'd locked up after she'd come in, he decided. He looked back to see her stop and gape out the living room window. Like a kid might, he mused, at her first eyeful of Disneyland.

So high, she thought in wonder. She had never been in a hut where the ground was so far below and so many people swarmed beneath. Their costumes were strange to her, strange and fascinating. But fascination turned to awe when she watched a cab zip to the curb, saw the woman leap out.

"She rose out of the belly of the yellow beast! How is this done?"

"You pay the fare, they let you out. Where the hell are you from?"

"I am from A'Dair. In my world, we have no beasts with round legs. I don't—wait." She closed her eyes, searched through the knowledge Rhee had given her. "Cars!" Those brilliant eyes opened again, smiled into his. "They are machines called cars and are for transportation. That is wonderful."

"Try to find one in the rain. Honey—"

"Yes, I would like honey, and bread. I am hungry."

"Right." He shook his head. "Coffee. Coffee first, then all questions can be faced. Come with me. I want you where I can see you."

She followed him into his tiny galley kitchen. While he measured coffee, she ran her fingers over the surface of the counter, over the refrigerator and stove. "So much magic," she said softly. "You must have great wealth."

"Yeah, rolling in it." He made a reasonable living, Harper thought. But he was what you could call between active cases at the moment. Maybe he could hold off on the guys in the white coats, see if she needed an investigator, and had enough to pay his retainer. "Jake didn't send you, did he?"

"I do not know this Jake." She peered at the side of the toaster, delighted with her own odd reflection. "I know no one in this world, save you."

"How did you get here, to my place?"

"Through the portal. It is . . ." She straightened, trying to decipher the knowledge, then to express it. "There are many dimensions. Yours and mine are two. The Bok stole a key and have entered yours. I have another." She drew the clear globe out of her pouch. "So I have followed. To hunt, to kill so that our worlds will be safe. You are to help me in this quest."

Poor kid, he thought. She was definitely a few fries short of a Happy Meal. "You can't just kill people in this world. They lock you up for that."

"You have no slayers to fight against evil here?"

He dragged a hand through his hair, then rooted out some

Extra-Strength Excedrin. Isn't that what his father had done? And what he himself had wanted to do as long as he could remember? To go after the bad guys, on his own terms?

"Yeah, I guess we do."

The woman was definitely in some sort of jam, even if it came out of her own oddball imagination. He would just keep her calm, ask some questions, see if he could dig out the problem. When he'd done what he could, he would make a few calls and have her taken someplace where she could get some help.

It would be the first good deed of his new decade.

"So, you come from another dimension, and you're here to hunt down some demons."

"The king of demons and three of his warriors have entered your world. They will need to feed. First, they will hunt for animals, the easy kill, to gather strength. Where are your farms?"

"We're a little short on farms on Second Avenue. So what do you do back in—where was it?"

"A'Dair."

He could run a search on the name on his computer, see if he could pinpoint where she'd come from. She didn't have a discernible accent, but the cadence, the rhythm of her speech sure as hell didn't say New York.

"What do you do back in A'Dair besides slay demons?"

"This is my purpose. I was born a slayer, trained, educated. It is what I do."

"Friends, family?"

"I have no family. She who raised me was killed by a tribe of Bok."

Mother killed, he thought. Trauma, role-playing. "I'm sorry."

"She was a fine warrior. Clud, sire of Sorak, took her life, and I have taken his. So there is balance. I have learned that she who bore me was another. Rhee, the sorceress. Her blood is in me. I think I am here, able to be here, because of that blood." She sniffed the air. "This is coffee?"

"That's right."

"It has a good scent."

He poured two mugs, offered one. She sniffed again, sipped, then frowned. "Bitter, but good."

To his surprise, she downed the entire mug in one swallow, then swiped a hand over her mouth. "I like this coffee. Dress now, Harper Doyle."

"How do you know my name?"

"It was told to me. We will hunt the Bok together."

"Sure. We'll get to that in a little while."

Her eyes narrowed. "You don't believe. You think I'm loose in the brain. You waste my time with too many questions when we should act."

"Part of what I do in my little world is ask questions. Nobody's calling you a liar here. Why shouldn't I believe you're a demon slayer from an alternate universe? I'm always getting clients from other dimensions."

She paced up and down the narrow room to work out the logic. He was mocking her, and this was not proper. Lesser warriors were not permitted to show a slayer disrespect.

Yet, she admired him for it even as she found his demeanor frustrating.

This was his world, Kadra reminded herself, one of wonders far beyond her ken. So her world would be beyond his. If she were in his place, she would not believe without proof.

"You must be shown. I cannot blame you for doubt. You would be weak and foolish if you didn't question, and the weak and foolish would be of no use to me."

"Darling, keep up that sweet talk and you'll turn my head."

She didn't have to understand the words to recognize the sarcasm dripping from them. A little impatient, a little intrigued, she held one hand up, and the other, with the globe in its palm, out.

"My blood is of the sorceress and the warrior. My blood is the blood of the slayer. I hold the power of the key."

She drew her mind down to the globe, drew the power of the globe into her mind.

Harper's kitchen wall dissolved as though it were a painting left out in the rain. Through it, he saw not the apartment next door but a thick, green jungle, a curving white ribbon, and a sky the color of pale blood under a fierce red sun.

"Holy shit," he managed before he was sucked into it.

3

The heat was enormous, a drenching, dripping wall of steaming water. It was a shock, even after the jolt of pain, the blast of blinding light. Even so, his bones felt frozen under his skin as he stared out at the tangle of towering green.

New York was gone, it seemed. And so was he.

Not a hangover, he thought, but some sort of psychotic event brought on, no doubt, by too much liquor and too many loose women.

As he watched, dumbfounded, a snake with a body as thick as his thigh slithered off into the high, damp grass.

"We can stay only a short time," Kadra told him, and her voice was dim, tinny, light-years away. "This is the west jungle of A'Dair, near the coast of the Great Sea. This is my world, which exists beyond yours. And the knowledge says, in balance with it."

"I've been drugged."

"This is not so." Annoyed now, she clamped her hands over

his arms. "You can see, you can hear and feel. My world is as real as yours, and as much in peril."

"Alternate universe." The words felt foolish on his tongue. "That's pure science fiction."

"Is your world so perfect, so important, that you believe it stands alone in the vastness of time and space? Harper Doyle, can you have lived and still believe you are alone? My heart." She pressed his hand to her breast. "It beats as yours. I am, as you are."

How could he dismiss what he saw with his own eyes? What he felt, touched—and somehow knew? Just, he thought, as he had somehow known her the instant their eyes had met. "Why?"

She nearly smiled. "Why not?"

"I recognized you," he managed. "I pushed that aside, clicked back into what made sense so I could deny it. But I recognized you, somehow, the minute I saw you."

"Yes." She kept her hand on his a moment longer. It felt right there, like a link. "It was the same for me. This is not something I understand, but only feel. I do not know the meaning."

And in some secret chamber of her warrior's heart, she feared the meaning.

"I'm standing here sweating in a jungle in some Twilight Zone, and it doesn't feel half as strange as it should. It doesn't feel half as strange as what's going on inside me, about you."

"You begin to believe."

"I'm beginning to something. I'm going to need a little time to process all the—"

She whirled, the sword streaking into her hand like a lightning bolt. A creature, no more than three feet high, with snapping teeth in both its mouths, shot out of the brush and leaped for Harper's throat.

Despite the shock of it, his instincts were quick. His hand

whipped down for his gun. It hadn't cleared the waistband of his jeans before Kadra's sword sliced through both heads with one massive stroke. There was a fountaining gush of vile green liquid that stank like sulfur.

Heads and body thunked, a grisly trio, onto the ground, then began to smoke.

"Loki demon," Kadra said as the three pieces melted away. "Small pests that usually travel in packs of three." She lifted her head, sniffed. "To your left. You will need your weapon," she added, and pivoted to her right as another of the creatures jumped through a curtain of vine.

Instinct had his finger on the trigger, and if that finger trembled a bit, he wasn't ashamed. He heard the slice of her sword through air just as the last—please, God—of the miniature monsters charged him.

He shot it between the eyes—all four of them.

"Christ. Jesus. Christ."

"This is good aim." Giving Harper a congratulatory slap on the back, she nodded over the smoking heads. "This is a fine weapon," she added, sending his Glock an avaricious glance. "When we go back to your world, you will provide me with one. It lacks the beauty of the sword, but it makes an enjoyable noise."

"Their blood's green," Harper said in a careful voice. "They have two heads and green blood. And now, how about that, they're just melting away like the Wicked Witch of the West."

"All demons bleed green, though only the Loki and the mutant strain of the Ploon are two-headed. On death, the blood smokes and the body . . . melts is not inaccurate," she decided. "You have witches in the west of your world who die like demons?"

When he only stared at her, she shrugged. "We have witches as well, and most of them the powers of life have instilled with good. My home is east," she continued. "Beyond the Stone Mountains, in the Shadowed Valley. It is beautiful, and the fields are rich. There is no time to show you."

"This is real." He took one long, deep breath and swallowed it all at once.

"Our time here is short. There is a clearing, and a village in it. Rhee lives there. We will go."

Since she set off in a punishing jog, he had no choice but to follow. "Slow it down, Wonder Woman. I'm barefoot here."

She tossed a scowl over her shoulder, but modified her pace. "You drank excessive spirits last night. I can smell them on you. Now you are sluggish."

"Alert enough to kill a two-headed demon."

She let out a snort. "A child with a training bow could do the same. Lokis are stupid."

As they ran down the narrow, beaten path, a flock of birds flushed out of the trees and into that odd red sky. He staggered to a halt. Each was its own rainbow—a bleeding, blending meld of pinks and blues and golds. And the song they sent up was like the trill of flutes.

"Dregos," she told him. "Their gift is their song, as they are poor eating. Stringy." She slowed to a trot as they came to the clearing.

He saw houses, small and tidy, most with colorful gardens in the front. People dressed in long, thin robes harvested out of them what looked to be massive blue carrots, tomatoes the size of melons, and long, yellow beans spotted with green flecks.

There were men, women, children, and each stopped work or play and bowed as Kadra came into view.

"Greetings, Demon Slayer," some called out.

She acknowledged this with what Harper supposed was a kind of salute by laying her fist on her heart as she walked.

Those long legs ate up the ground toward a small house with a lush garden and an open front door. She had to duck her head to enter.

Inside, a young girl stood by what he assumed was a cook-stove. She stirred an iron pot and looked up at them with quiet blue eyes.

"Hail to Kadra, Slayer of Demons."

"We come to speak with Rhee."

"She sleeps," the girl said and continued to stir. "She suffered a demon bite during the attack."

"She did not say." Kadra moved quickly, shoving open a door. Within, Rhee lay pale and still on a bed. The emotions that churned in her were mixed and confusing, and through them came one clear thought.

Mother. Will I lose yet another mother before my own end? "Is it the sleep of change?"

"No. She was not kissed, only bitten beneath the shoulder, as she tried to guard the keys. Nor was it a mortal bite, though she had pain and there was sickness. More than necessary, as she did not see to the wound quickly."

"She . . . spent too much time with me."

"Not too much, only what was needed."

"Your mother?" Harper looked through the doorway at the woman on the bed, and laid a hand on Kadra's shoulder. "Can we get her to a doctor?"

"I am Mav the healer," the young girl told him. "I tend to her. I have drained the poison, given her the cure. She must sleep until her body regains strength. She said you would come, Kadra, with the one from the other world. You are to eat."

Mav ladled out some of the thick broth from the pot. "And to wash in the falls. In this way, you will take some of this place with you into the next. You must be gone within the hour."

"Do you want to sit with her awhile?" Harper began. "Take some time with her?"

His hand caressed her shoulder, a gesture of comfort she had known rarely in her life. "There is no time." Kadra turned away from the doorway.

"She's your mother."

"She bore me. She set me on this path. Now I can only follow it."

She sat down at the table where Mav had put the bowls and a round loaf of golden bread. There was a squat pitcher of honey and another of water as white and sparkling as snow.

Because he was tired, hungry, and confused, Harper sat. This is real, he thought again as he sampled the first taste of the rich, spiced broth. It wasn't a dream, a hallucination. He hadn't just lost his mind.

Kadra tore off a hunk of bread, poured honey over it, and ate with a concentrated focus that told Harper she wasn't concerned with taste, only with fuel.

"Do you have family?" she asked Mav between bites.

"I have two brothers, younger. My mother who weaves. My father was a healer as well. Sorak, king of demons, killed him this morning."

"I was not quick enough." Grief thickened Kadra's voice. "And your mother is a widow."

"He would have killed us all, but you came. He fears you."

"He has cause. I regret that death touched you."

"He came for Rhee, for the key. Her powers are not as strong as they were, and he made demons from wizards so he might track her. She explained to me while I tended her so I might tell you."

Mav folded her hands and spoke as if reciting a story learned by heart. "The other, the world beyond with yellow sun and blue sky, is full of so much life, and most who live there have closed themselves off from the magic. They will not understand, they will not believe, and so the Bok will slaughter them. Flesh, passion. Innocence and evil. Sorak craves this, and the power he will gain from it. The power to destroy you."

"He will die there." Kadra drank the tankard of springwater quickly. "This is my vow, on your father's blood." She pulled out her dagger, sliced a shallow gash across her palm, and let her blood drip onto the table. "And on mine."

"It will comfort my mother to know it. But there should be no more bloodshed here." Mav reached in her pocket, took out a white cloth, and deftly wrapped it around Kadra's hand. "You must wash in the falls, for cleansing, then go."

When Kadra got to her feet, Harper sighed and got to his. "Thanks for the food."

Mav blushed, cast down her gaze. "It is little to give the Slayer and the savior. Blessings on you both."

Harper took one last glance at her. Kid couldn't be more than ten, he thought, then ducked out the doorway.

He had to double his pace to catch up with Kadra. "Look, just slow down a minute. I'm trying to keep up here, in more ways than one. I don't usually spend my mornings visiting alternate dimensions and killing loco demons."

"Loki."

"Whatever. So far you've jumped me, held a knife to my throat, threatened me with a sword, punched me in the face, and sucked me through some . . . wormhole in my kitchen. And all this on one lousy cup of coffee. This isn't your average first date."

"You do not have the knowledge, so you require explanations." She moved through the jungle at a brisk pace, eyes tracking, ears pricked. "I understand this."

"Beautiful. Then give them to me."

"We will cleanse in the falls, return to your world, hunt down the Bok and kill them."

He considered himself a reasonable guy, a man with an open mind, an active sense of adventure and curiosity. But enough was enough. He grabbed her arm, yanked her around to face him. "That's what you call an explanation? Listen, sister, if that's the best you can do, this is where we part ways. Send me back where I come from and we'll just put this all down to too much beer and fried food."

"I am not your sister."

He stared at her, at the faint irritation that clouded her glorious face. Helpless, he began to laugh. It rolled out of him, pumping up from the belly so that he had to bend over, brace his hands on his thighs as she cocked her head and studied him with a mixture of amusement, puzzlement, and impatience.

"I'm losing it," he managed. "Losing what's left of my mind." Even as he sucked in a breath, a spider the size of a Chihuahua pranced between his feet on stiltlike legs and gibbered at him. Harper yelped, whipping out his gun as he stumbled back.

But Kadra merely booted the enormous insect off the path. "That species is not poisonous," she informed him.

"Good, great, fine! It just swallows a man whole."

Kadra shook her head, then loped down the path. Keeping his gun handy, Harper followed.

Red sun, he mused as he looked up at the sky. Like, well, Krypton. If he followed comic book logic, didn't that mean that he, from a planet with a yellow sun, had superpowers here?

Concentrating, he took a little jump, then another. On the third, Kadra looked back at him, her face a study in baffled frustration. "This is not the time for dancing."

"I wasn't dancing I was just . . ." Seeing if I could fly, he thought, amazed at himself. "Nothing. Nothing at all."

He heard the roar like a highballing train. It grew, swelled, pounded on his eardrums as he jogged after her. She swung around a curve on the path, and he looked up.

In front of them, white water plunged from a height of two hundred feet or more. It screamed over the cliff, dived in a thundering wall, then pounded into the surface of a white river.

Flowers, some unrecognizable, some as simple as daisies, teemed along its banks. There, with the wild grass and wildflowers, with the sunlight spilling in rosy streaks through the canopy of trees, a unicorn lazily grazed.

"My God." The hand still holding the gun fell to his side. The mythical beast raised its regal white head and stared at Harper out of eyes so blue and clear they might have been glass. Then it went back to cropping the grass.

The beauty of it, the sheer wonder, wiped his temper away. Now I've seen it all, he thought. Nothing will ever surprise me again.

He realized the fallacy of that a second later when he glanced back at Kadra.

She'd stripped. The black leather lay piled on the bank, her sword, her dagger crossed over it. She'd pulled off her boots, her wrist sheaths, and was even now reaching up to lift the circlet from her hair.

She was, Harper thought, more mythical, more wondrous that the white-horned creature. Her body was curved and sleek, the color of the fresh honey she had poured over the breakfast bread. Her dark hair, arrow straight, rained over her shoulders, down her back, lay tauntingly over one magnificent breast.

His body tightened, his mouth went dry. For one blissful moment, he lost the power of speech.

"This is a sacred place," she began as she laid her circlet on her crossed blades. "No demon can cross its borders. Take off your clothing, put down your weapon. You may take no cloth or metal into the falls."

So saying, she dived.

It was a picture he knew would remain etched in his mind forever.

"Things are looking up," he decided, and peeling off his jeans, he jumped in after her.

The water was cool, sluicing the sweat from his body in one glorious swipe. When he surfaced, he felt the last nasty dregs of the morning's hangover sink to the bottom of the river. In fact, he realized as he struck out after Kadra and the falls, he didn't just feel clearheaded, didn't just feel good. He felt charged, energized.

She waited for him at the foot of the falls, treading the churning water lazily. Her eyes were impossibly green, impossibly brilliant.

"What's in this water?" he shouted.

"Cleansing properties. It washes away negative energies."

"I'll say."

She laughed, did a quick surface dive that gave him a brief and wonderful flash of her butt. Then she rose again, a vision of black and gold, under the pounding spill of the water. She climbed nimbly onto a plateau of rock, stretched her arms wide to the sides, and let the water beat over her.

He lost his breath, and despite the cool relief of the water, his blood ran hot. He hoisted himself up in front of her, laid his hands on her hips. Her eyes opened again, and her eyebrow quirked.

"You're the most magnificent thing I've ever seen. In any dimension."

"I have a good build," she said easily. "It's made for fighting." She bent her right arm, flexed her biceps.

"I bet it holds its own in other sports."

Though she couldn't ignore the trip of her own heart, or the quick click of response in her belly, she only smiled. "I enjoy sporting, when there's time for such things. You're very handsome, Harper Doyle, and I have a yearning for you that is stronger than any I have known before."

"Do you think you could pick one of my two names and stick with it?" Since she didn't seem to object, he slid his hands around her thighs, then over her silky butt.

"Harper is your title."

"No, it's my name. My first name." He really had to get a taste of that lush, frowning mouth. But as he dipped his head, she laid a restraining hand on his chest.

"I do not understand. Are you the harper called Doyle?"

"I'm Harper Doyle, and before this turns into a comedy routine, Doyle is my family name. Harper is the name my parents gave me when I was born. That's how it works in my world. I'm not *a* harper," he added as the light began to dawn. "I'm not, what, like a minstrel? Jesus. I'm a PI."

"A pee-eye? What is this?"

"Investigator. Private investigator. I . . . solve puzzles," he decided.

"Ah! You are a seeker. This is better. A seeker is more useful on a hunt than a harper."

"Now that we've worked that out, why don't we go back to me being handsome." He drew her closer so that her breasts—cool, wet, firm—brushed his chest. His mouth was an inch from hers when he went flying.

He landed clumsily, swallowing water on his own curse. She was still on the rocks when he came up and swiped the hair out of his eyes. She was grinning. "You made a good splash. It is time to go."

She dived, struck out for the bank. Oh, he was handsome, she thought as she hoisted herself out. Very handsome, and with a clever look in his eyes that made her want to join her body to his.

Something about him was making pricks on her heart, as if trying to find the weakness, the point of entry.

He would be a strong lover, she knew. And it had been a long time since she had desired one. If time and fate allowed, they would have each other.

But first, there was the hunt.

By the time he pulled himself onto the bank and put on his jeans, she was strapping on her sword. He didn't bother to think, just went with the moment. And tackled her.

She let out a surprised little grunt and studied his face with some approval. "I misjudged. You do have speed."

"Yeah, right, it'll help on the hunt. But right now . . ."

He lowered his head, all but tasting that beautiful mouth. And once more he went flying. But this time it was through the portal. The blast of light, and sharp, shocking pain.

He landed hard, with Kadra once more on top, on his kitchen floor. "Damn it!" He banged his head sharply on the base cabinet, felt the unmistakable shape of his gun dig into his bare back. "Give me some warning next time. A damn signal or something."

"You have your mind too much on sporting." She gave his shoulder a pat, then levered off him. Sniffed the air. "We will have more coffee, and plan the hunt."

"Okay, Sheena, let's reevaluate," he said as he got up.

"I am Kadra—"

"Shut up." He slapped the gun down on the kitchen counter while her mouth dropped open.

"You would speak so to a slayer?"

"Yeah, I'd speak so to anybody who busts uninvited into my house and keeps giving me orders. You want my help, you want my cooperation? Then you can just stop telling me what to do and start asking."

She was silent for a moment. She had a ready temper, something even her intense training hadn't completely tamed. To lose it now, she told herself, would be gratifying, but a sinful waste of time. Instead, she measured Harper, then nodded with sudden understanding. "Ah. You're talking with your man-thing. This is a common ailment in my world as well."

"This isn't my dick talking." Or at least, he'd be damned if he'd admit it. "I want answers. The way I see it, you're looking to hire me. That's fine. You want me to help you track down these . . . things. That's what I do. I find things, solve problems. That's my job. I work my way. Let's get that part straight."

"You are a seeker, and you require payment. Very well." Though she thought less of him for it, she wouldn't begrudge him his fee. "Come with me." She started out, turned when she saw him standing firm. "If you will," she added.

"Better," he muttered, and followed her into the bedroom, where she scooped up the leather pouch she'd tossed on the bed earlier.

"Is this enough?"

He caught the bag when she flipped it to him. Curious, he opened it. And poured a storm of gems onto the bed. "Holy Mother of God!"

"I am told these have value here. Is this so?" Intrigued, she stepped over to poke a finger into the pool of diamonds, rubies, emeralds. "They are common stones in my world. Pretty," she admitted. "Attractive for adornments. Will they satisfy your needs?"

"Satisfy my needs," he grumbled. "Yeah, they're pretty satisfactory."

He could retire. Move to Tahiti and live like a king. Hell, he could *buy* Tahiti and live like a god. For one outrageous moment, he saw himself living in a white palace by the crystal blue water, surrounded by gorgeous, scantily clad women eager to do his bidding. Drinking champagne by the gallons. Frolicking on white sand beaches with those same women—not clad at all now.

Master of all he surveyed.

Then his conscience kicked in, a small annoyance he'd never been able to shake. On the heels of conscience nipped the lowering admission that the fantasy he'd just outlined would bore him brainless in a week.

He picked a single diamond, comforting himself that it was worth more than he would earn in a decade.

"This'll cover it."

"That is all you require?"

"Put the rest away, before I change my mind." For lack of a better option, he stuffed the stone into his pocket. "Now, we're going to sit down. You're going to explain this whole demon deal to me, and I'll figure out our first move."

"They are out in your world. We have to hunt."

"My world," Harper agreed. "My turf. I don't go after anything until I know the score." He walked to his dresser, opened a drawer, and pulled out a T-shirt. "Normally I don't meet clients at home," he said as he pulled the shirt on. "But we'll make an exception. Living room." He headed out, took a legal pad from a desk drawer, then plopped down on the sofa.

However fantastic the client, however strange the case, he was going to approach it as he would any other. He made a few notes, then jerked his chin at a chair when she continued to stand. "Sit down. Bok demon, right? Is that B-O-K? Never mind. How many?"

"They were four. Sorak, demon king, and three warriors."

"Description?"

She sprawled in a chair, all legs and attitude. He looked more scholar than warrior now, working with his odd scroll and quill. Though she had never found scholar appealing before, this aspect of him was attractive to her as well.

He has brains as well as muscle, she thought. Intellect as well as brawn.

"Description," Harper repeated. "What do they look like?"

"They are deceptively human in appearance, and so often walk among people without detection. They are handsome, as you are. Though you have eyes blue as the marsh bell, and your hair is cropped short. Those who are foolish enough to be influenced by such things as beauty are easy victims."

"We've established that you're nobody's victim, baby. Be more specific."

She huffed. "They have good height, like you, but their build is less. It is more . . . slender. Hair and eyes are dark, black as a dead moon except in feeding or in attack, where they glow red."

"Glowing red eyes," he noted. "I'd say that's a fairly distinguishing mark."

"Sorak's hair curls." She demonstrated by waving a finger. "And is well groomed. He is vain."

"They outfitted like you?"

It took her a moment, then she glanced down at her hunting clothes. "No. They wear a kind of armor, black again, close to the body, and over this Sorak wears the tunic and cloak of his rank."

"Even in New York, body armor and tunics should stand out. Maybe there's something on the news." He picked up the remote and flipped on the television.

Kadra leaped up as if he'd set her chair on fire. Even before her feet were planted, her sword was out, raised high above her head in preparation for a downward thrust.

"Hold it, hold it, hold it!" He jumped and, as he might have done to save a beloved child, threw himself between the blade and his TV. "I don't give a rat's ass about what you did to the bathroom sink, but put one scratch on my TV and you're going down."

Her heart pounded in her chest, and her muscles quivered. "What is this sorcery?"

"It's not magic, it's ESPN." He hissed out a breath, then moved in to clamp his hands over hers on the hilt of the sword. She tipped her head back so their eyes, their mouths, lined up.

"It's television, which is arguably the national religion of my country. An entertainment device," he said more calmly. "A kind of communication. We have programs—ah, like plays, I guess, that tell us what's happening in the world, even when it's happening far away."

She drew a breath, slowly lowered the sword while she stared at the picture box where the machines called cars ran swiftly around a circle. "How is this done?"

"Something about airwaves, transmissions, cameras, stuff. Hell, I don't know. You turn the thing on, pick a channel. This is a race. You get that?"

"Yes, a contest of speed. I have won many races."

"With those legs, baby, I'll just bet you have. Okay, I'm turning on the news now so we can see if there are any reports on your demons. So relax."

"How can you use a thing when you have no knowledge of its workings?"

"Same way I can use a computer. And don't ask. I thought you said you knew about this world."

"I was given knowledge, but I cannot learn it all at once." It embarrassed her not to know, so she went back to sprawling in the chair, giving the television quick, suspicious glances.

"All right, we'll take it in stages. Just don't attack any more of my household appliances." He sat again, flipped the channel to the all-news station, then picked up his pad. "Back to your demons. Distinguishing marks? You know, like two heads, for instance?"

Feeling foolish, she sulked. He had nearly slain a spider with the weapon known as gun, but she had not made *him* feel loose in the brain. "They are Bok, not Loki."

"What makes them stand out? How do you recognize them?" Even as she threw up her hands, he tapped his pencil. "And don't say they are Bok. Draw me a picture."

Taking him literally, she reared up, snatched the pencil and pad. In fast, surprisingly deft strokes, she sketched a figure of a man with long, curled hair, a strong, rawboned face and large, dark eyes.

"That's good. But it's going to be tough to pick him out of the millions of other tall, slim, dark-haired guys in New York. Doesn't shout out demon to me. How do you recognize them— as a species, let's say."

"A slayer is born for this. But others might do so by their stench. They have a scent." She struggled for a moment in her attempt to describe it. "Between the ripe and the rot. You would not mistake it."

"Okay, they stink. Now we're getting somewhere. Anything else?"

"Teeth. Two rows, long, thin, sharp. Claws, which they show or conceal at will. Thick, blue, curved like talons. And when they are wounded, their blood is green. Now we hunt."

"Just settle down," he said mildly. He listened to the news reports with half an ear. The usual mayhem and gossip, but no frantic bulletins about man-eating demons on the loose in New York.

"Why are they here?" he asked her. "Why leave one world for another?"

"Sorak is greedy, and his hunger is great. For flesh, but also for power. There are more of you in this place than on our world. And you are unaware. They can move among you without fear of the slayer. They will feed, gluttonously. First on animals, for quick strength, then on humans. Those that he and his warriors do not consume, he will change so he can build a vast army. They will overtake the world you know and make it theirs."

"Whoa, back up. Change? What do you mean by change?"

"He will turn selected humans into demons, into slaves and warriors and concubines."

"You're telling me he can make people into things? Like, what, vampires?"

"I do not know this word. Explain."

"Never mind." Harper pushed himself to his feet to pace. For reasons he couldn't explain, the idea of having human beings turned into monsters was more disturbing than having them served up as demon meals. "How do they do it? How are people changed?"

"The Demon Kiss. Mouth against mouth. Tongue, teeth, lips. A bite, to draw blood, to mix it. Then the demon draws in the human essence, breathes his own into his prey. They are changed, and are compelled to hunt, to feed. They remember nothing of their humanity. This is worse than death."

"Yeah." The thought sickened him. "Yeah, it's worse. No way this son of a bitch is going to turn my town into his personal breeding ground." When he faced her, his face was set, and the warrior gleam in his eye gave Kadra her first real hope. "Animals, you said. Cats, dogs, what?"

"These are pets." She closed her eyes and searched the knowledge. "Such small prey would not please them. This would do only if the hunger was impossible. They prefer the flesh of the unicorn above all."

"Unicorns don't spend a lot of time grazing in New York. Horses?"

"Yes, horses, cows, goats. But there are no farms, you said. In the wild, they feed often on the lion or the ape."

"Lions, tigers, and bears? The zoo. We'll start there. As soon as we figure out how to outfit you so you blend in a little better with the general population."

Frowning, she looked down at herself. "I don't resemble the other females in your world?"

He scanned the breasts barely constrained by black leather, the long, lean torso, the swatch of leather over curvy hips. And those endless legs encased in boots. Not to mention a two-and-a-half-foot sword.

"I couldn't begin to tell you. Let's see what I can put together."

When she came out of his bedroom fifteen minutes later, he decided she did more to sell a pair of Levi's than a million-dollar ad campaign. And the old denim shirt had never looked better.

"Baby, you are a picture."

She studied herself in his mirror, and agreed. "It is tolerable hunting gear." Testing it, she executed several quick deep-knee bends that had Harper's blood pressure rising. "It will do." So saying, she picked up her sword.

"You can't walk around outside with that thing."

She glanced up, smirked. "So, do I slay demons with bad thoughts?"

"Aha, sarcasm. I like it. I've got something. Hold on." He went to the closet, shoved through it and came out with a long black coat. "A little warm for May, but we can't be picky."

"Why do people in your world cover up so much flesh?"

"I ask myself that question every day." He took another long look at her. Maybe, just maybe, if he'd been able to design his own ideal woman, he'd have come close to the reality of her. "You going to wear the little crown?"

Her hand went to the gold on top of her head. "This is the circle of my rank."

"You want to blend in?" He lifted the circlet off, set it aside. "Put on the coat and let's see."

Scowling, she dragged the coat on, turned to him. "You're still going to turn heads and star in a lot of male fantasies tonight, but you'll do."

Satisfied, he pulled on a battered bomber jacket, hitched it over his gun.

"I want one."

He noted her look at his Glock. "Yeah, I know. But I don't have one to spare." He slid on sunglasses, grabbed his keys. "Let's go."

"Why do you cover your eyes?"

"Styling, baby. I've got a pair for you in my car." He stopped at the elevator, pushed the Down button. "Try not to talk to anybody. If we have to have a conversation, let me handle it."

She started to object, but the wall opened. "A portal? Where does it lead?"

"It's an elevator. It goes up, it goes down. A kind of transportation."

"A box," she nodded as she stepped in with him. "That moves." Her grin spread when she felt the shift. "This is clever. Your world is very interesting."

The doors opened on three, and a woman and small boy got on.

"The elevator," Kadra said politely, "goes up and goes down."

The woman slid an arm around the boy and drew him close to her side.

"Didn't I tell you to keep quiet?" Harper hissed when they reached the lobby and the woman hustled her son away.

"I spoke with good manners, and made no threat to her or her young."

"Just stick close," he ordered, and took her hand firmly in his.

When they stepped outside, he thought it was a good thing he had a grip on her. She froze in place, her head swiveling right and left. "What a world this is," she breathed. "Blue sky, great huts, so many people. So many scents. There." She pointed to a sidewalk vendor. "This is food."

"Later." He pulled her along the sidewalk. "My car's in a garage a couple blocks over."

"The ground is made of stone."

He had to jerk her up when she bent over to tap a fist on the sidewalk. "Concrete. Men make it and pour it over the ground."

"Why? Is the ground poisonous?"

"No. It's just easier."

"How can it be easier? The ground was already there." She stopped again, mouth agape as an ambulance whizzed by, sirens screaming, lights flashing. "Is it a war?"

"No, it's transportation. For the sick or the wounded."

She digested this and other wonders on the two-block hike. The shops with their goods locked behind glass, the crowds of people in a hurry, the clatter and din of the machines that ran on the wide stone road.

"This is a noisy world," she commented. "I like it. What are these trees?" she asked, knocking a fist on a telephone pole.

"I'll explain later. Just say nothing."

Harper strolled into the garage with a death grip on Kadra's hand. He flipped a salute to the attendant, who was passing the time with a magazine. But one look at Kadra had the attendant gaping.

"Oooh, baby! That is *fine*."

"Why am I called baby here?" she demanded as he whipped into the stairway. "I am not new young."

"It's an expression. Endearment or insult, depending on your point of view." On the second level, he crossed the lines of cars and stopped at his beloved '68 Mustang. He unlocked it, opened the passenger door. "Climb in."

She sniffed first, caught the scent of leather and approved. She was already fiddling with dials and jiggling the gearshift when he got behind the wheel. "Don't touch." He slapped her hand away. She kicked her elbow under his jaw. "Cut it out." Shoving her arm down, he reached for her seat belt. "You need to strap in. It's the law of the land."

When he bent to buckle her up, he saw that she was still miffed. "You sure push my buttons," he muttered.

"This is an expression?"

"Yeah. It means—"

"I do not need an explanation. You are aroused by me."

"And then some." He trailed his fingers over her cheek. Then he opened the glove compartment and tossed a pair of wrap-around shades in her lap. "I guess we have to go kick some demon butt before we deal with our buttons."

4

She had a great deal to think about.

She was primarily a physical creature. When she was hungry, she ate. When she was tired, she slept. And all of her life, her purpose, above all others, had been to hunt.

It was a sacred trust, a sacred gift. She could laugh and weep, desire and dislike, dream and act. But over it all, through every cell in her body was the purpose.

She had been born, raised and trained for it.

But no slayer lived long if she didn't use her brain as well as her might.

Even with the wonder of her first car ride, the thrill of seeing the structures and the people, hearing the blasts of horns, of music, of voices, her mind still chipped away at the puzzle.

She had been sent to this place, and to this man. So their destinies were joined. She would protect him and his people with her life.

He was a seeker, and deserved respect. But as a slayer she

ranked highest, save for the sorcerer. And if Rhee had spoken true, she had that in her blood as well.

The man had no right to usurp her authority. He would have to be put in his place for it.

But he was correct. This was his world, and his knowledge of it exceeded hers. If he was to be her guide, then she must follow. However much it rankled.

She desired him, which both pleased and irritated her. Pleased because he was strong and handsome, amusing and intelligent—and he desired her in turn. Irritated because she was unused to experiencing a desire this keen without the time and means to act upon it.

And she was not prepared for what was tangled in and woven through that desire. Lust was appetite, which could be easily sated. But this longing fluttering inside her, like a wild bird fighting to be free, was stronger, stranger than any need of the flesh.

It distracted her, and she could not afford to be distracted. If the Bok escaped her, this world, and her world, were doomed.

"So, how'd you get into the slayer business?"

She turned her head, and even with the dark glasses, Harper felt the heat of her gaze. "It was a gift, given me at my creation. It is woven in my blood, in my bone."

"Let's put it this way. You didn't pop out of the womb with a broadsword in your hand and a little dagger clenched in your teeth."

"I was trained." She liked watching the lights turn colors. She'd processed their purpose herself because she was tired of asking questions. "To track, to hunt, in weaponry. To fight, to build my body, my mind, my spirit."

"How about your parents?"

"I know no father. It is the way of slayers."

"All slayers are women?"

"We are female, birthed by females, raised, trained, and tested."

"What do the guys do? The men."

"Males hunt, farm, become warriors, scholars, seekers like yourself." She shrugged. "Whatever path is open to them. Some, in protecting their land, their families, in battle or in defense of self, kill demons. But they are not slayers."

"Are there more like you back home?"

"There were ten, now there are nine. Four weeks past, Sorak killed one of us. A trap. He drank the blood of a slayer. That is how he had the power, the strength, to elude me, to get this far. She was Laris. She was my friend."

"I'm sorry." Harper closed a hand over hers. "He'll pay for it."

The gesture, the simple warmth and connection, moved her. "There is no payment rich enough. His death will have to do." She looked over quickly when he lifted her hand to his mouth, brushed his lips over her knuckles.

"A custom," he said, reading her shock. "Like an expression. Comfort, affection, seduction. Whatever fits."

Her lips curved. "In my world you would be thrashed for taking such a liberty with a slayer."

"We're in my world now, baby."

"And here the sky is different, and the ground. The customs. I enjoy many of the new things in this place. The drink called coffee, the elevator, and the car. I have not decided if I like the box called television or all your expressions, but I enjoy the sensation of your mouth on my skin."

He parked the car, turned off the ignition. "You got a man back home? A lover?"

"No."

"You're going to have one here." He climbed out, skirted the hood, and opened her door. "We'll walk for a while," he told her and took her hand again. "Stay close."

She let him lead. It gave her the opportunity to observe and absorb, to identify scents. Food came to her again—sweet, spiced, tart. Her stomach tightened in hunger. Perhaps traveling through the portal sharpened the appetites, she thought. If that were true for the Bok, they would already have fed at least once.

She caught the scent of animal among the human. Great cats, reptile, fowl, and more she couldn't identify. And then she saw them, exotic beasts, prowling or dozing in enclosures while people strolled past or stopped to stare.

It gave her a pang at the most elemental level. "It is not right to lock them up. They are not born for this."

"Maybe it's not," he agreed. He hadn't come to the zoo since childhood because it invariably made him sad. "I can't say I care for it either."

"This is a cruel thing you do here. This is a sorry place, this zoo. Is this what you teach your young?" she demanded, gesturing to a little girl being wheeled in a stroller by her parents. "That one species can be locked away for the amusement of another?"

"I don't know how to explain it to you. Civilization has encroached. There isn't as much room as there once was. In captivity, they're safe, I guess, and tended. They can't be hunted or taken as trophies."

"They are not free," was all she said, and turned away.

"Okay, maybe this was a bad idea. It's depressing, and the place is jammed. I wasn't thinking about it being Sunday. It doesn't seem like the time and place for a demon snack. Maybe we should try the animal shelter—dogs and cats. Or hit the stables."

She held up a hand, bared her teeth. "Bok," was all she said.

She was on the scent and ran like the wind. People scrambled out of her way, and those who caught a glimpse of the sword under her coat scrambled faster and farther.

It was a challenge to keep up with her under normal circumstances, but with the obstacle course of people, children, benches, and trash receptacles in the zoo, Harper's lungs were burning by the time he caught up.

"Slow down," he snapped. "You mow down innocent bystanders, we'll get arrested before we get where you want to go. And I can't begin to tell you how much fun the cops will have with your demon story."

"There!" She pointed to a building, seconds before a stream of people rushed out. Screaming.

She drew her sword as she raced through the doorway.

Whatever Harper had expected, it hadn't been this, this stench of blood and death, of fear and rot. In the cages, monkeys were wild. Screeching, screaming, leaping desperately from branch to branch.

He saw the blood and gore on the floor, tracked it with his eyes, and found—to his horror—a man, no, a demon, feeding savagely on a body. A human body.

When the demon lifted his head, his teeth, his eyes glistened red.

It all happened in seconds. The shock, the disgust, the fury. All of those vicious sensations burst through him as Harper drew his gun. And something hideous pounced on his back.

Claws dug into his shoulders, gouged as the thing that attacked him let out a predatory howl. He spun, ramming back into the wall. His gun flew out of his hand and slid across the floor. Cursing, he battered the thing against the wall as his own blood spilled hot down his back. He felt the rough edge of a tongue slide through it, slurp hideously.

Revolted, he flew back with his elbow, aiming high for the

throat, hammered down with his heel on the instep of a booted foot hard enough to hear bone snap.

There was a shriek, inhuman. Harper jabbed behind him with his fingers where he hoped to find eyes.

Now it screamed, and the claws released.

He saw what it was now, as he spun around. The face of a man, the eyes of a monster. It came for him, and Harper sprang into the fight.

It was limping from the bones he'd crushed, but it was still fast. Lightning fast. Harper whirled, and the thing hurtled past him. When it turned to charge again, he met its face with a flying kick.

Kadra fought her own demons, swinging her sword to block the slice of a curved blade, evading the swipe of claws as she carefully retreated. She gauged Harper's position by sound. She couldn't risk even a glance behind her. Out of the corner of her eye, she saw Sorak, behind the bars, grinning, grinning as he feasted and watched the battle.

Kadra flipped her dagger out of its sheath, managed to turn enough to judge Harper's distance and position. She feinted, thrust, then leaped to cleave the demon's sword arm from his body.

"Harper Doyle!" She shouted, then heaved him her sword as she snatched the sickle blade from the air to battle the next demon.

They fought back-to-back now, Harper wielding the sword, she slicing with the dagger and blade. Green blood mixed with red.

Still, she saw, Sorak watched.

"I will have you," he called out. "I will have your blood. I will have your body. I will have your mind."

"I am Kadra!" She almost sang it as she thrust through slicing claws and pinned the point of the dagger in the demon warrior's throat. "I am your death." She spun, prepared to leap into the other battle. And watched Harper's sword cleave his opponent's belly.

Through the smoke curling from the demon dead, she scooped the Glock up on the fly as she rushed to where Sorak fed and gloated. She saw only the quick flash of his teeth, the taunting swirl of his cloak as he bolted toward an open door on the side of the cage.

She fired, the explosions of sound roaring through the building. Even so, she could hear the demon's laughter. She vaulted over the safety rail, closed her hands on the bars of the cage where beasts lay slaughtered, and battered at the steel.

"Come on." Riding on adrenaline and pain, Harper wrenched her around. He shot the sword back into her sheath, snatched his gun and holstered it. "Put this away. Now," he snapped, handing her the dagger. "We're getting out, fast. There's no possible explanation for what just happened here, so we're not going to make one. Move!"

She ran with him, through the building, out the rear. He tugged the coat over her sword, wrapped an arm around her shoulders, and tried to look as normal as a couple could who had just battled a pack of demons.

"Keep it slow. Cops are already heading in." He heard the sirens, the shouts. They turned away from the noise and kept walking. How long had they been inside? he wondered. It had seemed like hours. But now he realized it had been only minutes.

"Can you track it?" Harper asked her.

Alone, on her world, the answer would have been yes. But here, with the crowds of people, the scents and sights so unfamiliar to her senses, she was unsure.

"He will go to ground now. He knew. He knew I would come

here. Sorak has more knowledge than I thought. Now he has fed, he has amused himself. He will rest and wait. He will not feed again in the daylight."

"Just as well. The place is going to be crawling with cops. Since we're covered with blood, and armed, we wouldn't get very far."

And he had a bad feeling that a lot of the blood was his own. He wouldn't be any good to Kadra in the next round if he was light-headed and shocky. First things first, he thought as he concentrated on staying upright. Get bandaged up, get steady. Then think.

"We'll hunt the bastard down and kill him with his belly full."

It was difficult to turn away from the hunt. But she had seen the demon attack him from the rear and knew he was wounded. She would not leave him behind.

"He has disguised his scent with the animals, and the humans. He will take time for me to find his lair." She steadied him when he swayed against her, and the hand she pressed to his shoulder came away smeared with his blood.

"How bad is your wound?"

"I don't know. Bad enough. Fucking claws. Went right through the leather. I've only had this jacket five, six years."

She turned her head to look at the gouges and was relieved to see the demon had torn more cloth than flesh. "It is not so bad. It was a good battle," she said with sudden cheer. "You fight well."

"Three out of four. It's just the one now."

"He will make more."

The horror of that seized Harper's belly. "We have to stop him."

"We will do what must be done. Now we go back to your hut.

Your wounds must be tended. We will rest, eat, think. We will be ready for the night."

Her unerring sense of direction took them back to his car. "Can I sit on the side with the wheel now?"

"No, you can't sit on the side with the wheel now. Or ever." Hurting, exhausted, he jabbed the key into the lock, wrenched open the door.

"Are all so selfish with their possessions here?"

"A man's car is his castle," Harper stated, and limped around to take the wheel. "Are you hurt?" he remembered to ask.

"No, I am unharmed." Realizing he might take this as a criticism of his skill, she took his hand as he had taken hers. "But I am a slayer."

"Kiss ass."

She cocked her head. The battle had lifted her mood. "This is another expression?"

He had to laugh, had to hiss in pain. On a combination of both, he started the car. "Yeah, baby, but it's one I wouldn't mind you taking literally."

5

Though sheer will kept Harper conscious, he was in considerable pain and woozy from the loss of blood by the time he pulled back into his slot at the garage. Kadra's idea of how to deal with the problem was to carry him.

He had just enough strength left to stop her from slinging him over her shoulder. And just enough wit to realize she could have pulled it off.

"No." Since his limbs had gone watery on him, he warded her off with a scowl. "I'm not being carried across the Lower East Side by a woman."

"This is foolish. You're injured. I am not."

"Yeah, yeah, keep rubbing it in. Just give me a hand."

When she frowned and held one out, he shook his head. "You're a literal creature." He slid an arm around her waist, let her take some of his weight. "Walk and talk," he told her. "Tell me more about this change."

"After the kiss of change, the victim falls into a trance—a sleep that is not a sleep, for one day. During the sleep, the demon blood mixes with the human's. The human becomes what has poisoned him, with the demon's instincts, his habits. His appetites."

Since Harper's breathing was ragged, she tightened her grip and shortened her stride. "When the human wakes he is demon, though some wake before the change is complete and are demi-demons. In either stage, the one who has changed is bound to the one who changed him."

"Is there a cure?"

"Death," she said flatly, and shifted her grip on him as they stepped outside. He was pale, she noted. And his breath was only more labored. It would have been easier to carry him.

But she understood a warrior's pride.

"Your hut is only a short journey. We will go at your pace."

"Just keep talking." His shoulder was going numb, and that worried him. "I need to focus."

"Why did you become a seeker?"

"I like to find things out. Without a PI license, it's called nosiness. With one, it's called a profession. Insurance fraud, missing persons, some skip tracing. I try to stay out of the marital arena. It's just humiliating for all parties to stand outside a motel room with a camera."

She didn't know what he was talking about, but she liked his voice. Despite his wounds, or perhaps because of them, there was grit in it. "Are you a successful seeker?"

"I get by." He looked around but couldn't quite pinpoint where they were. The sounds of traffic, the busy music of the city, sounded dim. She was the only thing clear to him now—the supporting strength of her arm, the firm curves of her body, the scent of the sacred waterfall that lingered in her hair.

It was as if both their worlds had receded and they themselves were all that was left.

"What must you get by?"

"Hmm?" He turned his head. He'd been right, he thought, there really was nothing but her. "I mean I do all right. I do regular legwork for a lawyer. Jake, the one I thought had hired you. He's got a sick sense of humor. That's why I love him."

He staggered at the curb, tried to orient himself when she steadied him. "It is this way." She turned the corner, glanced up and down the street. "Where is the well? You require water."

"Doesn't work that way here." But she was right about one thing. His thirst was vicious. He nodded toward a sidewalk vendor. "There."

With her arm banded around his waist, Kadra watched Harper exchange several small disks for a bottle. He fought the top off, drank deep.

"You must pay for water? Does it have magical properties?" She took it, drank. "Nothing but water," she said with some amazement. "The merchant is a robber. I will go back and speak to him."

"No. No." Despite the dizziness, Harper laughed. "It's just one of the acceptable lunacies of our little world. When water comes out of the tap, it's free. Sort of. When it comes out of a bottle, you pay on the spot."

She pondered this as they came to the intersection. She'd watched the way the people, the cars, the lights worked together. When the metal tree ordered the waiting group to walk, everyone hurried, often sliding and swooping between cars that jammed together and faced other metal trees with lights of amber, emerald, and ruby.

Everyone in the village played along.

She felt Harper sag, and pinched his waist ruthlessly to snap him back. "We have only . . ." She flipped back to his earlier term for the section of road. "One more block."

"Okay, okay." He could feel sweat running a clammy line

down his back. His vision was going in and out. "Let's talk about me. I'm thirty. As of yesterday. Unmarried. Came close a couple years ago, but I came to my senses."

"Had the woman bewitched you?"

"No." He had to smile at the term. "You could say that was the problem: she *didn't* bewitch me. This is a huge disappointment to my parents, who want grandchildren. As I'm an only child, I'm their one shot at it."

"Is it not possible in this place to make young without a life-mate? Can you not select a breeding partner for this purpose?"

"Yeah, you could, and a lot of people do. I guess I'm more of a traditionalist in that one area. If I have kids, I want them to have the package. You like kids?"

"I am fond of young. They have innocence and potential, and a special kind of beauty. In time I will select a breeding partner so that I may make life. It is a great honor to make life."

"I'm with you on that." Nearly there, he told himself. Please, God, we're nearly there. "Anyway, my parents live in New Jersey. Another world."

"Was Old Jersey destroyed?"

"Ah . . . no." His head was spinning now. Concentrate, he ordered himself. Just put one foot in front of the other. "Geography and world history lessons later. Let's stick with personal revelations. I didn't want to tie on my dad's cop's shoes, so I veered off into private investigation. I apprenticed with a big, slick firm uptown, but I didn't like the suit and tie brigade. Went out on my own about five years ago. I'm good at what I do."

"It's wasteful to be bad at what you do."

"You know, my dad would lap you right up. He'd like you," Harper explained, breathlessly now. "He was a good cop. Retired three years ago. He'd go for your sense of order."

He fumbled out his keys as they approached his building's entrance. She wanted to ask him why everything had to be locked, like a treasure box, but his face was dead white now.

She dragged him to the elevator, puzzled out the buttons. They had come down, so now they would go up. It pleased her enormously when the doors opened.

"Four," he managed. "Push four. If we have to call 911, I'm going to leave it to you to explain that I've been clawed by a Bok demon."

Ignoring him, and regretting that she couldn't fully appreciate the ride this time, she dragged him out when the doors opened again. She took the keys from him, selected the proper one, and unlocked his door.

"You don't miss a trick, do you? You'd make a damn good PI."

She merely booted the door closed behind them, then bending, lifted him onto her shoulder.

"Honey." His voice slurred. "This is so sudden."

She laid him facedown on the bed, peeled off his ruined jacket, then tore away what was left of his shirt.

His breath hissed through his teeth at the bright burn of pain. "Can you be a little more rough, Nurse Ratched? I live for pain."

"Quiet now." The wounds were deeper than she'd thought. Four ugly grooves and one jagged puncture. The blood that had started to clot flowed freely again. "This must first be cleansed. How do I fetch water?"

"Tap. Bathroom tap. The sink. Damn it. The white bowl—ah, the taller one," he added as he got an image of her scooping water out of his toilet. "Turn the handle."

She found the bathing room, and the sink. And was delighted when water gushed out. She soaked a towel and carried it sopping wet into the bedroom. She felt his body shudder when she laid it over his back.

He fought well, she thought again as she cleaned the wounds. And was stalwart in his pain. He had more than the strength of a warrior; he had the heart of one too. She remembered how his hand had whipped up and closed around the hilt of the sword she'd tossed him.

A good team, she decided. She'd never found a partner she could admire, respect, and desire.

She retrieved her supply bag, reached in for the vial of healing powder that all warriors carried. Her fingers brushed over the cloth Mav had wrapped around her hand.

Lips pursed, Kadra studied her own unmarked palm. Perhaps some of the healer's powers were still in the cloth. Quickly, she made a paste from powder and water.

"This will sting," she told him. "I'm sorry for it."

"Sting" was a mild word for the blaze that erupted under his skin when she spread the medication over his wounds. His hands fisted in the spread, his body jerked in protest.

"Only a moment," she murmured, wrenched by his pain. "It eats any infection."

"Does it chew through flesh while it's at it?" He spit the words out through gritted teeth.

"No, but it feels that way. It is no shame to scream."

"I'll keep that in mind." But he swore instead, softly, steadily, viciously, and earned more of the slayer's respect.

When the paste began to turn from sickly yellow to white, she breathed a sigh of relief. The infection was dying. Over the smeared wounds, she lay the thin healing cloth.

"If there is any magic in my blood," she whispered, "let it help him. Sleep now, Harper the valiant." She brushed her fingers through his hair. "Sleep and heal."

✱

He dreamed, strange, colorful dreams. Battles and blood. Storms and swords. Kadra, with her war cry echoing through dark, dank tunnels. The king of demons feasting on flesh in the shadows.

And he himself delivering the killing blow that sent green blood gushing.

In dreams he knew her body, the feel of those luscious curves under his hand, the taste of her skin, the sound of her moan. He saw her rising over him, warrior, goddess, woman.

He felt, real as life, the warm press of her lips on his.

And woke aching for her.

He sat up, instinctively reaching for the back of his shoulder. He found nothing, no wound, no break in the skin, no scar.

Had it all been a dream after all? One wild booze-induced dream starring the most magnificent woman ever created?

The idea that she was only in his mind depressed him brutally. What were a few Bok demons between friends, he thought as he pushed himself out of bed, when you had a Kadra in your life?

Was the only woman who'd ever stirred him on every level just a product of his imagination? Of wishful thinking? If he could only fall in love in dreams, why the hell did he have to wake up?

Back to reality, Doyle, he told himself, then took a step toward the bedroom door and nearly tripped over his leather jacket.

He scooped it up, fingers rushing over the battered material. Nothing, nothing in his life had ever delighted him more than seeing those bloodstained rips.

He tossed it aside and bolted for the door.

She'd changed back into her own clothes. And was sitting cross-legged on the floor, her nose all but pressed to the television screen, where the Yankees were taking on the Tigers.

"I like this battle," she said without turning around. "The

warriors in the white are beating the warriors in the gray by three runs. They are better with the clubs."

"Girl of my dreams," Harper said aloud. "She likes baseball."

"There were other images in the box." And each had startled and fascinated. "But this is my favorite."

"Okay, that does it. We have to get married."

She turned then, smiled at him. His color was back, and that relieved her. His eyes were clear, and held more than recovered health. The lust in them aroused her. "You healed well."

"I healed just dandy."

"I hunted among your stores," she told him. "You have little, but I like this food and drink." She gestured toward the bag of sour-cream-and-onion potato chips and the bottle of Coors.

"You're perfect. It's just a little scary."

"We must eat. Fighting requires fuel."

"Yeah, we'll eat. We'll order some pizza."

He looked hungry as well, she noted. But not for food. She rose smoothly. Her blood was already warm for him. "I'm pleased you are well."

"Yeah. I'm feeling real healthy just now. You can tell me how you managed that later."

"You do not wish to talk at this time." She nodded, stepped toward him. Then she circled around him to check his shoulder—and to admire his form. When she stopped face-to-face again, her eyes were level with his. "Do you wish to join your body to mine?"

He blinked once, slow as an owl. "Is that a trick question?"

"You have desire for me."

Charmed, perplexed, he dipped his hands in his pockets. "Is that all it takes?"

"No." She was never as sure of herself as a female as she was as a slayer. But this time, with him, she felt sure. "But I have desire for you as well. It is a heat in my belly, a burn in my blood. I want to join with you."

"I wanted you before I even met you," he told her.

"This is like a poem." And softened her under the skin. "You are well named. I cannot speak as cleverly, so I will say we have time for this and for food before we hunt again. And that our minds and bodies will be stronger for appeasing both appetites."

On those long, tantalizing legs, she walked past him into the bedroom.

Worlds, he thought as he followed her, were about to collide.

"Whoa. Wait. Hold on." She'd already stripped off her top, and was pulling off her boots. "What's the rush?"

She looked up, a crease between her brows. "Are you ready to sport?"

"Yeah. But we could take a minute to . . ." He stared at her, golden skin, naked breasts. "What am I saying?" He scooped her off her feet and made her laugh by tossing her on the bed.

She rolled, came up on her haunches. Saliva pooled in his mouth as she grinned at him. "You have energy. Good. Strip," she ordered. "We will wrestle first."

"You wanna wrestle?" He unbuttoned his jeans.

"It is stimulating," she began, then lowered her gaze. "You seem to be very stimulated already. I admire your body, baby." It pleased her to use one of his terms of affection. "I want to touch it."

"Are you sure you're not a dream, brought on by one too many bourbons and bumps?"

"I am real." Watching him, she stroked her hands over her breasts, cupped them. "Touch me."

When he came forward, reached, she rolled away laughing. And crooked her finger at him.

He dived.

She obviously took her wrestling seriously—he was pinned in under five seconds. "Two out of three," he said and put himself in the game.

They tumbled over the bed, hands gripping, sliding, legs scissoring. Bodies straining. He wasn't sure if he pinned her by skill or because she'd allowed it. He didn't give a damn. Not when she was sprawled under him, her hair spread out, her eyes hot and green.

"Let's call it a draw," he suggested, lowering his head.

Her hand shot out, wedged between them. "There can be no mouth on mouth. This is not permitted."

"Kisses are illegal in your world?"

"A kiss is a gift." Now it was she who was breathless, from the press of his body, from the knowledge that his lips were nearly upon hers. "One given in promise between those who mate."

"I had mating in mind."

"No, joining. Joining is . . . sport. Mating is for life."

He wanted that mouth, as much as he wanted to breathe. And he wanted her to give it to him. "In this world a kiss is a sign of trust, affection, love, friendship. All manner of things. When a man and a woman join here, a kiss is a part of the union. A pleasurable part. You've never kissed a man?"

"I've made no promise to a man with my lips."

Make one to me, he thought. "Let me show you the way it's done in my world." He brushed his lips over her cheek. "Let me have your mouth, Kadra."

The hand separating them began to tremble. "I can take no lifemate." She felt his breath on her lips, warm, seductive. "It is not permitted for a slayer in my world."

"This is here. This is now." He closed his hand over the one she still held to his heart. "Let me be the first. Let me be the only."

She could have resisted. She had the strength, and though she could feel it melting, she still had the will. But his lips were so lovely, so soft against her skin. The glide of them was like all the promises that could never be given.

And her own lips yearned.

His world, she thought as she yielded. She was in his world now.

Their lips met, silkily. And her breath rushed out in shock at the sensation. The intimacy, the sweet flavor, the smooth slide of tongue against tongue were more potent than any brew she had ever sipped.

With one drink, she was drunk on him.

"Again," she demanded, and dragged him down by the hair until mouth ravaged mouth.

He had thought a kiss a simple thing, just another part of the mating dance. But with her he was whirled into the glory of it. He sank deep into her, and deeper still, until the taste of her was a craving in his belly.

I've waited for you, she thought, bowing her body to his—a body that ached for his hands. How could I have waited for you when I didn't know you existed? How could I have needed you when you were never there?

But when his hands moved over her, she knew it was true. All the passion that was in her blood, all the passion newly discovered, she gave to him.

She was a fantasy come to life. All curves and sleek skin. Urgent hands and avid mouth. She raged beneath him, demanding more even as he gave. She was a feast who commanded him to feed.

Now when they wrestled, their breath was ragged and their skin damp. The mouth that had conquered hers rushed everywhere, tasted all of her.

When she crested, it was like a wave rising up inside her, spilling out on a throaty cry and pouring into him.

She rose above him, as she had in dreams. Woman, warrior, lover. She took him into her, closed around him, and throwing her head back, rode.

Joined, he thought dimly as his blood pounded. Everything inside him was joined with her.

He reared up, banding his arms around her, fusing his mouth to hers as they took each other over the brink.

6

No joining had ever been so intense or so pleasurable. None had caused her to feel this mysterious sensation that was beyond the physical. Nor to find herself both conquered and victorious.

Bards spoke of such unions, but she had never believed the words were more than romantic delusion.

And they were joined still, she realized. Wrapped tight, fused like two links in one chain. This was more than sport, she thought. She didn't wish it to end.

She rubbed her lips together, experimenting. His taste was still there—his flesh, yes—but it was more. His mouth, the intimacy of the kiss that had been like . . . feeding each other. She hadn't known such matters could have such heat, and yet be tender.

She had never known tenderness, nor had she believed she required it.

Small wonder that in the world she knew, a mouth kiss was reserved for lifemates and was part of the sacred vows that stretched for all time.

If he lived in her world, or she in his, could there have been a lifetime between them?

Thinking it brought such a pang, such a wrench of longing. She was a slayer, she reminded herself, and he a seeker. They could walk the same path only until their battle was won. Then they, like their worlds, would stand apart.

But until their time was ended, she could have what she could take.

"I like the kissing," she said, sliding her hands into his hair as she eased back to see his face. "I would like to do more if there's an opportunity to join again."

"Kissing isn't just for joining." Still lost in her, still steeped in the first heady brew of love, he brushed his lips across hers.

"What else? Teach me."

At the idea of tutoring her, his pulse kicked again. "At times like this, after making love—"

"Making love." Following his lead, she leaned in to rub her lips over his. "I like this expression."

"Sometimes, after, while a couple is still tuned to each other, they kiss to show how much pleasure they were given. It might be long and lazy, like this."

He drew her in again on a slow, gentle glide that brought a purr of approval to her throat. Soft, so soft, deep without demand. Sweet as a maiden's dream.

"Yes," she sighed. "Again."

"Wait. Sometimes, when passions have been roused and people are still caught in that last edge of the storm of them, the tone of the kiss reflects that. Like this."

He caught her to him, close and hard, and his mouth was like a fever on hers. Now she groaned and wrapped around him like rope. He felt the thrill of her on his skin, in his blood, down to the pit of his stomach.

"You make me want." Her voice was thick now, and her heart galloped as if she'd raced to the pinnacle of the Stone Mountains. "In ways I have never wanted."

"You make me need." He held her now, just held her. "In ways I've never needed. What are we going to do about this, Kadra?"

She shook her head. "What must be done is all that can be done."

"Things have changed. Things are different now."

If only they could be, she thought. With him, a joy she hadn't known was locked inside her could be free. "What I feel for you fills me, and empties me. I've never known this with another." Still, she made herself draw back from him. "The fate of two worlds is in our hands. We can't take each other and lose them."

"We'll save them. And then—"

"Don't talk of 'and then.'" She touched her fingers to his lips. "Whatever fate holds for us, we have now. It's a gift to be treasured, not to be questioned."

"I want a life with you."

She smiled, but there was sorrow in her eyes. "Some lifetimes have to be lived in a day."

He wasn't going to accept that. He was good at solving puzzles, Harper thought. He'd find a way to solve this one. He also knew when he was banging against a head as hard as his own. There were times for force, and times for strategy.

"Having a warrior goddess drop on me out of another dimension, visiting an alternate reality, fighting demons, making love. It's been a pretty full day so far." He tangled his fingers in her hair. "What's next on the schedule?"

Strength, Kadra thought, wasn't only a matter of muscle. It was a matter of courage. They would both be valiant enough to accept destiny. "We must hunt Sorak, but we will need food and planning time. He's the mightiest of his kind, and the most sly."

"Okay, we'll order that pizza and fuel up while we figure out our plan of attack."

Nodding, and grateful he hadn't pressed where she was now vulnerable, she rolled off the bed. "What is this pizza?"

No pizza on A'Dair, he thought. Score one for Earth. "It's, ah, a kind of pie. Round, usually," he said as he allowed himself the pleasure of watching her slip on the brief bottom half of her hunting costume.

"You're magnificent, Kadra. 'Beautiful' is too ordinary, too simple a word," he added when she stared at him. "Do men on A'Dair tell you that you take their breath away, that looking at you is like being struck blind by a force of beauty so strong it's painful?"

His words made her weak, as if she'd slain a thousand demons in one day. "Men do not speak so to slayers."

He rose. "I do."

"You are different." So wonderfully different. "When I hear the words from you, they make me feel proud. And shy. I have never been shy," she added, baffled. "It pleases me that you find me attractive to look at."

"Do you think that's all I meant? You are very attractive. You're right off the charts in that area. But then you add the courage, the brains, the compassion I saw in you when Mav told you of her father's death, the active curiosity, the sense of fun, the heart of a warrior. You're unique to any world, and I'm dazzled by you."

"No one has ever . . ." Her throat burned. "I need time to find the words to give back to you that are as fine and rich."

He took her hands, lifted them to his lips. "They were free. They don't require any trade or payment."

"Like a gift?"

"Exactly."

"Thank you."

He dressed, switched the TV to the news in case there were any updates. He started to call in the pizza order. Then he remembered it wasn't just his taste that had to be satisfied this time. "Okay, pizza can come with a variety of options. Meat, vegetables—stuff like onions, mushrooms, peppers, sausage, pepperoni. It's an endless parade. I usually get it pretty loaded. Is there anything you don't eat?"

"I don't care for the meat of the grubhog."

He let out a quick, huffing laugh. "Check. Hold the grubhog."

He called in the order—explained to her what a phone was—then went into the kitchen for a couple of beers. "It'll take about twenty minutes. Let's figure out what step we take next over a beer."

"I like the beer," she told him.

"Just one more reason we're perfect for each other." He tapped his bottle to hers. "So." He dropped down on the couch, stretched out. "You said Sorak would have a lair. What sort of digs would he look for? What's his habit in living arrangements?"

"Demons live belowground." She crossed her feet at the ankles, then lowered herself in one smooth move to the floor. "They like the dark after feeding. They will burrow, dig tunnels so they may travel under the ground."

She picked up the portable phone he'd set down and began to play with it.

"In the east, Laris and I once tracked a demon pack to a great lair, with many tunnels through the rock and dirt, with many chambers for stores and sleep and treasures. We slew the pack and destroyed the lair with fire. It was Clud's palace, and there I destroyed the king of demons. But Sorak, then prince, was not there. When he heard of this, he vowed to kill the slayers who had killed his sire, and to build a great new kingdom in a place where no slayer could defeat him. I have this."

She flipped back her hair to show him a thin hooked scar at the base of her neck. "Only a demon king can leave his mark on a slayer. This is Clud's. The last swipe of his claws before my sword took his heart."

"Impressive." Harper pulled down his shirt to expose the line of puckered skin on his shoulder. "Skip trace, with a bad attitude and a switchblade."

She nodded. "How did you kill him?"

"It doesn't work that way here—ideally. I kicked his ass, then turned him over to the cops and collected my fee. The authorities," he explained. "We put bad guys—our demons—in jail. In cages, like at the zoo today."

"Ah." She considered that, and found it just. Captivity was a living death. "Is the demon who broke your nose also in his cage?"

"Sucker punch," Harper told her, running his hand down the uneven line of his nose. "Yeah, he's doing a stretch. Pissant grifter going around snuggling up to rich women, then ripping them off, copping their jewelry, draining their bank accounts. Prick."

Kadra angled her head. "I like the way you speak. I find it arousing to listen to your stories."

"Oh, yeah?" He slid down onto the floor beside her, walked his fingers up her boot to her thigh. "I've got a million of them."

"Sporting must wait."

"I like your face. I find it arousing to look at your face." He touched it, just a skim of fingertips over her cheek. "When I was sleeping, I dreamed of making love with you. Then it happened, just the way I'd dreamed it."

"This is vision."

"Maybe." He thought of the blood and the battle, of the dark and the smoke. "One thing, before we get back on track. I've always liked working alone; that's why I went out on my own. I've liked living alone, which is why I've screwed up any potentially serious relationship with a woman. I never wanted a partner, until you."

She lifted a hand to his cheek in turn. A kind of joining, she realized, with only a touch. "I have been alone. It is the way of slayers. I never wished it otherwise, until you. They will write songs about you in my world. The great warrior from beyond A'Dair."

And when she listened to them by the fire, she thought, she would be alone again.

She let her hand drop away, then took a deep drink of her beer. "I tracked Sorak across my world and killed many of his warriors. He has sired no young, and with his death, the power of the Bok will be diminished. I thought he meant to build a lair in some far-off place, a fortress of great defense. But in my world. I did not know he meant to come to this place, to build his kingdom in yours."

"We won't give him the chance. You said he would burrow underground."

"Yes. The Bok require the cool dark when they rest."

"I've got an idea where he might've gone. The subway. We have a system of tunnels under the city, for transportation. The sewers are another option," Harper considered, "but I don't know why anyone, even a demon, would want to set up housekeeping in the sewers if he had any other choices. The trick will be pinpointing the right sector."

"What creatures of your world travel this subway, this underground route?"

"The variety is endless. Just people, of all walks. It's a

crowded city. It's another reasonably efficient and inexpensive way to get around it."

He spent the next few minutes explaining the idea and basic workings of the subway system.

"This is clever. You have an innovative and interesting culture. I would like to have more time to study it."

"Stick around, take all the time you want." He rose when his buzzer sounded. He went to the intercom by the front door, verified the pizza delivery, and buzzed the entrance door open.

"You keep a servant in that small box?"

"No." Amused when she came over to peer at it, he explained its function, then opened his door to the delivery boy's knock, paid him, and sent him on his way.

"Was that your servant?"

"No. I gave my servants this century off. He works for the place that makes the food. It's his job to bring it to people when they call on the phone. Hungry?"

"Yes." She sniffed. "It smells very good."

He set the pizza box on the coffee table. "I'll get some napkins—we'll need them—then you can see if it tastes as good as it smells."

When he came back she was sitting on the floor, the lid of the box open, poking a finger at the crust. "It is very colorful. Is this a staple of your people's diet?"

"It's a staple of mine." He lifted a slice, flicked strings of cheese with his finger. "You just pick it up with your hands and go for it." He demonstrated with an enthusiastic bite.

Following suit, Kadra brought a slice to her lips. She bit through pepperoni, through pepper, through onion into cheese and spicy sauce, down to the thin, yeasty crust.

The sound she made, Harper thought, was very like one she'd made during sex.

"I like this pie called pizza," she stated, and bit in again. "It is good food," she added, her mouth full.

"Baby, this is the perfect food."

"It goes well with the beer. It's like a celebration to have kissing and joining, then pizza and beer."

He knew it was ridiculous, but his heart simply melted. "I'm crazy about you, Kadra. I'm a goddamn mental patient."

"This is an expression?"

"It means I'm in love with you. I go thirty years without a scratch, and in less than a day I'm fatally wounded."

"Don't speak of death, even as an expression. Not before battle." She reached out, closed her hand tight over his. "It is bad luck. When it is done . . . When it is done, Harper, we will talk more of feelings."

"All right, we'll table it—if I have your word that when it's done you let me make my pitch."

Baffled, she frowned at him over what was left of her first slice. "Like in the battle of baseball?"

"Not exactly. That you'll let me tell you the way it could be for us."

"When it is done, you will make your pitch. Now tell me more of the subway."

"Hold on." He switched his attention to the televised news bulletin.

The reporter spoke of the attack at the zoo, the murder of the guard, and the mutilation of several animals. Witness reports were confused and conflicting, ranging from the claim of an attack by a dozen armed men to one by a pack of wild animals.

"They don't know what they're up against," Harper said quietly as the newscaster reported that the police were investigating the incident and that the zoo would remain closed until further notice. "They don't have a clue. I call them with the truth, I'm just another loony."

"It is for us," Kadra told him. "Rhee has said that we would fight this battle together. He must be destroyed here or driven back where he belongs. There must be balance again."

"Here." Harper rolled his shoulder where a demon had dug its claws. "We finish it here. New York style."

Kadra pondered the images on the television, the moving paintings of the zoo. "This subway. Does it go near the place where they keep the animals? Where we battled today?"

"There are possibilities."

"Sorak would like a lair near prey. It will be dark soon," she said with a long look at the sky through the window. "Then we hunt."

7

She balked at changing her hunting gear for jeans a second time, claiming they restricted her. He let it pass, figuring the long coat would cloak most of her . . . attributes.

The thing about New York, Harper thought, as they passed a guy with shoulder-length white hair, two nose rings, and a black leather jumpsuit, was there was always someone dressed weirder than you were.

He wore his ripped jacket, for sentimental reasons. And for the practical one that if he was going up against a demon again, there was no point to sacrificing another garment to the long blue claws.

He had his Glock in a shoulder holster, a backup .38 in an ankle holster, a combat knife sheathed at his back, and a switchblade in his left boot.

He'd have preferred an Uzi, but what he had on hand would have to do.

"I like my work," he told Kadra. "And I like to think it makes a difference to some of the people who come to me with problems." He paused to take a good look at his neighborhood—his city—his world. "But this heading out to save the planet stuff brings on a real high."

"You were born for it." When he glanced over at her, she shrugged. "This is what I believe. We are born for a purpose. How we live, how we treat others who live with us forms our spirit and determines if we will fulfill that purpose or fail. We were meant to face this night together. Meant for it from the moment we were created."

"I like that. And I'll take it one step further. We were meant for each other, too."

Meant to love each other, she thought, and to live alone in two different worlds. Her life had been filled with sacrifices, but none would bring the sorrow of the one she had yet to make.

Harper led Kadra down into the station for the train heading uptown. She would have vaulted over the turnstile if he hadn't blocked her.

"You have to use a token, then you walk through."

"These are very flimsy barricades," she pointed out as she bumped through. "Even a child could get over them."

"Yeah, well, it's . . . tradition."

"Like a ritual," she decided, satisfied. She heard the roar, felt the floor vibrate. "The earth trembles." She was prepared to drag him to safety when he grabbed her hand.

"It's just a train coming in." Still holding her hand, he pulled her onto the platform, where she studied the other waiting passengers.

It was a huge cave, strongly lit. She had never seen so much life, so much motion and magic in one place. "Your people have so many colors of skin. It's beautiful. You are blessed to have such richness of person, such variety." When she glanced back at him, she saw he was smiling at her in an odd way. "What is it?"

"Nothing." He leaned toward her, and to her utter shock, kissed her mouth.

"We cannot join here," she said in a hissing whisper. "It is a private activity."

"It wasn't that kind of a kiss. Remember, there are all kinds."

"I thought you were pretending."

"Is that a polite word for lying? On this side of the portal, people kiss all the time. Lovers, friends, relatives. Complete strangers."

She snorted. "Now I will say you are lying."

"Locking lips is practically a global pastime. And this one'll get you: people pay a fee to sit in a big, darkened room as a group and watch other people's images on a screen—a larger version of the TV, where you saw baseball. One of the things those images often do is kiss."

"I think you are a harper after all, because you tell fantastic tales with great ease and skill."

"Nothing in those knowledge banks about movies?"

She frowned, but tipped her head and searched through. When her eyes widened, lit with delight, he knew she'd hit on it.

"Movies." She tested the word. "I would like to see one."

"It's a date." He heard the rumble of the approaching uptown train. They had another date to keep first.

She liked the train that flew under the earth. She liked the way people crowded inside, bumping together as they clung to metal straps. There were colorful drawings to study and read. Some spoke of magical liquid that gifted the user with shiny, sexy hair. Another advised her to practice safe sex. There was a wall map provided for lost travelers, and yet another picture that boasted its elixir could transform the skin to make it sexually attractive to others.

Kadra leaned close to Harper's ear. "Is sex the religion of your world?"

"Ah . . . you could say a lot of people worship it. Why are you whispering?"

"No one is speaking. Is conversation permitted?"

"Sure. It's just that most of these people don't know each other. They're strangers, so they don't have anything to say."

Kadra considered it, and finding it reasonable, she tapped the shoulder of the woman standing beside her. "I am Kadra, Slayer of Demons. My companion in this dimension is Harper Doyle. Together we hunt Sorak."

The sound Harper made was somewhere between a laugh and a moan. "Rehearsing," he said with what he hoped was a non-threatening smile. "New play. Way, *way* off Broadway. Honey," Harper said to Kadra as the woman edged as far away as the press of bodies would allow, "maybe you should just talk to me."

"Making introductions is courteous."

"Yeah, well, you start chatting about demons, it tends to weird people out."

The train stopped. People poured off, people poured on. Kadra scowled and planted her feet. "As you said, how can they defend against Sorak if they are unaware of him?"

"I've thought about that. Thought about going to the cops. The National Guard." Frustrated, he dragged a hand through his hair. "Nobody's going to believe us, and the time we'd waste trying to convince them we're not candidates for a padded cell would only give Sorak more of an advantage."

"You said there were demons in this world, that you put them in cages."

"There are plenty of them. But they're a different type than you're used to fighting. They're not another species, they're us.

People come in a variety pack, Kadra. Most of them are good—at the core, they're good. But a lot of them aren't. So they prey on their own kind."

"To prey on your own kind is the greatest sin. You hunt these demons. Who else hunts them?"

"Ideally? The law. It just doesn't always work out. It'll take more than a subway ride for me to explain it to you. I don't always understand it myself."

"There is good and there is evil. The good must always fight the evil as the strong must always protect the weak. This is nothing that can change by walking through a portal."

He linked his hand with hers. Her vision was so clear, he thought. And her spirit so pure. "I love you," he murmured. "I love everything about you."

The warmth poured into her, flooding her belly, overflowing her heart. "You only know one day of me."

"Time doesn't mean a damn." The train jerked to a halt at the next station. "We'll be getting off soon. Whatever happens tonight, I need you to believe what I'm telling you now. I love you. My world was incomplete until you came into it."

"I believe what you say." It felt strange and right to press her lips to his. "My heart is joined to yours."

But what she didn't say, what she couldn't bear to say, was that her world would be forever incomplete when she left him.

"You're thinking that when this is over, we won't be able to be together." He put his hand on her cheek now, kept his gaze steady on hers. "That I'll have to stay in this world, and you'll have to go back to yours."

"There is only one thing that should be occupying our minds now. That is Sorak."

"When we get off this train, we'll worry about Sorak. Right now, it's you and me."

"You have a very domineering nature. I find it strangely appealing."

"Same goes. When this is over, Kadra, we'll find a way. That's what people do when they love each other. They find a way."

She thought of the globe in her pouch. The key that was hers only until the battle was done. The weight of it dragged on her heart like a stone. "And when there is no way to be found?"

"Then they make one. Whatever I have to do to make it work, I'll do. But I won't lose you."

"I can't stay in your world, Harper. I am a slayer, bound by blood, by oath, and by honor to protect my people."

"Then I'll go with you."

Stunned, she stared at him. "You would give up your world, the wonders of it, for me? For mine?"

"For us. I'll do whatever has to be done to have a life with you."

Tears swam into her eyes. She would never have shed one for pain, but one spilled down her cheek now. For love. "It is not possible. It would never be permitted."

"Who the hell's in charge? We'll have ourselves a sit-down."

She managed a wobbly smile. "It would take more than a subway ride to explain it to you. There are balances, Harper, that must be carefully held. I am here to right a wrong, and am given entrance by the power of Rhee's magic. When I have done what I've been sent here to do, I'll have no choice but to return. You will have no choice but to stay."

"We'll just see about that. Here's our stop."

"You are angry."

"No, this isn't my angry face. This is my if-I-can-fight-demons-I-can-sure-as-hell-fight-the-cosmos face." He gave her hand a squeeze. "Trust me."

She trusted no one more. If she had been permitted to take a lifemate, it would have been Harper Doyle. His strength, his honesty, his courage had stolen her heart. She would miss, for the rest of her life, his strange humor, his bravery, his skilled mouth.

When they had defeated Sorak, she would go quickly and spare them both the pain of leaving. And now she would treasure the time they had left as companions. She would relish the great deed they were fated to accomplish together.

The first order of business, Harper thought, was to get down on the tracks and into the tunnels while avoiding detection by the subway cops. He explained the problem to Kadra as they moved down the platform away from the bulk of the waiting commuters.

"Very well," she said, and solved the dilemma by jumping down onto the tracks.

"Or we could do it that way," he grumbled. He flashed his ID in the direction of a couple of gawking businessmen. "Transit inspectors."

Hoping they subscribed to the New York credo of minding their own business, he jumped. "Move fast." He took her arm. "Stay out of the light. Once we're into the tunnels our main goal is to avoid being smeared on the tracks by an oncoming train. Then there's the third-rail factor. See that?" He pointed. "Whatever you do, don't step on that, don't touch it. It'll fry you like a trout."

He pulled his penlight from his pocket as they followed the track into the tunnel. "There are some areas in the system where homeless people set up housekeeping."

"If they have a house to keep, they cannot be homeless."

"We'll save the tutorial on society's disenfranchised for later. Some of the people who manage to live down here are mentally unstable. Some are just desperate. What we're looking for, I figure, are the maintenance areas. Off the main tracks, where there's room to establish a lair."

"There is no scent of people or demon here."

"Let me know when that changes." He felt the vibration, saw the first flicker of light in the dark. "Train. Let's move."

He doubled his pace toward the recess of an access door, and pulling her up with him, he plastered himself to the door. "Think thin," he advised.

He held on as the roar of the train blasted the air, gritted his teeth as the air pummeled them. Through the train's lighted windows, faces and bodies of its passengers blurred by.

"It is more exciting to be outside the box as it flies by than to be inside it."

He looked over at Kadra as the last car whizzed past. "One of these days you'll have to tell me what you do for entertainment back in A'Dair. I have a feeling I'll be riveted."

He tried to keep a map in his head as they wound through the labyrinth. Twice more they were forced to leap for a narrow shelter as a train sped past. But it was Kadra who swung toward a side tunnel.

"Here. Sorak has been this way."

Harper caught no scent in the stale air other than the grease and metal of machines. "Can you tell how long ago?"

"Some hours past, but fresh enough to track."

She moved carefully, knowing the dangers of an underground ruled by a demon. She kept her voice low as they began to hunt. "The Bok sees as well in the dark as in the light. Perhaps better. He will fight more fiercely for his lair than he would even for food."

"In other words, that skirmish we had this morning was just a preview of coming attractions."

She thought she was beginning to understand his odd expressions, so nodded. "Tonight, it is to the death."

She whirled, coat billowing, as she laid a hand on the hilt of her sword. Though he had heard no sound, the beam of Harper's light picked out a shadow in the dark. He'd nearly drawn his gun when he recognized the uniform.

"Transit cop." He said it under his breath to Kadra. "Let me handle this. Hey, Officer. Riley and Tripp from the *Post*. We're cleared to do a feature on—"

He broke off as the figure took one shambling step toward him and his stiletto-like teeth gleamed in the narrow beam of light.

The teeth parted, row after monstrous row. The hands, tipped with bluing claws, lifted. But the eyes—the eyes were still painfully human.

"Help me. Please, God, help me." And with a sound trapped between a sob and a howl, he leaped.

Kadra's dagger shot through the air and into his throat with an ugly sound of steel piercing flesh. The blood that trickled out of the wound was a thin reddish green.

"The change was not complete with this one," Kadra stated.

"He was still human." Furious, Harper dropped to his knees and tried to find a pulse. "Goddamn it, he was still a human being. He was a fucking cop. You killed him without a thought."

"He was neither human nor demon, but trapped between. I ended his life to save yours."

"Is that all there is?" Harper's head whipped around, and his gaze burned into hers. "Life or death? He asked for help."

"I gave him the only help I could. Do you think it gives me pleasure? With his death, one of my people dies. That is the balance." She crouched, pulled his dagger free. "That is the price."

"We could have gotten him to the hospital. A blood transfusion, something."

"That is fantasy!" She shot her dagger home. "He was dead the instant Sorak kissed him." She gestured toward the body as it began to smoke. "Infected with demon blood. There was nothing to be done for him, in your world or in mine. If Sorak has found one human to change, he has changed others."

She glanced toward the dark maw of tunnel. She would rather face it, even if her own death waited inside, than the hot accusation in his eyes. "If you are unable to do what must be done, go back now. I will go on alone."

"He asked for help. He was scared. I saw the fear." Now all Harper could see was a blackened skeleton. "And he never had a chance." Sickened, Harper got to his feet. "We'll finish it together."

"This is the way. I smell blood, some still fresh." She walked deeper into the tunnel.

8

They moved in the dark, guided by the thin beam of Harper's penlight and Kadra's instincts. And they moved in silence.

She had killed a man—and to Harper the charred remains they had left behind in the tunnel were still a man. She had done so with the same cold efficiency she had used to destroy the hideous little two-headed monster in A'Dair.

In the zoo he'd found her brutal focus fascinating, admirable. Even sexy. But there they had fought beasts—savage and hungry and alien despite their form.

This had been a man. How could she be so certain that his lunge forward had been an attack instead of a plea?

"You said it takes time for the transformation," Harper began.

"In my world." She snapped the words out. "I can't know—no one can know—how the change happens in yours. No demon has ever traveled from my world to yours until now. In A'Dair, the demon carries his victim off, into a lair. For twelve hours the human sleeps, a changing sleep that is like death. Only during this period is there any hope of being saved, and even that hope is small. Once the demon wakes, it is too late. The change is irreversible even if he is not complete. He is demon. And he feeds."

"If there's a different time frame here, maybe there's a different structure to the change."

"He waked. He walked. He would have fed on you if he had not been stopped. The blood was already mixed, Harper. His death was a mercy. What was still human inside knew."

She hadn't known love could be painful. She hadn't known that when your heart lay open to another it could be so easily wounded. But hers was, and the hurt ran down to the bone: he had looked at her as if she were the monster.

She didn't want to speak of it. She wished to push it aside and do only what she had come to do. But the ache in her heart was a distraction.

"Every human death is a death inside me." She spoke quietly, without looking at him. "I cannot save them all. I would give my life if that would make it otherwise."

"I know that." But they both heard the doubt in his voice.

The pain of it sliced through her, made her careless, made her vulnerable to what leaped at her out of the dark.

It was snarling, teeth snapping. Its claws swiped, scoring her neck as she whirled to block.

It was old and female. And it was mad. It skittered back, impossibly fast, like a spider, into the shadows. Kadra freed her sword and, going by scent and sound, struck out.

It cackled. That was the only way to describe the sound it made as it attacked Kadra from behind.

Harper's bullet caught it in midair. Blood gushed, that awful hue of mixed red and green, as it thudded to the ground, arms and legs drumming.

An old woman, Harper thought as he stared into the crazed and dying face. One of the pitiful who so often slipped through society's fingers and into its bowels.

She was old enough to be his grandmother.

"You did not kill her." Kadra crouched beside him. "You did not end her life, and you must not take the weight of it. Sorak killed her, and you ended her torment. You slayed the monster. The woman was already dead."

"Do you get used to it?"

She hesitated, nearly lied. But when he lifted his head and looked into her eyes, she gave him the truth. "Yes. You must, or how could you pick up your sword day after day? But there is regret, Harper. There is sorrow for what is lost. The demon has no regret, no sorrow. No joy or passion, no love. I think when thy feed on us, they hope to consume what it is that makes us human. Our heart, our soul. But they cannot. All they can take and transform is the body. The heart and soul live on in another place. And that place is locked to them."

"So Sorak's come here. Maybe he thinks he'll have better luck eating souls in this dimension."

"Perhaps."

The woman was all but ashes when Harper looked at Kadra again. "I'm sorry about before. I didn't want to believe it could happen, that we could be used this way. It was easier to blame you for stopping it than Sorak for starting it."

"There will be more."

"And we'll both stop it." He reached out, touched a fingertip to the claw marks on her neck. "You're hurt."

"Scratches, because I was careless. I won't be a second time."

"Neither will I." Not with the battle, he thought, and not with her. He took her hand as they got to their feet. "Let's find this bastard, and welcome him to New York."

Harper kept his Glock in one hand, the knife in the other. The tunnel curved, and a dim light glowed at the end of it. He heard the rumble of a train behind them, but ahead there was silence.

He could see signs of human habitation now. Broken glass, an empty pint bottle that had held cheap whiskey. Food wrappers, an old tennis shoe with the toe ripped out.

"His lair." Gesturing with her chin, Kadra slid her sword out of its sheath. "He is not alone."

"Well, why don't we join the party?" He turned the knife in his hand. "We've brought our host some nice gifts."

She stripped off the coat, flung it aside. "He will not be pleased to see us."

The tunnel widened. There was more debris from the life that had chosen to spread underground. Spoiled food, battered boxes that might have served as shelter. A headless doll. And as they drew closer to the light, a splatter of blood against the dingy wall.

The first three came out in a mad rush, all claws and teeth. Harper fired, sweeping his aim left to right. There was a stench of something not human as one threw the wounded at Harper, then came in like a missile beneath the body. Its teeth fixed in his calf as he sliced upward with the knife.

The teeth continued to grip his leg like a vice even as the thing began to smoke. He cursed, kicked, and felt both cloth and flesh tear as the demi-demon struck the tunnel wall.

He spun clear to see that Kadra had already killed the third, and a fourth that had tried to use the cover of their attack for one of his own.

She wasn't even winded.

"That was too easy," she commented.

"Yeah." He limped over, gritting his teeth against the burning pain of the bite. "That was a real breeze."

"He toys with us." Now she pulled out the healing cloth. "He insults us. Bind your wound."

He knelt, quickly tied the cloth around his bleeding leg. "And just how is sending four advance men with really nasty teeth an insult?"

"He knew we would destroy them. Four, not fully changed, are child's play."

"Yeah." Grimly he tightened the knot on the cloth. "I'm feeling real childlike at the moment."

"He wants us in there. Wants to watch the battle. The smell of blood feeds him almost as much as the taste."

"Okay." He tested his weight on the injured leg. It would have to hold. "Let's go give his majesty a real five-star meal."

She drew her dagger, checked the balance of both blades, then nodded. "For your world and for mine. To the death."

"Let's make that Sorak's death."

They charged.

Kadra caught a blur of movement above, and went into a roll that sent the demon flying over her head. She ran him through with one thrust, pulled her sword out clean before his body hit the ground. Using her hips, she reared up, shot her boots into the next attacker's face. And was on her feet, hacking and whirling.

She heard gunshots and, pivoting, saw Harper slay two demi-demons on his left and set to meet another on his right with his blade.

She spun clear, slicing with her sword, and positioned herself so they fought back-to-back.

"Sorak is close!" she shouted. "I smell him."

"Yeah." Sweat dripped into Harper's eyes and was ignored. "So do I."

He shot a bony, bald demi-demon who still wore a torn and

faded New York Mets T-shirt. As the demon smoked and died at his feet, Harper scanned the tunnel.

He couldn't think about who they had been, he told himself, only what they had become.

"I don't see any more of them."

Still back-to-back, they circled. "Sorak!" Kadra shouted. "Come and meet your fate."

As if on cue, light flashed into the tunnel. Through the glare of it, three demons charged.

"He's used the portal. He's brought more through."

Harper fired, and when the Glock clicked on empty, he used it as a club. His leg screamed as he sprang off it to launch himself into a roundhouse kick. The demon barely staggered, shoving Harper so that his wounded leg buckled. He skidded over the floor, and lost his breath and the gun when the demon landed on him.

For the second time, he felt the bite of claws. Screaming in rage, he plunged the knife into the demon's throat, snarled like an animal himself when the thick green spewed onto his hands and face.

When he crawled out, covered with blood, he saw Kadra fighting both of the remaining demons.

Her blades flashed like lightning. She blocked the sickle sword that one of them swung at her, then plunged her dagger into his belly while she hacked her blade through the second demon.

"Next time," Harper said as he limped toward her, "I get the two-on-one."

Winded, she nodded. "Next time."

The smoking blood hazed the air. She peered through it, pointed her sword at Sorak. His claws and face were smeared with the blood of the body that lay at his feet.

He had fed, and fed again, she realized, and would have the strength of ten.

Still, her stance was cocky, her voice a sneer. "You should have brought an army, demon king. We would have littered this place with your dead."

"I brought better than an army." Sorak reached back and hefted a small girl by the scruff of her neck. She let out a sobbing squeal as her little legs kicked in the air, two full feet off the ground.

Leering, Sorak skimmed his teeth over her throat. "The young are so sweet to the taste. How much for her life?"

Kadra lowered her blade. Though her hand was steady, her heart stumbled in her chest. "Will you bargain your life with a human child's? Is not a king worth more?"

"I was not speaking to you, Kadra, Slayer of Demons." Sorak lifted his other hand, and the gun.

Subway cop, Harper thought on a jolt of panic. Sorak had taken the gun from the transit cop, and he had been too angry to notice the empty holster.

On an oath, Harper shoved Kadra aside as Sorak fired. As she fell, blood streaming from her temple, the sword clattered to the ground.

"No. Goddamn it, no!" Harper fell to his knees, gathering her up, checking quickly for a pulse.

"I was born for her death." Sorak shook the child until she began to wail. "Tell me, Harper Doyle, were you born for death?"

She was alive, he told himself. And slayers healed quickly. He would do whatever he could to give her that time, and to save an innocent child from death. Or worse.

He got to his feet, the knife gripped in his hand. "For yours. I was born for yours."

"Approach me and . . ." Sorak ran a blue claw teasingly

down the girl's round cheek as her wails became the mewling sounds of a trapped animal. "I tear her to pieces. How much for the child, Harper Doyle? How much are the young worth in this world?"

Her eyes were blue, Harper noted. Glassy as a doll's now, filled with shock. "How much do you want?"

"You will do. Your life for her life. I would enjoy taking what is the slayer's and making it mine. Throw down your blade, or the child dies now."

"And Kadra?"

Through the stinking smoke Harper saw the gleam of jagged teeth. "Do you think your life is worth both of theirs?" Sorak stepped forward, and Harper could see blood coming from wounds of the claws sliding down the girl's white neck. "I could kill you where you stand with this weapon. But it would be . . . unsporting. Make the bargain, or watch while I give her my kiss."

There was no bargaining with monsters. Even knowing that, Harper could see no choice. "Set her down, let her go. A knife isn't much good against a gun. You're smart enough to know that. In this world, using a kid as a shield is a sign of a coward. I thought you were a king."

"I am more than king here. I am god." Carelessly, he tossed the girl on the floor, then drew out the globe. The portal burst open. "Run, little human child. Run quickly, or I will take you after all."

She ran, weeping. The portal snapped shut behind her.

"And now." Grinning, Sorak streaked forward in a move so fast that Harper had no chance to evade or defend. Using the back of his hand, Sorak struck Harper in the face with a blow so vicious that it threw Harper back against the wall. The knife spurted out of his hand like wet soap.

With the wall bracing him, Harper slid to the ground.

"You are mine now. A warrior slave in my army, in this world. I will rule here."

"Fry in hell," Harper choked out as those claws closed over his throat. In his mind, he called out to Kadra to wake, to save herself from the horror that was coming.

"Soon you will see what it is to be as I am. To lose those weaknesses that make you human." Sorak leaned close, his mouth only a fetid breath away from Harper's, his gleaming teeth bared. "I will give you the slayer when you wake, and we will feed on her together."

He knew pain, agony beyond imagining as that mouth, those teeth closed over him. The shock of it ripped through his system, tore at his sanity as those keen blue claws tore through flesh until he felt his own heart prepare to burst.

The hand that had been fighting to reach the gun in his boot convulsed, dropped limply to the ground.

He had visions of fire and smoke, of blood and brutal death. Torment and anguish. With them came a lethargy that weighed his limbs down like molten lead.

Through the smoke, through the pain, he heard Kadra scream his name.

His trembling fingers closed over the gun. His numb arm moved, slowly, slowly, in exquisite pain to bring it between their bodies. Without being fully aware of where the muzzle was pointed, he fired.

9

When Kadra came to, her vision was smeared with blood and pain. Her body knew a thousand stings and aches from the battle. Her ears still rang from it.

And her first thought as she pushed to her knees was: Harper.

The air was clogged with smoke and stink from the blood of a dozen demons and demi-demons. She remembered the child and her heart jerked. Burying her pain, she picked up her sword, gripped it in both hands.

The sound she heard now, slicing through the filthy air, was one of greed, one of bitter glory. Whirling, she swung the sword high over her head.

She saw, huddled by the dripping wall, Sorak, his regal cape unstained as he gifted the bleeding Harper with his evil kiss.

Fear, rage, horror gushed through her and poured out in a single urgent cry that was Harper's name.

She ran, screaming still, the point of her blade pointing toward the ceiling, where it caught the dim light and glinted like vengeance.

The gunshot was a small sound, a muffled crack like the rap of a fist on wood. Sorak's body jerked, and his head lifted with a kind of baffled shock. He pressed a hand to his belly where his blood spilled between his slender blue-tipped fingers.

"I am king of the Bok." Sorak watched in confusion as his own blood poured. "I am god here. I cannot be destroyed by human means."

"Wanna bet?" With what little strength he had left, Harper fired again. "You lose," he managed before his head slumped.

Kadra leaped between them as Sorak collapsed. She whipped her sword down, the point at its heart. "He has killed you. Harper the warrior has sent you to hell."

"And I have made him mine." His grin spread. "And you, Kadra, Slayer of Demons, must destroy what you love or be destroyed by it. I have won."

"He will never be yours. That is my vow." With all of her strength, she rammed the sword home. Leaving it buried in Sorak's body and in the stone beneath, she dropped to her knees beside Harper.

There was blood, his own and Sorak's, on his face. The healing cloth around his wounded leg had soaked through. His eyes were already going dim.

But they met Kadra's now with something like triumph. "He's done."

"Yes." The slayer's fingers shook as she brushed Harper's hair from his face. "He is finished."

"Mission accomplished, huh? The kid." He closed his eyes on a wave of agony, a flood of impossible fatigue. "The kid got back through the portal."

"You traded your life for hers." For mine, she thought. And for mine.

"She couldn't've been more than two. I couldn't stand there

and let him . . . Christ." He had to gather strength just to breathe. "Your head's bleeding."

"It's only—"

"A scratch. Yeah, yeah. Got a few of my own." He bore down, fought to clear his vision so he could see her better. "Baby, I'm pretty messed up here."

"I will get you to a healer."

"Kadra." He wanted to take her hand, but couldn't lift his arm. "Bastard kissed me. It works faster here, the change. We can't be sure how fast."

"You will not change. You will *not*." Tears ran down her cheeks unchecked. "I will take you back, through the portal. To Rhee, the sorceress."

"I'm going under. I can feel it." He was cold, cold to the bone. Losing, he knew, the warmth of his own humanity. "We can't take the chance. You know what you have to do."

"No." She gripped his face with desperate hands. "No."

"I dropped the gun. Get it for me, let me do it myself."

"No." She pressed his face to her breast and rocked. "No, no, no."

The smell of her flesh brought comfort, but under it, creeping under it, was an ugly, alien hunger that horrified him. "Don't let me change. If you love me, end it. Let me die human." He pressed his lips to her heart. "I love you. Let that be the last thing we both remember from this. I love you."

He went limp. Panic filled her, a wild weeping as she shook him, slapped him, called to him. But he was in the changing sleep, a kind of living death, and could not be reached.

"No. You will not take him." She leaped up, whirled to where Sorak had died. All that was left was her sword, still in the stone, and the globe the demon king had stolen. She scooped up the globe, then with a piercing battle cry, wrenched her sword free.

Tears streamed down her stony face as she dropped down beside Harper again, wrapped her arms around him.

But when the portal opened and the light burst over them, it took them to a world she had never seen.

The room was white. Through a wall of glass were trees of crimson and sapphire against a pale gold sky. Framed by it, robed in white, stood Rhee.

"Help him." Kadra laid Harper between them, stretched out her arms in pleading. "Save him."

"I cannot."

"You have power."

"So do we all. Child—"

"Do not call me child." Furious, primed for battle, Kadra leaped to her feet. "Some are saved from the changing sleep through sorcery. I have heard the tales."

"It is beyond my means to save him."

"You say we share blood, but you refuse the one thing I have ever asked of you. You sent me to him."

"Not I, but destiny."

"Destiny," Kadra spat out. "Who weaves a destiny that asks a man to fight what is not his war, to risk his life in a battle not his own? This he did. He fought with me, and for me. He destroyed the Bok king when I failed. He laid down his life for a child who was not his own. And for this courage, for this valor, he is repaid by becoming what he fought against. Who asks such a sacrifice?"

"There are no answers to the questions you ask. What did he bring to you, what was your gift to him?"

"Love."

"Then there is a way. Courage and strength," Rhee said as she stepped forward. "Vision and love. With these there is a way for you, only you, to save him."

"How? Whatever it is, I will do. A quest, a battle? Tell me, and it is done."

"A kiss."

"A kiss?"

"A gift of breath, of life and love. If your love is true, if it is pure, one to the other, the power of that kiss, of the love in it, will overcome the evil of the demon's."

"Can it be so simple?"

"Nothing ever is," Rhee said with a smile. "You must be cleansed first. I will help you, and tell you the rest."

"There is no time." Her heart lurched as she gestured to Harper. His fingernails were a pale blue. "He is already changing."

"Time stops here. That I can give you. He will remain as he is while we prepare."

★

"There is choice," Rhee said while Kadra bathed. "There is great risk."

"I am a warrior," Kadra replied.

"You must be woman and warrior now."

"So I bathe in scented oils, wash my hair with jasmine blossoms. I have no patience for such matters."

"Rituals." Rhee's lips curved as she held out a thick white towel. "Do you not sharpen your sword before battle? This is not so different. Not all warriors are female, daughter, but all females should be warriors. He will need all you are if he is to survive this."

"If I fail, may he stay here? Sleep, as he is sleeping now?"

Gently, Rhee touched Kadra's hair. "Would you wish that for him? An eternity of nothing?"

"I cannot let him change. It was the last thing he asked of me, to take his life so he might end it as a man."

"And will you?"

"I will not let him die a beast. I will not fail him. If I use my sword to end it, I will never lift it again."

This, Rhee thought, was what I wished for you. Beyond valor and might, beyond battle cries and quests, a love so deep it is a drowning pool.

"These are choices that only you can make. There is one more. The magic that passed from my blood to yours is strong. But more potent is the magic you found in your own heart. Trust it."

Rhee closed her hands around her daughter's arms. Arms, she thought now, that had learned to lift a sword and to embrace a man who was her equal. "Give yourself to it without hesitation. If you waver, if you doubt and still do this thing, he may live. You may not."

Rhee offered a long white robe. "Wear this."

"Strange garb for battling life and death." Kadra put it on, belted it. "If my love isn't strong enough, I die."

Rhee folded her hands because they longed to reach out, to touch, to soothe. "Yes. I gave you to your fate once before. And my arms ached from emptiness. I watched you, in my way, as you grew, as you became. And I was proud. But my arms were empty. Now, I give you once more to your fate."

"Did you love the man who was my father?"

"With everything I am. And yet I could not save him. I could only watch while he was taken from me. He would have been proud, as I am, of the life we made together in you."

"Mother," Kadra said when Rhee turned to the arched opening. And she stepped forward, let herself be gathered close. Let herself hold.

"You found kindness," Rhee murmured. "And forgiveness.

They will make you stronger." She held tight one moment more, just one moment more. "Be strong, my daughter. It is time."

She led Kadra back into the white room. Now Harper lay on a bed that was draped with thin white curtains. A garden of white flowers surrounded it. Dozens of slender, milky tapers added a quiet light.

He wore a white shirt and trousers. His face, while deathly pale, was unmarked.

Kadra parted the bed curtains. "His wounds."

"This much I could do. His flesh is healed, as yours is."

"He is beautiful. He is . . ." My life, she thought. "I have only known him a day, yet he has changed me forever."

"You changed each other. And that change will be stronger than the one Sorak put inside him. You must believe it."

"A sword is not enough." Kadra glanced over. "Is this my lesson?"

"You have always had more than a sword. Sorak is dead. To-gether you have accomplished this great feat, and both our worlds are safe. For this gift, each of you is granted passage into both worlds. As you choose."

"How can this be? The balance—"

"Love makes its own balance." Rhee walked to a table where each of the globes stood on a small pedestal. One emer-ald, one ruby.

"The emerald is your stone, and its key opens the portal to the world you knew. The ruby is his, and its key opens to his world. I must leave you. What you do now is between only you two. I will always be with you. Kadra, Slayer of Demons, your fate is again in your own hands."

Rhee held up her arms and vanished.

"This I must do without sword or dagger." Still, she took her circlet from the table, placed it on her scented hair. "But I am what I am. And all I am is yours, Harper Doyle."

She stepped to the bed, placed a hand on his cold cheek. The words were inside her, as if they, too, had been sleeping. "I love you with heart, with soul, with body. In all worlds, in all times. Come back to me."

And bending, she laid her lips on his.

Love and life, she thought as she breathed both into his mouth. Life and love. Strong as a stallion, pure as a dove. She drew the poison in, gave him her breath. Gift of heart and soul take now from me, and from the Demon Kiss be free.

Pain vibrated through her, but she kept her lips warm and gentle on his. Dizzy, she braced a hand beside his head, and gave.

I would die for you, she thought. I would live for you.

When his mouth moved under hers, when he stirred, she slid bonelessly to her knees beside the bed.

Outside, the sky deepened, gleamed gold, and the jeweled trees shimmered.

Harper dreamed of swimming, fighting through a black and churning sea that was swallowing him whole. He broke through its icy void, searching for her, battling the greedy waves that sucked him back.

Until he slid into a warm white river, floated there. And woke speaking her name.

She lifted her head, and felt no shame at the tears as she gripped his hand. "Yes. Yes, yes." She pressed his hand to her cheek, kissed it, then taking his hand, she laughed in relief at the healthy color in his skin and nails. "Baby," she said, relishing the term, "I am with you."

He saw only white, the gauzy draperies, the glow of candles through them, the richness of the flowers. Then he saw her as she rose up beside him and again laid her lips on his.

"If this is hell," he said aloud, "it's not so bad."

"You are not dead. You live. You are unchanged."

He sat up, amazed at the energy running through him, the absolute freedom from pain. "How?"

"Love was enough."

"Works for me. Where are we? What did you do?"

"We're in yet another dimension. Rhee the sorceress . . . my mother, brought us. She healed us."

"And what, exorcised the demon?"

"That was for me. A kiss waked you, and brought you back whole."

"Like Sleeping Beauty? You're kidding."

She leaned back. "You look displeased."

"Well, Jesus, it's embarrassing." He scooped his hair back, slid off the bed.

"You would rather die, with pride?" Though part of her understood the sentiment perfectly well, it still rankled. She who had never believed in romance had found the event desperately romantic. The kind of moment the bards write of. "You are ungrateful and stupid."

"Stupid, maybe. Ungrateful, definitely not. But if it's all the same to you, let's just keep this one portion of the experience completely to ourselves."

She jerked a shoulder, lifted her chin. And made him smile. "You saved my life, and you made me a man. Thank you."

Now she sniffed. "You are a brave warrior and did not deserve the fate Sorak intended for you."

"There you go. My ego's nearly back to normal now. And can I just say you look gorgeous. Incredible. In fact, there's an expression in my world about how you look right now. It goes something like, wow."

"Ritual foolishness," she replied, flipping a hand at the robe.

"I love the way you look. I love you, Kadra."

She sighed. "I know. If the love between us was not strong and true, you would not have waked so I could be annoyed with you." She looked away from him, deliberately, when he came to her, when he wrapped his arms tight around her.

So he kissed her cheek, kissed her temple where a bullet had grazed. "I thought I had lost you, and that was worse than thinking I'd lost myself."

Yielding, she turned her lips to his. "Harper Doyle."

"Kadra, Slayer of Demons."

She eased back, her eyes solemn despite the humor in his. "Do you wish me to be your lifemate and bear your young?"

"You bet I do."

"This is what I wish as well. This is not a traditional path for a slayer."

He lifted a hand to skim a finger over her circlet of rank. "We'll make new traditions. Stay with me, Kadra. Be with me. We'll stay here, wherever this is. It doesn't matter."

"This is not our place." She stepped back, gestured to the two globes. "The one on the emerald stand opens to my world. The ruby to yours. I believed that to keep the balance we must each go back, must each remain in the world where we came from. But, I have vision."

She looked back at him. "My mother is a sorceress, and her blood is my blood. I see what I once refused to see. I have magic inside me. I must practice with this as I once practiced with a sword. Until I am skilled."

"Slayer and sorceress. I get a two-for-one."

"There can be no balance when love is denied and refused. We are meant, so we will be."

"Choose," he told her. "I'll live in any world, as long as it's with you."

She picked up the bag that held their things, tossed it to him. She lifted her sword. And, crossing to the table, she lifted the globe that rested on a ruby stand.

"The Bok have lost their king, and the slayers who are my sisters will rout them, and continue the fight against all demons. But there are battles to be fought in your world, demons of a different kind to be vanquished. I wish to fight with you there."

"Partners, then." He took her hand, kissed it. "We make a hell of a team."

"And I like the pie called pizza, and the beer. And even more than these, the kissing."

"Baby, we were made for each other."

He swung her into his arms, crushed his lips to hers. When the portal opened, and the light washed in, they leaped into it together.

And went home.